"It is obvious [...] that it can only [...] before you get embroiled in some real scandal...."

"I will do no such thing!" Imogen replied.

"It will be unavoidable, if you will go about kissing men on moonlit terraces. It is about time somebody took you in hand!"

"I am well able to take care of myself! I do not need some man to *take me in hand* as you put it."

"On the contrary. You need a very strong man to keep you in line. I know only too well what you are capable of."

"How dare you! You were the one who grabbed me, and... mauled me about."

"You kissed me back," the viscount pointed out. "And you enjoyed it."

* * *

The Viscount and the Virgin
Harlequin® Historical #1012—October 2010

London, 1814

A season of secrets, scandal and seduction!

A darkly dangerous stranger is out for revenge, delivering a silken rope as his calling card. Through him, a long-forgotten scandal is reawakened. The notorious events of 1794, which saw one man murdered and another hanged for the crime, are ripe gossip in the ton. Was the right culprit brought to justice or is there a treacherous murderer still at large?

As the murky waters of the past are disturbed, so servants find love with roguish lords, and proper ladies fall for rebellious outcasts until, finally, the true murderer and spy is revealed.

Regency Silk & Scandal

From glittering ballrooms to a Cornish smuggler's cove; from the wilds of Scotland to a Romany camp—join the highest and lowest in society as they find love in this thrilling new eight-book miniseries!

Annie Burrows

THE VISCOUNT AND THE VIRGIN

HARLEQUIN®

TORONTO • NEW YORK • LONDON
AMSTERDAM • PARIS • SYDNEY • HAMBURG
STOCKHOLM • ATHENS • TOKYO • MILAN • MADRID
PRAGUE • WARSAW • BUDAPEST • AUCKLAND

Recycling programs
for this product may
not exist in your area.

ISBN-13: 978-0-373-29612-5

THE VISCOUNT AND THE VIRGIN

Copyright © 2010 by Annie Burrows

www.eHarlequin.com

Printed in U.S.A.

Author's Note

Writing is usually a solitary occupation. Many writers refer to the place where they go to write as their "cave." A place where they shut themselves away, and weave their fantasies into tangible works that they can present to the reading public.

So it was a totally new experience to collaborate with five other authors on an entire series of stories, which would share an overarching theme, as well as several major characters. It seems ironic that a historical series such as this one could not have been produced in the time we were allotted without all the technology available to twenty-first-century writers. Of particular help was the file sharing made available to us by Yahoo. We posted maps, documents and even pictures of actors on whom we based the appearances of our heroes. And of course, we needed to keep tabs on who was up to where, and doing what with whom at any given time, which we did by e-mail. To date, we have exchanged over 2,500 e-mails.

It has been an amazing experience for me as a writer to take part in this continuity series. First, I came to admire the creative powers of my fellow writers as we started out by bouncing ideas off each other. And then, as the stories and characters began to take shape, the others all impressed me so much with the depth of their knowledge about the period, the breadth of the resource materials they made available to me and, not least, the unstinting support and good humor that carried us through several sticking points.

I hope you enjoy reading this series as much as I have enjoyed taking part in the creation of it.

Look for *Unlacing the Innocent Miss* by Margaret McPhee, coming November 2010 in Silk & Scandal.

To the other "Continuistas"—Louise Allen, Julia Justiss,
Margaret McPhee, Christine Merrill and Gayle Wilson.
It has been a wonderful experience working with you all.
I am so looking forward to sitting down, and reading this
entire series through from beginning to end.

Available from Harlequin® Historical and
ANNIE BURROWS

One Candlelit Christmas #919
"The Rake's Secret Son"
The Earl's Untouched Bride #933
The Viscount and the Virgin #1012

Look for Annie Burrows's
A Countess by Christmas
Coming December 2010
from Harlequin Historical

Chapter One

January, 1815. London

Imogen Hebden knew it was no use blaming the Veryan sisters when her first ball ended so disastrously.

Not that it was all that much of a ball. There was scarcely anyone in town so soon after Christmas. But that, as her aunt had pointed out, was all to the good. Imogen could experience the flavour of a select Ton gathering at Mrs Leeming's soirée without exposing herself to anyone that really mattered.

Still, Imogen had been really pleased when a gentleman had actually asked her to dance. Even though it was with the rather wooden expression of a man bent on doing his duty by the night's resident wallflower.

Mr Dysart had looked bored throughout the set, and the moment the music had ended, accorded her a very stiff bow, and hightailed it to the card room.

That had been when she noticed that one of the three sets of ruffles on her skirt had come adrift and was hanging down in an untidy loop at the back. She did not think Mr Dysart had been responsible. She would have felt it if he had trodden on her hem. Besides, he had maintained a good arm's length from her at all times. No, it was far more likely that she had snagged it on the chair leg when she had leapt up in response to her first invitation to dance at her first, sort of, ball.

She had begun to make her way to the retiring room so she could pin it up, when the Honourable Miss Penelope Veryan, flanked on one side by her younger sister Charlotte, and on the other by her friend Lady Verity Carlow, had moved to block her path.

'I do hope you enjoyed your dance with Mr Dysart,' Penelope had cooed, with a smile that did not reach her eyes. 'But I do feel I should warn you not to place too much hope in that quarter. He is a particular friend of mine, and only asked you to dance because he knows *we* are taking an interest in you.'

Mr Dysart's behaviour now made perfect sense. Lots of people were keen to curry favour with the wealthy and influential Veryan family. It was a little disappointing to learn that Mr Dysart had not sought her out for her own sake. But at least now, she would not have to pretend to like him when she ran across him again. It was strange, but during the whole year she had been living with Lady Callandar, though she had been introduced to a great many people, she could not say she liked any of them all that much.

'I suppose you expect me to thank you,' mused Imogen aloud, though she was not at all sure she was grateful for Penelope's interference. She thought it might have been preferable to have sat on the sidelines all night, rather than have a man dance with her only because he sought Penelope's good opinion or, rather, that of her father, Lord Keddinton.

There had been a flash of anger in Penelope's eyes, but with her customary poise, she quelled it almost at once.

'How is your court dress coming along?' hastily put in Lady Verity.

Imogen turned to her with relief. Although she had absolutely nothing in common with the supremely fashionable Lady Verity, who never seemed to think about anything but dresses and parties, at least there was not an ounce of malice in her.

'I have had the final fitting,' Imogen replied.

'Do you not like it?' Charlotte pounced on Imogen's less than enthusiastic response. 'I heard that Lady Callandar hired the very *best* modiste, and spent an *extortionate* amount on yards and yards of the most *exquisite* Brussels lace!'

Imogen could not help bristling at Charlotte's implication that no matter how much money was spent on her, or how skilled the dressmaker, she would never manage to look anything but a sad romp. Especially since Charlotte was correct.

The flimsy muslin gowns that Imogen's aunt dressed her in, with their straight skirts and delicate ruffles, permitted no activity more strenuous than strolling to the shops. And in Imogen's case, not even that. Why, she seemed to be able to part a shoulder seam between leaving her bedroom and arriving in the breakfast parlour. And as for her hair…

Well, it went its own way no matter how often Pansy, the maid her aunt had provided her with, was called to rearrange it. Charlotte's ringlets, she noted enviously, fell decoratively *around* her face, not into her eyes. If only her aunt would permit her to just keep her hair long and braid it as she had done before! But no. Fashionable young ladies had their hair cut short at the front. And so poor Pansy had to wield the curling tongs, tie in the bandeaus and jab in the pins.

Which reminded her: that torn flounce still needed pinning up.

'I look perfectly frightful in my court dress,' admitted Imogen with a wry smile. 'Now, if you will excuse me...' And she began once more to press towards the exit.

The other girls fell into step beside her, Charlotte linking her arm, which obliged her to match their languid pace.

'Just wait until you try walking backwards with that train!' chortled Charlotte. Penelope uttered a tinkling little laugh, shaking her head at the impossibility of Imogen performing such a feat.

'Oh, I am sure you will manage it, given time and plenty of practice,' put in Lady Verity kindly.

Penelope made a noise which expressed her extreme doubt. They all knew Imogen could not survive half an hour in a ballroom without tearing her gown. How on earth was she going to cope with all the rigmarole of a court presentation? Sidling through doorways with panniers strapped to her hips, backing away from the royal presence with yards and yards of lace train just waiting to trip her up?

Imogen was still managing to hang onto her composure, when Penelope brought up the subject of her headdress.

'Have you practised getting into a carriage yet?' she

asked, all feigned solicitude. 'I presume you have bought your feathers. Or at least—' she paused, laying a hand on her arm, obliging Imogen to come to a complete standstill '—you do know how tall they usually are?'

And that had been the moment when disaster struck. Irritated by Penelope's patronizing attitude, Imogen had swung round, replying, 'Of course I do!'

Charlotte had let go of her arm, and naturally, Imogen had taken the opportunity to demonstrate exactly how tall those infernal plumes were.

'They are this high!' she said, waving her free arm in a wide arc above her head.

And her hand had connected with something solid. A man's voice had uttered a word she was certain she was not supposed to have understood. She had whirled round, and been horrified to discover that the solid object which her hand had struck had been a glass of champagne, held in the hand of a man just emerging from the refreshment room. All the champagne had sprayed out of the glass, and was now dripping down the front of an intricately tied cravat, onto a beautifully embroidered, green silk waistcoat.

'Oh! I am so sorry!' she had wailed, delving into her reticule for a handkerchief. 'I have ruined your waistcoat!' It really was a shame. That waistcoat was very nearly a work of art. Even the stitching around the buttonholes had been contrived so that the buttons resembled jewelled fruit peeping out from lush foliage.

She pulled out a square of plain muslin—highly absorbent and just the ticket for blotting up the worst of the spill. So long as not too much soaked into the gorgeous silk, his valet would be bound to know of some remedy to rescue it. Why, Pansy could make the most obdurate stains disappear from even the most delicate of fabrics!

But her hand never reached its intended target. The gentleman in the green waistcoat grabbed her wrist and snarled, 'Do not presume to touch my person.'

Stunned by the venomous tone of his voice, she looked up, to encounter a glare from a pair of eyes as green as the jewels adorning his waistcoat. And just— she swallowed—as hard.

It was only the hardness of those eyes, and perhaps the cleft in his chin, that prevented her from immediately applying the word *beautiful* to the angry gentleman. She took in the regular, finely chiselled features of his face, the fair hair cut in the rather severe style known as the Brutus, the perfect fit of his bottle-green tailcoat, and the immaculately manicured nails of the hand that held her wrist in a bruisingly firm grip. And all the breath left her lungs in one long, shuddering sigh. She had heard people say that something had taken their breath away, but this was the first time it had ever happened to her.

But then she had never been so close to such a breath-takingly gorgeous specimen of masculinity before.

She pulled herself together with an effort. It was no use standing there, sighing at all that masculine beauty. A man who took such pains over his appearance was the very worst sort of gentleman to have spilled a drink over! Determined to make some form of reparation for her clumsiness, Imogen feebly twitched the handkerchief she was still clutching in fingers that were beginning to go numb.

'I only m-meant—' she began, but he would not let her finish.

'I know what you meant,' he sneered.

Ever since he had arrived in town, matchmaking mamas had been irritating him by thrusting their daughters under his nose. But worse, far worse, were the antics of enterprising girls like this one. It was getting so that he could not even take a walk in the park without some female tripping over an imaginary obstacle and stumbling artistically into his arms.

By the looks of her, she was yet another one of those girls from a shabby-genteel background, out to snare a wealthy husband who could set her up in style. Definitely not a pampered lady who had never done anything more strenuous than sew a seam. He could feel the strength in her wrist, as he held her determined little fingers away from their target.

It never ceased to amaze him that girls could think that running their hands over him would somehow make a favourable impression. Only two nights earlier, he had been disgusted by the apparently prim young miss who was seated next to him at dinner running her hand along his thigh under cover of the tablecloth. Just as this hoyden was attempting to run her hands over his torso, under cover of mopping up the drink she had thrown over him.

He glared down into her wide grey eyes, eyes which told him exactly what she was thinking. They were growing darker by the second. And her lips were still parted from that shuddering sigh.

To his shock, he experienced a reckless urge to yank her closer and give her the kiss those parted lips were begging him for.

Instead, he flung her from him. 'I am sick to death of the lengths *your kind* will go to in order to attract my notice.' And sickened to find that, in spite of his better judgement, his body was responding to *this* girl's far-from-subtle approach.

'My kind of…attract your…what?' she sputtered.

'Do not think to dupe me by a display of outraged innocence, miss. And do not presume to approach me again. If you were a person worthy of notice, you would have been able to find a more orthodox way of effecting an introduction and making me aware of your charms.'

Imogen stood, open-mouthed, while those hard green eyes raked her quivering form from top to toe with such insolence she felt as though he might just as well have stripped her naked.

'Such as they are,' he finished, with a sneer that left her in no doubt of his low opinion of her.

'Well!' she huffed.

One of his companions raised a lavender-scented handkerchief to his lips to conceal his smirk as the green-eyed exquisite turned and stalked away. The others sniggered openly.

Penelope and Charlotte flicked open their fans and raised them to their faces, but not before Imogen caught a glimpse of a pair of smiles that put her in mind of a cat that has a live bird under one paw.

'Oh, dear,' said Lady Verity, a frown creasing her normally placid brow as her friends turned their backs on Imogen and sauntered away, their noses in the air. 'How unfortunate. He seemed to think…'

'Yes, he made it quite plain what he thought. Odious man! Who does he think he is?'

'I have no idea, but he seems to be someone of con-sequence…'

'Someone who thinks a great deal of his own consequence, you mean,' Imogen muttered darkly, taking in the arrogant set of the blond man's shoulders as he strode towards the exit. 'How dare he talk to me like that!'

Lady Verity was beginning to look perturbed. And Imogen realized she was clenching her fists and breathing heavily and, worst of all, scowling. All three things a lady should never do. Particularly not in a ballroom.

Oh, heavens, she thought, swinging to look towards the chaperon's bench, where her aunt was sitting, monitoring her every move.

She took a deep breath, smiled grimly at Lady Verity and said, 'I think I had better go and rejoin Lady Callandar.'

Lady Verity dipped a curtsy and went off after her friends, while Imogen braced herself to face her aunt's exasperated brand of censure.

Not that her aunt's face showed so much as a hint of disappointment that her niece had just demonstrated she was completely unfit to mix in polite Society. Nothing, but nothing would induce the woman to betray any kind of emotion in a public place. No, the unbearably gentle scolding would wait until they were in their carriage and on their way home, where nobody could overhear.

It began, as Imogen had known it would, the very moment the flunkey closed the carriage door on them.

'Oh, Imogen—' her aunt sighed '—I had such hopes for you when Mrs Leeming extended you an invitation to this small, select gathering—and what must you do but squander this opportunity by making an exhibition of yourself with one of, if not *the* most eligible bachelor in town! Everyone took notice of the way Viscount Mildenhall stormed out—' she shook her head ruefully

'—and by now I am sure nobody is in any doubt that it was because you threw your glass of champagne over him!'

She wished her aunt would give her space to explain that far from throwing *anyone's* drink over the rude, arrogant fop, the whole thing had been an accident… although now she came to think of it, she wondered if it really had been an accident that she had been standing there, waving her arms about, at precisely the moment a supremely eligible viscount had been emerging from the refreshment room with a drink in his hand. Given the cruelty of the smiles as they had strolled away, she wouldn't be a bit surprised to learn that Penelope Veryan had set the whole thing up. With Charlotte's help.

But she knew it would be pointless to say a word against the Veryan girls. Her aunt was bound to simply point out that if *she* were not such an ill-disciplined, hurly-burly creature, who could be so easily goaded into waving her arms about like a windmill, the viscount's waistcoat would have got away scot-free.

And her uncle, she huffed, folding her arms in exasperation, was even more blind where the sisters were concerned. He was always telling Imogen to observe their manners, and use the example of those 'perfect' young ladies as her pattern. It was because they always listened to him with their heads tilted to one side, their eyes wide with admiration, whatever nonsense he spouted. And because they moved gracefully, dressed beautifully and had such polished manners. Oh, yes, they were exceptionally careful to conceal, from powerful men like Lord Callandar, their love of playing spiteful tricks on those less fortunate than themselves!

Well, if that was what it meant to be a young lady,

she was glad her new guardians thought she was not one! She would never sink to the kind of unkind, sneaky behaviour those cats indulged in!

'And when I think of the lengths,' her aunt went on, 'Mrs Leeming went to, to get him there at all! She will be furious with me! He has only recently come into his title, and is up in town for the express purpose of finding himself a bride with all due speed to ease the last days of his poor dear father, the Earl of Corfe. And Mrs Leeming has two daughters she particularly wished to bring to his notice.'

No wonder he was a bit conceited, thought Imogen, if he was the son of an earl on his deathbed. Especially if he was used to females flinging themselves at him because they all knew he was in town in search of a wife. But to bracket her in their company, just because she had waved her arm about… why, she had not even known he was standing behind her! What, did he think she had eyes in the back of her head?

He might be breathtakingly handsome to look at, but if he could not tell a genuine accident from a deliberate ploy to attract his notice, he obviously had the brains of a peacock, as well as the strutting gait of one!

'What were you thinking?' her aunt continued. 'No—' She closed her eyes, and held her hands up in a gesture of exasperation that had become all too familiar to Imogen over the past year. 'On second thoughts, it is pointless asking you that! Not after the constant stream of excuses you have come up with ever since Lord Callandar brought you into our home on the death of your stepfather.' She opened her eyes, eyes that were now filled with such sadness it brought a lump to Imogen's throat.

'It is *such* a pity my husband did not remove you from—' she took a quick breath, and mouthed the words 'That House,' before continuing in a normal tone '—much sooner. You should have come to us the moment your mother died. Or even a year or so later, when it was the proper time to bring you out. *Then* I might have been able to do something with you. You were young enough *then*, perhaps, to have had some of your faults ironed out.'

She heaved a sigh. 'Of course, although one can sympathize with your poor dear mother, for she never really recovered from—' she pursed her lips and squeezed her eyes shut again '—that Dreadful Tragedy, nevertheless—' her eyes snapped open '—she should not have permitted you to run wild with those Bredon boys.'

'My brothers,' Imogen could not help blurting. She knew that girls were not supposed to argue with their elders and betters. But sometimes she felt so strongly that she simply could not hold her tongue. Her uncle had informed her, less than one week after taking her in, that it was her most deplorable fault.

'Properly reared young ladies,' he had said, the corners of his mouth pulling down in chagrin, 'should never set their own ideas above that of *any* gentleman. In fact, they should not even have them!'

'Not have ideas?' Imogen had been astounded enough to reply. 'How can that be possible?' She and her brothers had been used to having the liveliest of conversations around the dining table when they were all home. Even her stepfather had enjoyed what he termed a stimulating debate from time to time.

'*Step*brothers,' her aunt was firmly correcting her. 'They are not blood relations.'

Imogen flinched. When Hugh Bredon—the scholarly man she had grown up to regard as her father—had died, his second son, Nicomedes, had done his utmost to disabuse her of the notion she had any legal claims on him.

'My father never adopted you,' he said coldly. 'In the eyes of the law, you are not my sister. And therefore it would be quite inappropriate for you to make your home with me now.'

Nick, who was training for the law, had already given her the devastating news that the Brambles—the house where she had grown up, the place she had thought of as her home—would have to be sold to pay off the debts Hugh had racked up in the latter years of his life.

'What is left over is to be divided equally between myself, Alaric and Germanicus.'

She had felt as though Nick had struck her. 'What about me?' she had asked in a scratchy voice. *How could he have left everything equally between the three sons who had left her to nurse their father through his last, protracted illness?* Not that she blamed any one of *them*. Nick was too busy with his law books. Alaric was away with his regiment, fighting in the Peninsula. And Germanicus was a naval lieutenant serving with his squadron in the Caribbean.

No, it was Hugh's attitude she found hard to swallow.

She had listened with mounting hope as Nick proceeded to witter on about widow's jointures and marriage settlements, slowly grasping the fact that her mother, at least, had not intended her to be left completely penniless. She had, in fact, bequeathed her only surviving child quite a tidy sum.

Though Nick had not been able to quite meet her eye as he explained that it *was* to have been hers when she reached her twenty-fifth birthday.

'Unfortunately, my father somehow got access to it and made some rather unwise investments.'

From the look on Nick's face, Imogen had gathered he had squandered the lot.

'What must I do then, Nick?' she had asked with a sinking feeling. 'Seek employment?' She would probably be able to get work in a school. One thing about growing up in the household of a man who devoted his life to studying antiquities was that there had never been any shortage of books. She could teach any number of subjects, she was quite sure, to boys as well as girls.

'No, not as bad as that,' Nick had assured her. 'Your mother's family have agreed to take you in and, once your period of mourning is over, to give you a Season. If you can make a match your uncle approves of, he will make up what you would have received from your mother upon your majority into a respectable dowry.'

And so, though the prospect of having to endure even a single Season had her shivering with dread, she had been packed off to live with Lord Callandar, her mother's brother, and Lady Callandar, his wife.

At least it had not been like going to live with total strangers. Though she had never met them, Lord Callandar had written to his sister Amanda punctiliously on her birthday and Imogen's, every year.

It had never crossed anyone's mind to approach her real father's family, not considering their obdurate attitude towards her mother. They had laid the blame for what her aunt termed the Dreadful Tragedy firmly at her door. Imogen had never had any contact with them at all.

'Are you attending me, Imogen?' her aunt snapped, rapping her wrist with her fan so smartly that it jerked her out of her reverie. 'And sit up straight. Hands in your lap, not folded in that insolent manner!'

Imogen flinched to hear her aunt sounding so annoyed, and dutifully corrected her posture. She was truly sorry that she had turned out to be such a disappointment to her aunt and uncle, who had each shown her a great deal of kindness, in their own way. Her uncle had spent an extortionate amount of money trying to make up for what he saw as the deficiencies in her education. He had paid for deportment lessons and dancing lessons, and encouraged her aunt to buy her more clothes than she had believed it was possible for one girl to wear in a lifetime. And that had just been to cover her mourning. They had shopped all over again when she went into half mourning, and again when it was time for her to begin moving about in society a little.

And yet she had never felt at all happy in the Herriard household. It might have had something to do with the fact that she still had vague, shadowy memories of the short time she had lived there before, in the aftermath of the Dreadful Tragedy. Her grandfather seemed always to have been angry, her mother always weeping. And nobody would tell her where her big brother Stephen had gone. Her grandpapa had roared at her that she was a naughty girl for even mentioning him, and said that if she so much as spoke his name again, he would have her beaten. A feeling of utter isolation had frozen her to the spot on a part of the landing that she could still not pass without a shiver. For Stephen had always been the one to scoop her up when the grown-ups were fighting and take her away somewhere she could not hear the raised voices.

There was nobody to stand between her and this large, angry man, and it had terrified her. Even the nursery had been no refuge for the frightened little girl. Without Stephen, it had just become a bleak and empty prison cell. She had the impression of being left for days on end behind locked doors, although she was sure even her grandfather could not have been that cruel. He must have ensured she had at least a nursery maid bring her something to eat!

But no matter how hard she tried to resist them, those unhappy memories came swirling round her every time she crossed the threshold of the grand house in Mount Street.

It was not helped by the fact that once her mother had married Hugh Bredon, her life had undergone such a drastic change. Instead of incarceration and isolation, she had spent her first years at the Brambles learning to fish and shoot and ride, so that she could keep up with her magnificent new big brothers. She did not think she had run wild, precisely, over the ensuing nineteen years, though towards the end of her time there, she definitely had far more freedom than her aunt and uncle deemed appropriate for a young lady. She had thought nothing of saddling up her mare or harnessing the gig to go on errands or visit friends, entirely unaccompanied. And then, after her mother had died, she had taken over the running of Hugh's household.

Her Uncle Herriard, she knew, would never have trusted a sixteen-year-old girl to run his household for him. Her stepfather might never have shown her much affection, but he had reposed a great deal of confidence in her abilities. Hugh had only checked the household accounts for the first few months she was in charge, and though he never praised her, he never complained about the way she ran things, either. All he wanted was to be left in peace to get on with his studies, and she had taken great pride in ensuring that he could do so.

But she had to face facts. When it came right down to it, Hugh Bredon had never quite thought of her as his own daughter. It was as though he was unable to forget that she was the result of his wife's first disastrous marriage to Baron Framlingham.

Imogen's shoulders slumped. 'I am sorry to be such a disappointment to you, Aunt,' she said dejectedly. 'It is not that I am not *trying* to behave as you would wish…'

'I know,' her aunt agreed. 'That is what is so particularly exasperating. It is so hard to discipline you for faults you just cannot help having! They are so deeply ingrained, that…' She sighed. 'If only you were as pretty as your mother,' she said, for what seemed to Imogen like the thousandth time.

The very first time Lady Callandar had seen her, she had blanched and said, 'Oh, dear! How very unfortunate!'

With her wildly curling hair and intelligent grey eyes, Imogen was, apparently, the very image of her father, Kit Hebden.

'*Knowing* eyes,' her uncle had said disparagingly. 'That was the thing about Framlingham. Always looking at you as though he knew something you didn't.'

'Anyone who knew him will take one look at her,'

Lady Callandar had wailed, 'and say she is bound to turn out exactly like him!'

'Then you will just have to make sure,' her uncle had said sternly, 'that she never gives anyone cause to think it!'

'Imogen, dear,' her aunt had said sympathetically, once her uncle had stormed from the room, 'you must not let your uncle's manner upset you. You are—' she had floundered for a moment, before her face lit up with inspiration '—just like a lovely rose that has rambled in all the wrong directions. Your uncle may seem to be severe with you, but it is only because he wants to see you blossom.'

And from that day forward, her aunt had set about pruning her into shape.

'If you could only learn to carry yourself with the poise of Penelope or Charlotte!' her aunt had advised her, time after time. 'People might gradually stop talking about the thorny issue of your mother's Dreadful Disgrace!'

Although the shocking scandal in which her mother and father had been involved had happened over twenty years earlier, Imogen's emergence into Society had reminded people of it.

Her mother had taken a lover. Not that there was anything unusual in that, in her circles. But feelings between William Wardale, Earl of Leybourne, and Baron Framlingham had apparently run high. They had got into a fist fight. And only weeks later, the earl had brutally stabbed Imogen's father to death. As if that were not bad enough, it turned out that both men had been involved in some form of espionage. The Earl of Leybourne had been found guilty not only of murder, but treason. He had been stripped of land and titles, and hanged.

No wonder people stared at her and whispered behind their fans, whenever she walked into a room!

She was not pretty, she was not rich, she lacked poise and she had a scandal attached to her name. Mrs Leeming had been one of the very few Society matrons prepared to give her the benefit of the doubt. But Imogen had just ruined her chance to demonstrate she was nothing like either of her parents, by getting embroiled in that scene with Viscount Mildenhall.

The promises of invitations her aunt had managed to cajole, bribe or bully from her other intimates would probably dwindle away altogether now.

'Perhaps,' she ventured timidly, 'we should abandon the attempt to find me a husband.'

She had already begun to suspect that she would be completely miserable married to the kind of man her uncle would approve of. The more she learned about fashionable Society, the more she understood her mother's willingness to accept her banishment to the wilds of Staffordshire under the aegis of the somewhat reclusive Hugh Bredon. He may have had his faults, but he had never treated Amanda like a piece of topiary that needed constant clipping to maintain an artificially decorative shape.

Her aunt shot her a darkling look, but made no reply, for the carriage was slowing down.

If she ever did have any children, Imogen decided, mutinously, ignoring the footman's outstretched hand and jumping down from the carriage, she would make sure each and every one of them knew they were loved exactly as they were, be they boys or girls. She would

never try to stifle their personalities or make them feel
they had to constantly strive for her approval.

Though, she thought despondently as she trailed up
the front steps behind her aunt, it was not likely that she
ever would have children of her own.

No man that Lord and Lady Callandar considered
eligible would want to ally himself to a girl who could
bring so little credit to his name. She only had to think
of the disdain she had read in the viscount's eyes, the
mockery in those of his friends, to know she was never
going to measure up.

'In here, if you please,' said her aunt, making her way
across the hall to the sitting room. She waited in silence
while a footman hastily lit some candles, banked up the
fire, enquired if they wanted any refreshment and then
withdrew.

'Sit up straight,' she then urged Imogen, who had
slumped down on the sofa. 'Just because you have suffered a little setback, there is no excuse for forgetting
your posture!'

Imogen sat up straight, mentally bracing herself for
yet another lecture about how young ladies ought to
behave.

'Now, Imogen, I have not taken you into my home
and drilled you into the ways of Society, only to have
you fall at the first hurdle! I do not despair of seeing
you make a creditable alliance before the end of the
Season.'

Imogen had a depressing vision of endless balls where
she sat on the sidelines, watching the prettier, wealthier
girls whirling round with their admiring partners. Or
dancing with dutiful, bored men like Mr Dysart. Of
picnics and breakfasts where she endured the spiteful

comments of girls like Penelope and Charlotte, while the matrons whispered about her father's terrible fate, and the bucks sniggered about her mother's scandalous conduct. Of always having to rein herself in, lest she betray some sign that she took after either of her scandalous parents.

And then she looked at the determined jut of her aunt's jaw. Her poor, beleaguered aunt, who had so determinedly taken up the cudgels on her behalf.

The last thing she wanted was to become a lifelong burden on her aunt and uncle. 'If…if I have not received a proposal by the end of the Season, though, I could always go and teach in a school somewhere. For you surely cannot want me living with you indefinitely.'

'That is for Lord Callandar to decide. Though I am sure it would make him most uncomfortable to think of a Herriard teaching in a school!'

'But I am not a Herriard,' Imogen pointed out. 'I am a Hebden.' It was why Hugh Bredon had not wished to adopt her, after all. Because she was the spawn of the notorious Kit Hebden.

'Nobody will be in the least surprised that you could not make anything of me. Though I am sure everyone can see that you have done all you could to try and make me more…' she waved her hands expansively, then frowned '…make me less…'

Her aunt sighed. 'That is just the trouble, is it not? You are what you are, niece, and I am beginning to think no power on earth will ever make a jot of difference.'

'I am sorry, Aunt.' She bowed her head as she tugged off her evening gloves, one finger at a time. The backs were sticky with dried champagne. 'I do not want you to be ashamed of me. I do not ever wish to cause you any trouble.'

'I know that, dear,' her aunt replied on yet another sigh. 'But trouble seems to find you, nonetheless.'

Chapter Two

Imogen was in the sitting room, with her tambour on her lap, trying extremely hard to look as though she did not think decorative embroidery was the most pointless exercise ever foisted upon womankind.

Sitting indoors on a sunny day, embroidering silk flowers onto a scrap of linen, when real crocuses would be unfurling like jewelled fans in the park not two hundred yards from her door…just in case somebody chose to pay a visit! Not that anybody ever came to see her. Still, when her aunt was 'at home' a steady flow of callers made their way through this room. And her aunt insisted that they saw Imogen sitting quietly in her corner, applying herself to her embroidery, so that they could go away with a favourable impression of her.

Not that Imogen could see what was so praiseworthy about stitching away at something that was never going to be of any practical value.

'Lady Verity Carlow,' her aunt had explained, as

though delivering a clincher, 'sits for hours at a time plying her needle.'

Well, huffed Imogen, so had she, back in Staffordshire, when she had some useful sewing to do. She had made all her brothers' shirts, hemmed miles of linen and darned thousands of socks. And she had not minded that at all. Particularly not when one of the boys came to read aloud to her while she did it.

Her mind flew back to the days when she and her mother would sit with the mending basket, by the fire in the cluttered little parlour of the Brambles. And just as she was recalling how the boys would lounge like so many overgrown puppies around their feet, her uncle's butler, Bedworth, stunned her by opening the door and intoning, 'Captain Alaric Bredon.'

While Imogen was still reeling from the coincidence of having the butler announcing a visitor with a name so like that of the boys she was thinking of, Bedworth opened the door a little wider, and she saw, just beyond his portly figure, in the scarlet jacket with the yellow reveres and cuffs of his regiment, his shako held under one arm, and a broad grin creasing his weather-beaten face, her oldest—and favourite—stepbrother.

'Rick!' she squealed, leaping to her feet, scattering her silks, tambour and pincushion in all directions.

Captain Bredon met her halfway across the room, dropping his shako as he spread his arms wide to sweep her into his embrace.

'Midge!' he laughed, lifting her off her feet and twirling her round as she flung her arms round his neck.

'Oh, Rick, c-can it really be you?' She was so happy to see him. It was absurd to find tears streaming down her face.

'When did you get back to En-England?' she hic-cupped. He had missed his father's funeral. The letter informing him of Hugh Bredon's death had not caught up with him for several weeks. She had hoped he might have been permitted time to come home, but his com-manding officer had thought pushing Bonaparte's troops back into France had been far more important. *'You have Nick there,'* he had written back to her. *'Trust him to do what is best for you. After all, he is the legal brains of the family.'*

And Nick had dealt with everything with extreme punctiliousness. But, oh, how she wished Rick had been there on that day when she had felt as though she had lost everything at a stroke!

Now that he was here, she found herself burying her face in his shoulder, letting go of all the grief she had bottled up for so long.

'Rick, Rick,' she sobbed. 'I have m-missed you so much.'

'Imogen!' shrieked her aunt, preventing Rick from making any reply. 'Have you lost all sense of decorum?'

'But this is Rick, ma'am, Rick, my brother—'

'I had gathered that,' her aunt snapped. 'But that is no excuse for indulging in such unseemly behaviour! And as for you, young man, I will thank you to put my niece down!'

Rick did so with alacrity. He had just tugged his jacket back into place and taken a breath as though to tender an apology for offending his hostess, when they all heard a carriage drawing up outside.

Lady Callandar flew to the window, said a rather unladylike word, then rounded on Imogen and Rick.

'Up to your room, this instant!' she barked at Imogen. 'And as for you—' she swooped on Captain Bredon's shako and thrust it into his hands '—out! Now! No arguments!'

Imogen had caught a glimpse of the carriage when her aunt had twitched back the curtains, and she recognized Lord Keddinton's crest on the door panel. The very last people she wished to face, in her present state, were Penelope and Charlotte Veryan. Hitching her skirts up in one hand, while dashing tears from her face with the other, she ran from the room and up the stairs.

She heard booted feet echo on the hall's marbled tiles, then Rick's bewildered cry of 'Midge?'

She turned and looked down. Rick had one foot on the bottom step, as though he meant to follow her.

'Oh, no you don't!' said her aunt, erupting from the drawing room in a froth of Brussels lace and righteous indignation. 'This is a respectable household. I will not permit Imogen to have young men in her room.'

'But I am her brother, ma'am,' he protested.

'No! You may think of yourself in those terms. But you are not related in the slightest.'

Somebody rapped on the front door, making them all freeze for a second. Rick took one last questioning look up at Imogen, who shook her head, silently begging him to understand. She could see him weighing up his options and in the end, choosing discretion. He removed his foot from the lower step, then made for the front door, his expression grim.

Torn between gratitude he was not making a stand and grief that he was retreating, Imogen backed noiselessly along the landing.

Bedworth, who had been biding his time beside the

porter's chair, opened the front door to permit Rick to leave and the visiting ladies to enter.

Imogen tiptoed to her room, where she sank onto her bed, guiltily aware that only her aunt's quick thinking had saved her from becoming the subject of yet more gossip.

The next morning, when Imogen went down to breakfast, she found a carefully worded note from Rick beside her plate. With some trepidation, she passed it to her aunt.

'He wishes to take you out for a drive in the park this afternoon?' she said, squinting at the letter through her lorgnette. 'Quite unexceptionable. You may send him back a note to the effect that you accept his invitation.'

Imogen felt faint with relief. She had spent the whole of the previous night in a state of sleepless agitation. What if her aunt had taken such exception to Rick's lack of manners, she had reported the whole scene back to her uncle? He might forbid her stepbrother to call ever again! Even though Rick was an officer now, he was not exactly what Lord Callandar would call 'top drawer.' Her mother had, she learned soon after coming to live in Mount Street, married beneath what he expected of a Herriard on both occasions. First to an impecunious baron with an unsavoury reputation, and then to a mere 'mister.'

Though at least it had shed some light on Nick's apparent defection. He must have been astute enough to realize he would not receive a warm welcome in such an elevated household as Imogen now inhabited. *That* was why he had never called!

'You will wear the dark blue carriage dress, with the silver frogging. And the shako-style bonnet with the cockade. It will make a charming picture, beside his own uniform.'

Imogen blinked at her aunt in surprise. She knew Lord Callandar disapproved of her stepbrothers, and had thought Lady Callandar shared his opinion. Whenever she mentioned them, it was as 'those Bredon boys' with her nose wrinkling up in distaste.

She gave Imogen a straight look. 'I can see how fond of each other you are. I do not wish to make you unhappy, niece, by preventing you from seeing something of him during the short time I daresay he has on leave.'

'Thank you, Aunt,' said Imogen as meekly as her thundering heart would permit.

'Besides,' said her aunt, laying the note down next to her plate, 'I cannot see how even *you* could manage to get into trouble, sitting beside a gentleman in his carriage. Do you happen to know what kind of carriage he has?'

Imogen was certain he had no carriage of any description. He would hire something. Her stomach turned over. She only hoped he had the funds to procure something that was not too run-down. Nor too dashing. It would have to strike just the right balance to satisfy her aunt's notions of propriety.

'And I hope,' her aunt said with a hard gleam in her eye, 'that now you are over the initial excitement of seeing him, you will manage to behave with the requisite decorum. You cannot go letting young men pick you up and swing you about in drawing rooms like a bell. Nor is it seemly to weep all over them. You know how very important it is that you do nothing to increase the speculation already rife about you!'

'I won't, I promise you,' said Imogen, leaping to her feet and going to give her aunt a swift kiss on the cheek. Her poor, dear aunt was doing her utmost to protect her from malicious gossip. She fully accepted that Lady Callandar could have done nothing but send her to her room the day before and explain to the visitors that she was indisposed. And to get rid of Rick before he said or did something that would have provided those cats with ammunition to have used against her.

'I shall be as prim and proper as…as Lady Verity Carlow!'

'That I very much doubt,' said her aunt tartly, her hand going to the spot on her cheek that Imogen had kissed. But there was a softening to her eye which told Imogen that though she might *say* a proper lady should not indulge in such unmannerly displays of affection over the breakfast cups, she was not unmoved by it.

It seemed to take forever before Bedworth was finally announcing the arrival of Captain Alaric Bredon and showing him into the sitting room.

He bowed stiffly to her aunt, his normally laughing brown eyes wary. Lady Callandar accorded him a regal nod. Imogen dipped a curtsy and managed to *walk* across the room to his side.

And then they were off.

Rick led her to a sporting curricle whose paintwork gleamed golden in the wintry sunshine. A wizened groom was holding the heads of two magnificent matched bays.

'Oh, Rick.' Imogen sighed, taking his arm, and rubbing her cheek against his shoulder, after he had settled her on the bench seat and tucked a rug over her knees. 'I am so glad you have come back.' The groom sprang up behind and the horses shot forward, giving her the excuse to clutch his arm tighter. 'I was half afraid, after the reception you got yesterday, that my aunt had scared you off.'

Rick gave a contemptuous snort, which the horses interpreted as a signal to go a bit faster. Imogen kept a firm hold of his arm while he brought them back to a pace more suited to the traffic they were negotiating.

Then he said with mock severity, 'I have held raw recruits steady in the face of an approaching column. Do you think a frosty reception from a lady of a certain age could rout me? No, I just decided upon a tactical retreat. It went against the grain to leave you when you were so terribly upset. But I know your aunt has the power to banish me from your life permanently, should I truly offend her. Couldn't risk that! Thought it best to regroup.'

'You did so brilliantly,' she said, giving his arm an affectionate squeeze. Then she remembered she was supposed to be behaving with extreme propriety at all times, and straightened up guiltily, looking about her to see if there was anyone who might have recognized who she was and start tattling.

'I say, Midge, do you get scolded like that all the time? Just for hugging a fellow?'

Imogen coloured up. 'I cannot go about hugging gentlemen, Rick. Have you forgotten what tales my father's family spread about my mother?'

'Pompous toad, the man who took the title after your father,' growled Rick. 'Has done his damnedest to erase the association your father brought to the name by being exceptionally priggish. And as for slandering your mother all over town—don't know how he thought he could get away with that! Why, anyone who ever met her would know it was ridiculous! Amanda have affairs!' He snorted again, in spite of the effect it had on the horses before. 'A beautiful woman married off to a dry old stick like my father might have been excused for looking for a bit of excitement elsewhere, but there was never any such thing, and well you know it!'

'Yes, but that is just it,' she countered. 'Very few people ever did meet her after she married Hugh. She never showed her face in Society again. It left Baron Framlingham free to say whatever he liked.'

Rick frowned, either because he was at a loss to know what to say or because he was concentrating on getting through the park gates.

Once they were safely bowling along the broad carriageway and there was no further risk to the gleaming paintwork, Imogen continued in a subdued voice, 'There is no escaping the truth, though, that she did take a lover.'

'Only the one!' he retorted, as though that made it acceptable. And then, hot in defence of the woman who had mothered him throughout his formative years, 'And only because your father drove her to it by making her so miserable! My father never blamed her for any of it. Said she would have done better to have married the Earl of Leybourne in the first place. Courted her at one time, so he told me. Why didn't she marry him? After all, she must have carried a torch for him for years, if she…'

He petered out, with the look of a man who had just

realized he was engaging in a rather improper conversation with an innocent young female.

'My father swept her off her feet,' replied Imogen dryly. 'Not only did it satisfy his sense of mischief to win her from a man of higher rank, he had his eye on her fortune. Then again, he hoped marrying into such a respectable family might hoodwink certain people into believing he would reform. But of course, he did no such thing. Mama said—' And then she realized it was not at all the thing to repeat any of the stories her mother had told her. They had been delivered as a warning, when Amanda knew she was not going to live long enough to steer her daughter through the shoals of the Marriage Mart herself.

'He was a shocking rake,' was all Imogen could bring herself to say. 'Very indiscreet.'

At that moment, they passed a barouche carrying a group of particularly haughty matrons, whose eyes widened to see her riding in a sporting curricle—with a dashing military man as her only escort.

'People watch me with their beady little eyes—' she indicated the retreating vehicle with a wave of her hand '—just hoping to see some signs of flightiness in me. With my mother branded as some kind of temptress who lured two noblemen to their doom, and my father notorious for his legions of mistresses, it is hardly surprising people expect the worst of me. Aunt Herriard has to be extremely strict with me, Rick. To make sure nobody has even the slightest reason to say I am tarred with the same brush.'

'I am amazed she let you come out with *me* this afternoon, then,' he said wryly.

'I was not sure, until the moment we saw you draw up

in this rig, that she might not think better of it, either!' Imogen laughed. 'But it hit exactly the right note. Wherever did you get it?'

'Oh, I borrowed it off Monty. You remember Monty?'

'Remember Monty! Of course I do!'

Rick had not been on active service for long before Monty's name began to crop up in his correspondence to Midge. It turned out that whenever a packet of mail arrived for the officers, they tended to share news from home with each other. Right from the first, she had scattered little sketches throughout her text, to illustrate the events she was describing. The pictures of the butcher chasing a recalcitrant pig through several paragraphs before meeting its inevitable fate beneath her signature had proved a particular hit. After that, everyone in Rick's unit began to look forward to his receiving letters from his dear little Midge. Especially Monty, who never seemed to receive any mail of his own at all.

Appalled to learn that a young man who was serving his country had no support from his family, Midge had begun to include short messages specifically for him. And he had returned his own personal greetings.

'He is in town?' she said, half turning to him.

From the very first, her heart had gone out to the lonely young lieutenant, serving alongside her brother. Fancy being in a strange country, fighting battles, and nobody from home writing to him!

Later, as she had got to know him better through Rick's accounts of his exploits, she began to think there was no finer or braver officer than Lieutenant Monty, saving her own dear Rick, of course. She was genuinely pleased for him when he got made up to captain and asked Rick to tell him so. In his turn, he had sent her, via Rick, his condolences when first her mother and then her stepfather had died.

But then, not long after making major, he had sold out. And for the past few months, she had heard no news of him at all.

'Yes, he is in town, and a good job too. Entirely thanks to him we are enjoying this outing. Told me exactly how to turn your aunt up sweet—you know, sending round a note, applying in writing for permission to take you out—oh, how to do everything in form! Capital fellow, Monty!'

'I do wish I could meet him—' she sighed '—though I don't suppose Uncle Herriard will think him a suitable person for me to associate with. Not if he is one of *your* friends.'

'Oh, I don't know,' Rick darted her a sideways look. 'He comes from a very respectable family. And he has money. Dash it, you must be able to tell that at least from the pair harnessed to this rig!'

She observed the paces of the high-stepping matched bays for several minutes before venturing, 'I don't suppose he will be anything like I have imagined him anyway. I am bound to be disappointed.'

He had probably run to fat now that he was not on active service. Not that she would hold that against him. No, she would *prefer* him not to be as handsome as she had always imagined him. Handsome men, her mother had warned her over and over again, were not to be trusted. Particularly if they had charming ways about them. A girl could easily be deceived by such a man. Her own father was a case in point. By the time Amanda had become a widow, she told Imogen, she had learned it was better for a woman to look for the worth of a man in his character, not in his appearance. Hugh Bredon may have been much older than her, and somewhat dull, but he would never have dreamed of breaking a woman's heart just for sport.

'You won't be disappointed by Monty,' Rick assured her, his grin spreading. 'Tell you what, why don't I see if I can get up a party with him and some of the other officers kicking their heels in town this week. Do you think your uncle would permit you to come to the theatre with us? Monty's family has a private box.'

'Oh, I do hope so. That sounds wonderful!' An evening spent with Rick's friends! For a few hours, she might be able to be herself, rather than her aunt's prim and proper creation.

'I will see what I can do then. Hope I am not speaking out of turn,' he said, his shoulders stiffening, 'but it does not seem to me as though you are very happy, living with your aunt and uncle.'

Imogen sighed again. 'Their one ambition is to see me married well. But because of the scandal attached to my name, I am not getting many invitations to the kind of places where I might meet the sort of man they would think eligible. And when I do go, I nearly always manage to disgrace myself.'

'You? I cannot believe that!'

'Oh, Rick, it is kind of you to say that. But it is the truth. Why, only last week, I knocked a full glass of champagne all over a viscount.'

'Well, that's hardly disgraceful behaviour,' Rick objected. 'Anyone can have an accident.'

Imogen wanted to hug him for dismissing the incident

so lightly. But she needed to make him understand why it had preyed on her mind so much.

'Yes, but the viscount was furious with me for ruining his splendid waistcoat. He…he swore at me, and stormed out of the ballroom, which in turn made the hostess angry too. He was a much sought after guest, while I am just…'

'Popinjay!' Rick interrupted. 'He cannot be much of a man if he gets in a miff over a little bit of drink spilled on his clothing. And what kind of blackguard swears at a female, I should like to know!'

'Quite,' Midge mused. She had always accepted she had been at fault in spilling the drink, but *his* behaviour had certainly not been that of a true gentleman.

She began to feel a little better about herself and sat up straighter. She might be a sad romp, but Viscount Mildenhall had the most abominable manners. But just because he was wealthy and titled, nobody would call him to book for his boorish behaviour.

She knew that for a fact. In the days since what she thought of as *the champagne incident*, she had glimpsed him at one or two functions. He was always surrounded by a court of fawning females and obsequious males. If ever he caught her looking at him, his face would twist into an expression of contempt that made something inside her shrivel.

Well, she was not going to waste another minute trying to work out how she could counteract the viscount's mistaken impression of her. Viscount Mildenhall was exactly the kind of man her mother had warned her about. Too handsome by half. Full of his own consequence. And to be avoided like the plague.

Men like Rick or Monty would never bother about

getting a little bit of champagne on their clothes. Why, they must have been covered in mud, and blood, and worse, time without number. And men like that, real men who had fought and bled and starved to serve their country would not go strutting about a ballroom rigged out in satins and silks, either, looking down their noses at lesser mortals with expressions of disdainful boredom.

'Well, I will only have to endure a few more months in town, anyway,' she confided. 'I will only be having one Season. It is pointless for my aunt and uncle to persist in trying to marry me off. Even apart from the scandal attached to my name, I am a bit long in the tooth to attract a husband.'

At five and twenty, she was long past the age most girls had their first Season. No wonder *certain people* assumed she was so desperate she would deliberately knock a drink over an eligible man just to attract his attention.

'Nonsense!' scoffed Rick. 'You are just a slip of a girl.'

'To you, perhaps, but not to men on the hunt for a bride. Anyway, enough talk about marriage. I will probably never get married. It was not my first plan, you know. I told Nick I would rather look for work. And that is what I shall do.'

'You would rather work than marry?' said Rick, aghast. 'And what as, might I ask?'

'Oh, as a governess, I expect. I…I like children.'

'Yes, but you should have your own, not get paid to mind somebody else's! Midge, have you got some aversion to marrying? Have your mother's experiences frightened you that much?'

Imogen wondered if that could be true. It struck her that whenever the question of her having a Season had cropped up, she had always declared she would rather stay at the Brambles and look after her family. But after a moment's reflection, she shook her head. 'It is not marriage itself I am afraid of. Mama was content with Hugh. As content as she could have been with anyone, after what she went through.'

Imogen sighed. Amanda had been grateful, all her life, for Hugh's willingness to offer her the protection of his name, in return for a generous settlement from Grandpapa Herriard. She always felt that he had rescued her from an intolerable situation. Her world had been lying in ruins. The shock of having her lover arrested for murdering her husband had caused her to lose the baby she was carrying. She had lost her independence, too, when Imogen's grandfather had hauled her back to the house in Mount Street when, to cap it all, somebody had broken into the Framlingham residence and ransacked part of the ground floor. She could not show her face in public, for the gossips were tearing her reputation to shreds. Almost out of her mind with grief and guilt, Amanda had submitted to the family doctor who had administered copious quantities of laudanum.

Imogen thought that it was probably during those days that she had been left for such lengthy periods in the nursery. It was certainly about that time when her baby brother, Thomas, contracted the illness that killed him.

The doctor's response was to sedate her mother even more heavily.

That was when Grandpapa Herriard had taken the

drastic measure of writing to his widowed friend Hugh to beg him to get his only daughter out of town.

'He had three young sons,' Amanda had often told her, her eyes welling with tears, 'for whom he had little time and even less patience. They missed their mother, and I missed my boys. We all comforted each other.'

'She was a wonderful mother to us,' said Rick, as though completely attuned to her thoughts, 'and I know you would be too. The way you took us all on after she went…'

'I did not *take you on*, as you put it. I just love you all. You are my brothers,' she declared, lifting her chin mutinously.

'How would you like it if your brother took you to Gunter's for some hot chocolate?' He smiled down at her. 'Would your aunt think that was improper?'

'I expect so.' Imogen grinned sheepishly. 'But I should love it above all things. What will you do with the curricle, though?'

'Oh, Monty's groom can take it back. You won't mind walking home, will you?'

'Not with you,' she smiled. 'I know you will set a spanking pace. I have not had a good brisk walk for months!'

'Ah, Midge,' said Rick. 'What was Nick thinking, to send you to live with a parcel of relatives who seem to want nothing more than to crush you?'

'He did not have a lot of choice. They were the only ones who would have me. Oh, don't let's talk about such gloomy things. Tell me what you have been up to.'

So he spent the rest of their time together regaling her with anecdotes of his time with the forces occupying Paris.

'You would like Paris, Midge,' he said reflectively. 'Pity we cannot find you a serving officer to marry while I am over here, and then you could come back with me.'

'I should love that! But—' her face fell abruptly '—I do not think my uncle would grant me permission to marry a soldier.'

Rick let the subject drop, but a thoughtful frown creased his brow as he made his way to Monty's house in Hanover Square, after escorting Imogen home.

A footman took him straight upstairs to a dressing room, where he found his friend lounging on a sofa, a valet on a low stool before it, buffing his nails.

'Ah, Rick!' Monty smiled, nodding towards a side table that held a selection of crystal decanters. 'You won't mind helping yourself, while my man finishes?'

Rick made for the table, but then paused, fiddling with one of the stoppers, his frown deepening.

'Not had a pleasant afternoon with Midge?'

'Not entirely,' Rick scowled, pouring himself a small measure and then walking with it to the window. 'I need your advice.'

Monty dismissed his valet. 'How may I be of service?'

Rick flung himself into a chair and gazed moodily into his glass.

'My family has left Midge in a pickle. Up to me to get her out of it. Thought I could trust Nick to handle things, but what must the stupid cawker go and do but tell her the truth. You know our house had to be sold to cover my father's debts? Well, anyone with an ounce of sense would have split the proceeds four ways and let Imogen think she was entitled to it. It isn't as if the money makes all that much difference to us. We all have our careers. We can make our own way in the world. But no. Nick had to tell her that father left her with next to nothing! Then packed her off to a set of starchy relatives who seem intent on crushing all the spirit out of her. And now she says she's too long in the tooth to attract a decent sort of husband with such a paltry dowry, and she's thinking about becoming a governess!'

'A fate worse than death,' Monty agreed, only half joking. 'My brothers have seen off three of the poor creatures since I sold out, and the Lord alone knows how many they dispatched before that!'

'Midge would be wonderful with boys like your brothers, I should think. Probably thoroughly enjoy taking 'em birds—nesting. That's half the problem. Grew up following us around like a little shadow… well, you know that's how she got her nickname. Nick said she was like a cloud of midges you just couldn't shift no matter how many times you swatted them away!' He chuckled. 'Plucky little thing, she was. Gerry said she must have rubber bones. Why, when I think of the trees she fell out of, and the horses she fell off and the streams she fell into…and never cried! That was why, when she burst into tears all over me yesterday…well, it shook me up, I can tell you.'

Monty poured himself a brandy, and took the chair opposite Rick's.

'Well, I am not going to let her become a governess. Going to find her a husband myself! That is why I came to you.'

'Indeed?' said Monty coldly.

'Well, her aunt's not going to succeed, not by throw-

ing her in the way of society types who want a wife to
be a decoration to hang off their arm.'

'I take it you are warning me that Midge is not very
decorative.'

Rick looked affronted. 'She is pretty enough. In her
own way. It is just that she doesn't go in for all that flut-
tery feminine nonsense. You know, batting her eyelashes
and sighing up at you and so forth. She would never do
anything that smacks of insincerity. Straight as a die,
she is.'

'Let me get this straight,' said Monty. 'She has no
dowry to speak of, she is past the first flush of her youth,
and is happier climbing trees than dancing quadrilles.
Is that it?'

Rick grinned. 'That just about sums her up!' Then
his expression grew serious. 'Monty, you have been in
town for a while now. You know who is about. And you
said you were bored. Well, this will give you something
worthwhile to do. Dammit, Monty, you know what a
warm, sweet, loving girl she is. We need to find her
someone who will appreciate her for what she is.'

Monty gave him a peculiar look.

'Are you suggesting that I should fill the role?'

'You!' Rick's jaw dropped. 'Absolutely not! Not
now you've sold out. A bit above our touch now you've
stepped into your brother's shoes. Your family will want
you to marry somebody with money and connections,
won't they? And I'm sure you will be holding out for a
diamond of the first water. All Midge has to offer any
man is a warm heart. No, no, the kind of fellow that
would suit Midge would be a serving officer. You would
never hear her complaining about the hardships of following the drum. She would just fling herself into the

role of taking care of her household on the march, and relish every challenge.'

Something about the set of Monty's shoulders altered. 'Forgive me. For a moment I thought you were trying to set me up with your sister.'

Rick burst out laughing.

Monty grinned sheepishly. 'I know. It is just that recently, I have begun to feel…' he shivered '…hunted. You have no idea the lengths some females will go to in order to hook a viscount on their line. The most mousy, unkempt of creatures fling themselves in my path…'

Rick looked very pointedly at Monty's silk knee breeches, then at the rings that sparkled from almost every finger. 'If you will dress so extravagantly, what can you expect?'

'Oh—' his expression soured '—for people to show their true colours, of course.'

Monty had still been seething from the interview he had endured with his father, when he had first arrived in town. He had spent months trying to prove that he was well able to take up his position as his father's heir. But nothing he did or said had made any difference. Nor would his father listen to a word of criticism against the steward, who was bleeding the tenants dry to line his own pockets. So far as he could see, it would take only one more bad harvest to have the lot of them rising up in protest at their lot.

'You have spent too long abroad.' The earl had sneered when he had voiced his concerns. 'This is England, not revolutionary France. Your brother knew these people, and he never noticed anything amiss.'

His older brother had been cut from the same cloth as his father, though, that was the trouble. Piers had been

indulged and pampered from the day of his birth. He felt
the whole world existed only to provide his pleasures,
so saw nothing wrong with letting his tenants endure
hardship, so long as the rents that funded his luxurious
lifestyle came in on time.

'You would do better to go up to town to get yourself
a wife. It is heirs I need from you, not interference in
the management of my estates!'

He had never felt so worthless in his life.

And it might have been perverse of him, but his
reception in town had made him feel ten times worse.
People knew he had a title and wealth, and that was all
they cared about. Dandies aped every ridiculous kick of
fashion he instigated. The more jewellery he wore, the
more the women's eyes lit up. The more obnoxiously he
behaved, the more they fawned round him, until it was
hard to know who he despised more: them or himself.
It was only with an effort that he managed to shake off
the feelings of disgust with himself—and the world in
general—and say to Rick, 'Will you dine with me before
coming on to Lady Carteret's rout? A tedious affair,
but for several reasons, I am obliged to go. Once I have
shown my face, we can go on to Limmer's.'

'Why not?' Rick replied, draining his glass and
setting it down on the table. 'I have no other engage-
ments tonight. And I have heard you keep an excellent
cook.'

'It is one of the few benefits of civilian life,' agreed
Monty, 'that I can now have as much to eat as I want,
as often as I want.'

'Then let us get started, Monty,' said Rick. 'Or am I
being presumptuous? Do I need to *My Lord* you these
days?'

Monty shuddered eloquently. 'You cannot believe how glad I am to have somebody in town who knows me as Monty. Whenever anybody calls me by my title, I get the urge to turn round to see if my brother has walked into the room. And I find myself going to greater and greater lengths to demonstrate that I am nothing like the former Viscount Mildenhall.'

'So that explains why you are playing the dandy these days.' Rick grinned, eyeing his friend's brocaded waistcoat. 'Can't tell you how relieved I am. Was beginning to think I didn't know you any more!'

'Sometimes, lately,' he admitted, thinking of how very tempted he had been by that chit who had thrown her drink over him, 'I hardly know myself.'

If it had been on just that one occasion, he could have put it down to a momentary aberration. But since that night, he always knew when she was at any function he attended. The nape of his neck would prickle, and he would turn and find those knowing eyes fixed on him, and instead of feeling the contempt for her that her behaviour deserved, he would want to stalk across the room, free all that luxuriant hair from the pins that were scarcely restraining it, yank her into his arms and yield to the temptation of those seductively parted lips. He was beginning to think she, or some woman like her, could offer him a temporary respite from his torment. If he could just bury himself in that tempting little morsel for an hour or two… But then what?

By making such a girl his mistress, he would only prove his father right. Only a worthless rogue would ruin a girl from his own class.

Even if she was asking for it.

Chapter Three

'Now, Imogen, I need hardly tell you that it is quite a feather in your cap to receive an invitation to Lady Carteret's. Nor how important it is that you do absolutely nothing to raise eyebrows tonight.'

'No, Aunt,' replied Imogen meekly.

She was quite sure she would have no problem at all tonight affecting the slightly bored expression that was de rigueur for young ladies. She *would* be bored! Nobody talked about anything but dresses, and who was the latest arrival in town and how much money they had.

How on earth her aunt expected her to find out enough about a man to decide she wanted to marry him, when nobody spoke about anything that mattered, she had no idea!

As soon as they entered the house, Imogen understood why she had been invited. Lady Carteret was obviously one of those women who would enjoy boasting that her event had become a sad crush, even though the Season had not yet properly begun. The rooms were already crowded and hot, but since it was only just February, nobody dreamed of opening any windows. All she could do was ply her fan as energetically as she dared.

'Midge!' cried a beloved voice, making her glance up from her perusal of her so-far-empty dance card. 'I thought it was you! My, don't you look splendid!'

Imogen ignored the reference to her appearance, which was entirely due to her aunt's generosity and good taste. Tonight's white gown, the debutante's uniform, had been lifted above the ordinary by the addition of a silver gauze overdress. The material was so delicate that Imogen was scared to sit down, never mind fling her arms round her brother, which was what she really wanted to do.

'Oh, Rick! How glad I am to see you.' She smiled. 'You won't mind dancing with me, just the once, will you?'

'I should love to,' he replied gallantly, 'And I am quite sure Monty will do the same. He is here tonight, you know. That is how I come to be mixing in such exalted company. Hanging on his coat-tails!'

'Really?' Imogen's heart lifted still further at the prospect of finally coming face-to-face with her brother's friend.

'Really,' Rick assured her. He scanned the crowded room rapidly, a frown darkening his features. 'Can't think where he has got to, though. Was stood just over there a minute or so ago. Tell you what, Midge, you wait here, while I go and find him.'

'Even better, Rick, why don't I go and wait out on the terrace and you can bring him to me there. I need some fresh air.'

'Yes, dashed stuffy in here,' he agreed, running his finger round the inside of his rigid stock. 'Tell you what, I will fetch you a glass of champagne, while I am at it. In fact, that is probably where Monty's gone—to get a drink. He was complaining about the crush and the heat himself.'

Imogen smiled at the sight of Rick shouldering his way through the throng. It was amazing how heartening it was to have a gentleman eager to fetch her a drink. And to know there was another one, to whom she would shortly be introduced, who was already kindly disposed towards her.

Having enquired of a footman how she could make her way outside, she ambled along the corridor that led to the back of the house, picturing to herself what Monty would look like. He would be neatly and soberly dressed, she was sure. Even though he was now quite well off, according to Rick, she could not see a man who had been a serving soldier ever leaning towards dandyism. She pushed open the door that led outside, deciding he would definitely be slightly portly by now. After the deprivations of campaigning, he would probably make the most of having as much food as he wanted. She would not mind that at all. He would be…cuddly, she decided, trailing her way dreamily across the flagstones to rest her hands on the balustrade. He might have a limp, given the number of times he had been wounded. Not, of course that Rick had ever told her the specific nature of any of those wounds. But he would definitely have scars upon his person. He might be a little self-conscious about them. But she would tell him they did not make him any less attractive to her. She would tell him they were his badges of courage…

A slight movement from the garden below alerted her to the fact she was not alone outside.

'Why, if it isn't the girl who ambushed me with a champagne glass,' a hated voice drawled, as Viscount Mildenhall emerged from the shadows and made his way up the steps to her side. 'How very persistent you are.'

'Persistent? Oh!' She gasped as it dawned on her that the viscount had assumed she had come outside in pursuit of him. 'How dare you!'

'I dare because women like you will stop at nothing!' He came right up to her, his eyes flashing green fire. 'Set up one more scene like this, just one—'

'I have not set up any scene, you arrogant pig! Are you so vain you think the whole world revolves around you?'

'So, what *is* your excuse for coming out here, not two seconds after I left the ballroom?' He laughed mockingly. 'Discovered that you show to advantage in moonlight, have you? But it is too late to attempt to charm me with those starry eyes and that dreamy air. You may think you look like some kind of romantic vision in silver tissue, Miss Hebden. But I have seen you watching me with a calculating gleam in your eyes—'

The only thing she had been calculating was how to right the wrong impression he had gained of her. But since her drive with Rick, she had decided she no longer cared what the arrogant fop thought of her.

'I wanted,' she replied, drawing herself up to her full height, 'to get some fresh air. If I looked starry-eyed, it was because I was thinking of another gentleman. Had I known *you* were out here, it would have been the last place I would have come. All you have to do, if you do not wish to remain in my presence, is to return to the ballroom.'

He took one pace in the direction of the doors, then stopped and whirled back to her with a face like thunder.

'And I suppose you will come in right behind me, with your gown disarrayed, telling tales that I have taken advantage of you. Hoping to force my hand...' The only way Miss Hebden was going to get a husband was by utilising such unscrupulous means. It infuriated him to think she had made him her target. That she had somehow sensed, in spite of the pains he had taken to conceal it, that she might have some chance of success. Because, even though he despised her methods, he could not deny that she was never very far from his thoughts. And that those thoughts were, invariably, highly salacious.

Imogen had taken all she could stand. The accusation, coupled with the expression of contempt on his face was like a bellows, fanning her simmering antipathy into searing flame. She lashed out at him, her open palm cracking across his cheek with a noise like a whiplash.

It silenced him, but only for a second. 'You vicious little...' His hand went to his reddening cheek. 'You will pay for that.'

Before she could make a move to stop him, Viscount Mildenhall pulled her into his arms and kissed her. Her cry of protest was swallowed under the insistent pressure of his mouth. His arms clamped her own to her sides, so that although she struggled with all her might, she was quite unable to break his hold.

At first she was far too angry to feel scared. Then after only a few seconds, she discovered that there was something wickedly fascinating about being kissed, thoroughly kissed, by an utterly determined man. She stopped struggling as some essential, deeply buried aspect of her femininity came leaping to life in acknowledgement of his masculinity. Her lips softened and parted. With a low growl, Viscount Mildenhall plunged his tongue into her mouth, taking the experience onto a whole new level.

Her mind reeled. Her heart pounded. Her stomach did an excited little flip.

And Viscount Mildenhall, sensing her capitulation, brought one hand round to the front of her gown and cupped her breast.

His audacity shocked her.

'What are you—' She gasped, her eyes widening in dismay. 'You cannot—'

'It is what women who pursue men get,' he sneered. 'Exactly what they deserve. Since the night you made a play for me at Mrs Leeming's, I have made it my business to find out about you. Did you know that men are making wagers about how long it will be before you follow—' he delved inside her bodice '—in your mother's footsteps?'

Then he fastened his lips to her neck.

Imogen felt as though she was splitting in two.

She hated the scathing way he had spoken of her mother. She knew the casual way he was fondling her breast, as though she was a light skirt, was grossly insulting.

Yet the sensuality of that caress was sending rivers of desire coursing through her veins. Her body wanted to arch into his, entwine itself around him.

'Please, please,' she heard herself moaning. 'Kiss me again.'

The viscount raised his head and smiled at her. With such contempt it roused what remained of her pride.

When he lowered his mouth to take the kiss she had begged for, she bit him.

'What the—!' He reared back, and Imogen, who had been taught well by Rick, struck him in the face, first with her right fist, and then her left.

There had not been room for her to take a really good backswing. It was shock, she expected, that sent him reeling backwards. And a stroke of luck that his shoulder slammed into an ornamental urn—that turned out to be full of sandy loam. Which cascaded all over him as it rocked on its plinth.

She made good her escape while he was still struggling to prevent it from toppling onto the flags below the terrace.

She had only just got inside when she careered full tilt into Rick, who had a glass of champagne in each hand. He did not spill a single drop when she crashed into him, she noted somewhat hysterically as she clung to him. He merely raised his arms in the air, absorbing the impact of her body with a slight grunt.

She felt him turn and put the drinks down, then put his arms round her as he asked, 'What the devil has happened?' He put her from himself, then looked down at her with concern. His eyes snagged on the front of her gown, and narrowed. 'Has some man tried to take advantage of you?'

For the first time, Imogen noticed that the flimsy material was torn. It must have happened when she wrestled herself out of the viscount's hold.

His face darkened. 'I shall kill him,' he growled, making for the outside door.

'No, Rick! Don't say such a thing!' She grabbed his arm and hauled him round. 'If you get into a fight over this, everyone will say I am just like my mother, luring good men to their doom! Don't you see?'

His eyes flicked from her to the door and back again.

'Dammit, Midge,' he growled, 'it's my job to bring the fellow to book.'

'No,' she countered. 'It is your job to protect me. And you won't do that by making a fuss about… about…' she swallowed down her outraged pride '…a mere trifle. All you will do is stir up even more gossip.'

She glanced over her shoulder then, fearful that the viscount would come storming into the house after her. He would be bound to act in such a way that nothing she could say would stop Rick from murdering him!

'It won't be just my chances for a good marriage I will lose. I won't even be able to get employment in a respectable household. Oh, please, Rick, can you not just take me home and pretend this never happened?'

He reached out and, with one gloved finger, touched a spot on her cheek.

'I say, is that blood?' he hissed through gritted teeth. 'If the fellow has really hurt you, Midge, no matter what you think, I will have to call him out!'

'Blood?' She blinked, bewildered for a second. 'Oh, I should think that is probably his. I bit him.'

'You…bit him?' Rick looked startled.

'Yes, and then I hit him, both hands, just as you taught me. One—two!' She mimed the punches for his edification.

He looked a little mollified. 'Don't suppose you laid him out, by any chance?'

'No,' she admitted ruefully. 'Though I have put a mark or two on his face, and ruined his coat.' She remembered the look on his face when soil had rained down on him, and couldn't help smiling. She had hit his most sensitive spot. His vanity. No wonder he had not come indoors yet. He would not want anyone to see him covered in dirt!

She came out of her daze to find Rick rearranging her shawl so that it concealed her torn bodice.

'Come on then,' he said, putting one arm comfortingly about her shoulders. 'I shall take you home.'

It was only then that she realized she was going to have to give an excuse for leaving so suddenly.

'My aunt!' she cried, stopping dead in her tracks. 'I cannot go back into the ballroom looking like this!'

'Don't you worry,' Rick said, ushering her inexorably along the corridor that led towards the front hall.

'I shall tell her you have a headache or something. Females are always falling ill at events like this, aren't they?' Rick pressed Imogen into a chair, and strode across to a footman who was eyeing them indolently. 'Hi, you, fellow! Take a message to Lady Callandar, will you? Tell her I've had to take Miss Hebden home. Sudden indisposition.' He lowered his voice. 'And tell Viscount Mildenhall I will catch up with him later, at Limmer's. Had to escort my sister home.'

'Lady Callandar that Miss Hebden is indisposed,' repeated the footman, pocketing the coin Rick pressed into his palm. 'And Viscount Mildenhall that you will be at Limmer's, after taking your sister home.'

Satisfied he had the message correct, Rick hurried back to Imogen's side.

She barely registered him shepherding her out of the front door and into a waiting cab.

Oh, how right her mother had been to warn her to beware of exchanging furtive kisses with rakes by moonlight! She hated the viscount. She really did. And yet, when he had swept her into his arms, the emotion that had been uppermost had not been revulsion at all. But excitement.

The feel of Viscount Mildenhall's tongue sweeping into her mouth had been as intoxicating as champagne. Exhilarating bubbles had fizzed through her whole body, bringing it to life in a way she had never imagined could be possible.

She raised her fingers to her mouth, suddenly understanding her mother's downfall in a way that had always, until tonight, completely baffled her.

Because she had never experienced the power of desire before. This was why Amanda had turned down the chance of a match with her worthy suitor! Because she could not resist the thrill of Kit Hebden's wicked brand of lovemaking!

She shivered, suddenly scared. For it was not only her mother's blood that ran through her veins. She was Kit Hebden's daughter too. Kit, who never once tried to subdue that side of his nature, but had given it full rein. Kit, who was never content with one woman, especially not the one he had married.

Were the gossipmongers right about her, after all?

She reached for Rick's hand across the seat, and grasped it.

Now that she was exposed to handsome, experienced rakes like Viscount Mildenhall, would it only be a matter of time before everyone found out that she really had inherited Kit Hebden's lascivious nature, after all?

Once Viscount Mildenhall had finished brushing the dirt from his jacket he sat down on the stone coping of the balustrade. It was over. He surrendered. When Miss Hebden came back outside, no doubt with her chaperon and any other witnesses she managed to round up, he would inform anyone who cared to listen that yes, he would marry the hussy.

It scarcely mattered what he thought of her. It had not been the behaviour of a gentleman to half ravish an unmarried girl. He pulled a handkerchief out of his pocket, keeping his eyes fixed on the door through which Miss Hebden had fled, and dabbed at the blood seeping from his lower lip. Now he must pay the price for letting the base side of his nature get out of hand.

He grimaced. It would serve his father right. The earl had given him a lengthy lecture about the type of female he wanted him to bring back to Shevington as his bride. Though his father, with three abysmally miserable marriages under his belt, was the last person qualified to dish out marital advice.

How ironic it was that his father had already specified that on no account was he to marry for love! 'If she should die in childbirth, you will feel like a murderer,' he had said. 'And if she proves faithless, it will break your heart. Just pick a woman with the right connections that you feel interested in bedding. And then, once you have got her pregnant, you may leave her here, return to town and reward yourself by taking a pretty mistress. Or two.'

Well, he was interested in bedding Miss Hebden all right! Yes, it would serve his father right if he did bring her into the family. He would positively enjoy flaunting that scandalous creature under his father's nose!

He shifted his weight as the cold from the stone parapet seeped through his silken breeches. Where *was* the girl? It could not have taken her this long to round up reinforcements, could it?

He got to his feet, and began to pace up and down. He did not like the feeling of being played like a fish on Miss Hebden's line. But in a way, it would be a relief to get the issue of marriage settled. Once he had her name on the marriage lines, he would have reason to return to Shevington, and this time, he would brook no nonsense from his father's steward. He would let the man know that he knew what he was up to. He would visit every single tenant on all his father's vast holdings and let them know that things would change once he was in the saddle. That until that time, he would do his damnedest to see that none of them suffered unnecessarily. And as for the matter of his brothers…

Yes, marrying Miss Hebden would have its advantages. Not least of which would be getting her flat on her back, where she belonged.

But he was damned if he was going let her think he would dance to her tune! He cocked his ear to listen to the strains of the music filtering out onto the terrace; if she did not get herself back out here by the time the minuet was finished, he was leaving! Why should he freeze to death, awaiting her pleasure? He had given her a sporting chance to get the matter resolved tonight.

The last strains of the minuet faded away, and Viscount Mildenhall strode to the door, his face set. He had an appointment to meet Rick at Limmer's. He would enjoy one last night of freedom, and then, in the morning, he would make an appointment with her guardian, when he would offer to make an honest woman of her.

If such a thing were possible.

Imogen passed a restless night.

She may have escaped Lady Carteret's house with nobody any the wiser, but the vile viscount was bound to want to exact some form of revenge for his waistcoat, his jacket and his lower lip. She could not see him doing it by simply telling everyone what had passed between them on the terrace, since he might come out of the retelling looking a little ridiculous. But he would think of something.

She would never dare show her face at any Tonnish gathering again!

But she could not just sit back and wait for the viscount's next move.

She had not fully appreciated, until he had hauled her into his arms, just how close to the brink of disaster she stood. But now she understood her nature better. She would have to take drastic steps to prevent herself from tipping over the edge.

It would mean leaving London. To protect her uncle and aunt. Because, while she resided under their roof, everything she did reflected on them.

She could, she eventually decided, seek Lord Keddinton's help. He had, after all, made a point of taking her to one side, not long after she arrived in London, and telling her in an undertone that if ever she found herself in difficulties, she could apply to him for assistance. He explained that this was because he felt a particular fondness for her, on account of the close friendship he had enjoyed with her father.

She had not, she recalled ruefully, been all that grateful for such an assurance at the time. For one thing, she had felt offended at his assumption she would get into the kind of trouble her aunt and uncle might not be able to deal with. For another, his claim to have been a friend of her father had set her back up. She had never heard anything good about the man who had sired her. And then again, if Lord Keddinton was such a good friend, why had she never even heard of him before arriving in town?

She had mouthed all the right words, but had not been able to repress a shiver as she had shaken his long white fingers from her arm. There was something so very…dessicated about the man. His smile had held no warmth. She had not been able to look straight into his cold, pale eyes for more than a fleeting moment. On top of everything else, his faintly supercilious air had made her aware how very gauche and countrified and ignorant she was.

But since that first, inauspicious meeting, she had revised her opinion of him. For he had demonstrated the friendship he claimed, by instructing his daughters to include her in their social set. Which, considering her reputation, was a risk in itself. And while she had never warmed to either Penelope or Charlotte, there was no denying that they had become frequent callers. The fact that all their 'helpful hints' made her feel wretched was hardly their father's fault.

And he had not exactly been a friend of her father's either.

'I expect,' her aunt had explained, 'he began to feel responsible for your welfare after he worked with Lord Narborough to smooth things over after the Dreadful Tragedy. Robert Veryan, as he was then, only held a junior post in the Home Office when your father was called in to help with some mystery that others were finding hard to solve. Say what you like about Kit Hebden—' she had nodded sagely '—his mind was exceptionally sharp. As is Lord Keddinton's. He has risen to his present exalted office solely due to the brilliance of his mind and the energy he devotes to his work. It is whispered—' she had lowered her voice conspiratorially, though there were only the two of them in the room '—that he is soon to receive an earldom. If he declares he is your friend, Imogen, you may think yourself a *very lucky girl*. Just a hint from him, in the right quarters, and, well...' She had spread her hands expansively.

Yes, Imogen decided, just as dawn was breaking, she *would* take Lord Keddinton up on his offer of assistance. With all the connections he was supposed to have, he was bound to be able to find her a post somewhere as a governess. And deal with her uncle's objections. It would mean confiding in him something of what had happened. And her fears of creating havoc in the Herriard household. But somehow, she sensed that he was a man well used to receiving—and keeping—secrets.

She was not sure exactly when she would be able to arrange an interview with Lord Keddinton, though. She yawned. Nor how long it would take him to arrange for her departure from London.

The next morning, when she found a note from Rick beside her breakfast plate, her heart leapt into her throat. Had he challenged the viscount to a duel after all? With trembling fingers, she broke the seal, and discovered that all he wanted to tell her was that Monty was arranging a trip to the theatre for that very evening. With immense relief, she passed the note to her aunt.

'A trip to the theatre?' Her aunt regarded her doubtfully while Imogen fiddled nervously with her teaspoon. 'Are you sure you are quite up to it? You had to leave Lady Carteret's early last night. And you still look a little wan. If your head is still paining you…'

'I am feeling much better, thank you, Aunt. And providing I have a rest this afternoon, I am sure I shall be quite well by this evening.'

She so wanted to see Rick and assure herself he was not going to get mixed up with the vile viscount. And he was not going to be in the country for very long.

'This Monty person, whose box it is, does he come from a good family?'

'Rick says so, Aunt. It was his curricle Rick borrowed to take me driving in the park.'

'Must be well-to-do, if his family has a box. And his address?'

'Hanover Square.'

'Hmm. I suppose it can do no harm, so long as I accompany you.'

Imogen exhaled the breath she had been holding. If she had to go out anywhere tonight, she would feel far safer in the theatre, with Rick and his friends, than at some Ton gathering where she might run into the viscount again! And as the day wore on, she began to wonder if Rick's notion—to match her up with a serving soldier who could remove her from England altogether—might not have some merit.

It would not be the match they had hoped for, but surely her aunt and uncle would prefer to tell people she was married, rather than working as a governess in some rural backwater?

And most of Rick's friends, she suspected, would be younger sons from the kind of families that were not likely to care very much about scandals that had happened twenty years ago.

It might work! If only, she thought despondently, she could induce one of them to propose to her. She did not have much confidence in her own powers of seduction. But she only had to drop a hint to Pansy that there was likely to be a special gentleman at the theatre that night for the girl's eyes to light up with missionary zeal. She pulled out the evening gown whose bodice was so low, Imogen had never agreed to wear it before. Even now, she eyed it with some trepidation. Then lifted her chin. Desperate straits called for desperate measures. Besides, the gown could not be as shocking as she considered it, or her aunt would never have purchased it for her.

It was not long before she was standing before the mirror, staring in shocked awe at the exposed mounds of her breasts and the shadowy outline of her legs through the diaphanous skirts. She flicked open her fan and looked at her reflection over the top of it, in the coquettish way she had seen other girls employ. Could she really bring herself to simper up at some poor unsuspecting gentleman like that?

Bother the viscount for forcing her into a situation where she felt obliged to resort to such stratagems! She snapped her fan shut and tossed it onto the bed as Pansy held out yet another brand-new pair of evening gloves. The ones she had worn the night before had been beyond repair. Ladies' gloves, she sighed, were just not designed to withstand bouts of fisticuffs.

Only Rick's response, when he saw her descending the stairs, managed to ease her conscience somewhat.

'You look as pretty as a picture!' he declared, bussing her cheek.

'Really?' Imogen flushed with pleasure. The gown could not be too revealing, then, or her brother would have certainly let her know. Of course, she did not really believe she was as attractive as he had implied. She was not a beauty, like her mother. But she knew she was not an antidote, either. She smiled wryly. By the end of the evening her hair would most likely have escaped the bandeau into which Pansy had restrained it, and would be rioting all over the place. But at least she could start the evening out feeling as though she looked like a fashionably eligible young lady.

'Here, let me help you on with your cloak,' he said, taking it from the footman who was hovering with it over his arm.

'Your aunt about?' he murmured into her ear as he draped the fur-lined mantle round her shoulders.

'She will be down shortly, I expect.' Her conscience niggled at her again. Would she be feeling so glad to be covered up, if her gown was not verging on the indecent?

'Good. Wanted a word.' He tugged her into the drawing room and pushed the door to. 'It's like this.' He looked briefly uncomfortable. Then he took a deep breath and plunged in. 'Glad you've made an extra effort tonight. With the dress, and the fancy thing in your hair, and all that. Because, you see, I was talking to Monty last night, and the upshot is, he's willing to help you. Find a husband that is. The fellows he's rounded up for tonight are both on the lookout for the kind of wife who would accept they have careers in the Army.'

'He…what?' She sat down quickly on the nearest chair. 'Are you r-roasting me?'

'No! Would not make a jest of a thing like that! He said he feels as though he knows you, through all those letters you used to write to me, and that you deserve to find happiness with a man who will appreciate you, rather than some fashionable—' he broke off, looking guiltily towards the door, through which her aunt might enter at any moment. 'You ain't angry with me, with us, are you? Just trying to help.'

'No, oh, no, I am not in the least angry,' she exclaimed as she gave him a fierce hug. 'How can I thank you! Best of my brothers!'

His cheeks flushed. 'It is nothing. Sure Gerry would do something, if he were here. So would Nick, if you could get his nose out of his books long enough to alert him to the fact that all's not right with you.'

No, she sighed. Neither of them would ever be likely to stir themselves on her behalf. Rick *was* the best of her brothers. He had always been the one to check her over for broken bones when she fell out of a tree, while Nick would cluck his tongue impatiently and Gerry would roar with laughter.

Before either of them could say another word, they heard her aunt coming down the stairs. They went to join her in the hall, and embarked on the kind of light-hearted chatter suitable for a party bound on an evening of pleasure. All the way to the theatre, she felt as though she was floating on air. This was the first stroke of good luck she'd had in an age. Even if the gentlemen she met tonight did not take to her, it sounded as though Monty would be prepared to help her find the kind of man she could enjoy being married to. Perhaps, he might even take one look at her, and… Her heart skipped a beat. How wonderful it would be if Monty himself, the hero of all her girlhood dreams, took a shine to her. If *he* proposed and whisked her away from London, just when she was most in need of rescue!

She could not stop smiling, all the way up the stairs to the upper tiers. Though her heart was beating so fast that it made her feel a little shaky. By the time they reached the door to Monty's private box, she was clinging to Rick's arm for all she was worth.

And it was just as well. For the first person she saw, when the door swung open, was none other than Viscount Mildenhall. He was lounging against one of the pillars that supported the gilded ceiling. Very soberly dressed, for him, in a dark coat, plain waistcoat and only one ring adorning his little finger.

The castles she had been building in the air came crashing down about her in ruins. However much Monty might want to help her, the Viscount would prevent any man he considered a friend from getting entangled with her!

Viscount Mildenhall met her horrified gaze with lowered brows. Then he looked at Rick. Then at the way she was clinging to his arm. Then back at Rick.

'Rick,' he drawled, pushing himself off the pillar and coming forward with his hand outstretched. 'Welcome. And this is?' His eyes flicked to Imogen again, his features now fixed in an expression of polite enquiry.

'My sister!' said Rick, as though it must be obvious.

'Your sister,' he repeated, looking at her long and hard.

Imogen bristled. What was he doing acting as though *he* was the host tonight, the arrogant pig! It was Monty who had invited them! And then, to her horror, Rick said, 'She has been really looking forward to meeting you properly, at last.'

Imogen felt heat flood to her cheeks. If that was not enough to destroy her reputation in this man's eyes, she did not know what would. He had already accused her of pursuing him. Though nobody else seemed aware anything was wrong, she could tell from the way his eyes glittered he thought she was so brassy she had even roped her brother into her schemes.

She lifted her chin and glared at him. 'I was not in the least keen to meet *you*, Viscount Mildenhall. My brother told me he was to introduce me to an ex-officer from his regiment.' She scanned the other occupants of the box again, wondering which one of the young gentlemen it could be. Neither of them looked in the least like the Monty of her imagination.

'You already know each other?' Rick asked, glancing down at her in surprise.

'We have crossed each other's paths, once or twice. But we have never been formally introduced,' said the viscount.

'Well, then, Monty, let me do the honours. This is my sister, Midge. Well, my stepsister, Miss Imogen Hebden, I suppose I should say, to be perfectly accurate. And her maternal aunt, Lady Callandar.'

'M-Monty?' Imogen's eyes swivelled back to Viscount Mildenhall and widened in horror. '*You* are Monty? B-but—'

At exactly the same time, Lady Callandar rounded on her. '*This* is your brother's friend Monty?'

Finally, even Rick picked up on the fact there was something amiss.

'Oh, ah, well, suppose I should have explained he's Viscount Mildenhall, nowadays.'

'The family name is Claremont, as I am sure you are aware, madam,' he said to Lady Callandar, bowing stiffly from the waist. 'My brother officers still tend to use the name by which they have always known me. I started off as Lieutenant Monty, then Captain Monty, and so on. In Captain Bredon's defence, we have not seen each other since I took the title after my older brother died last year.'

Lady Callandar began to talk to him. About what, Imogen did not know. There was a funny roaring sound in her ears.

Rick led her to a chair at the front of the box, then helped her off with her cloak, while Viscount Mildenhall performed the same office for her aunt.

She felt naked without her cloak. Even more so when the viscount's eyes swept over the curves of her exposed bosom, reminding her of the way his hands had stroked there, to such devastating effect, only the night before. He looked up, then, and their eyes met.

Imogen gasped at what she saw in them. He was remembering too!

He had raised his hand to his jaw, and was fingering his lower lip, drawing her horrified attention to the raised scab, and the purplish bruise she had put there.

She tore her eyes from his and gazed dizzily down

into the stalls below. She had never been scared of heights before, but now she felt as though she was teetering right on the brink of an abyss.

All the viscount had to do was give her one little push, and she would go plunging down into social ruin.

Chapter Four

Nothing on the stage could hold Imogen's attention. There was far too much drama playing out right there in the darkened box.

After the initial shock of meeting her, the viscount recovered his customary aplomb remarkably swiftly, introducing her to his other guests—the men she now had no hope of marrying—as though nothing was amiss.

Only she noticed something odd in the way he did not give her full name, but instead presented her as 'The sister of my good friend, Captain Alaric Bredon,' before correctly introducing her aunt as Lady Callandar.

He did it to prevent them knowing Rick was related to the scandalous Miss Hebden, no doubt. And she was, reluctantly, grateful to him.

Though he was still furious with her. She could tell by the way the air between them seemed to positively thrum whenever she glanced his way.

When the curtain fell for the interval and everyone

rose and began to chat to each other, he took the opportunity to draw her aside.

'You will not say one word to your brother about what has passed between us,' he bit out. 'He has introduced you to me, in all good faith, believing you to be the innocent young creature who grew up with him in Staffordshire. He has no idea how much you have changed, and I have no intention of being the man to disabuse him.'

She felt an overwhelming sense of relief that he was going to put aside his desire for vengeance because of his friendship with Rick.

'Thank you,' she breathed. 'I would not have Rick hurt for the world. Indeed, I would never have come tonight and put him in this situation, had I known that you were Monty.' She took a good, long look at him then, riddled with confusion. She would never have guessed that Monty could be the same man as Viscount Mildenhall. The Monty Rick had written about had been dashing, courageous and honourable. Whatever could have happened, to turn him into this vain, rude, slimy…

His eyes narrowed under her scrutiny. She wondered if he could tell what she was thinking about him. But then he nodded and said, 'I believe you. For my part, I never connected the sister Rick described to me with the Miss Hebden I know. Why *is* your name Hebden—' he frowned '—and not Bredon?'

'Because Rick's father did not care to adopt me and give me his name.' She stared past him, to where Rick was chatting happily with one of the other young men. Out of the corner of her eye she could see her aunt quizzing the other. 'Well,' she added bitterly, 'I should think you can understand that. You, above all people, know the kind of things that are said about my parents.'

When they all took their seats again, after the interval was over, Imogen found to her dismay that she had been manoeuvred into a chair next to Viscount Mildenhall.

He ignored her for the entire second act with magnificent disdain. Every time she glanced up at him, his face was turned towards the stage, his whole demeanour indicating that the actors were far more interesting than the presumptuous female who had inveigled her way into his box.

While, to her growing annoyance, Imogen could think of nothing *but* him. Even though he was a despicable worm, being able to feel the heat of his body—so close to hers—and smell the indefinable scent of him made her whole being thrum with awareness. She could not stop thinking about the way his tongue had swept into her mouth, the way he had held her, dominated her. It made her stomach turn over and her heart speed up. When she knew a well-brought-up young lady would feel nothing but revulsion for a man who had treated her so insultingly, it was galling to admit that merely sitting next to him in the dark was making her hanker for more of the same.

She squirmed in her chair, a seething mass of insecurity and thwarted longing, counting the minutes until she could escape from the arrogant, handsome brute lounging in the chair next to hers. As soon as the last curtain came down, she leapt to her feet and made for the sanctuary of Rick's side.

There was the inevitable hiatus before they could leave, during which Viscount Mildenhall came across to where she was standing clinging to Rick's arm, and said, 'I shall call to take you for a drive tomorrow, Miss Hebden.'

Imogen's heart sank. The expression on his face was so forbidding she could see that while he tooled his vehicle round the park he fully intended to give her a stern lecture upon her manners and morals, before warning her to forget any notion she might have of marrying any of his friends!

But she would have to endure the scold, if that was what it took to get him to abandon any plans he had to ruin her socially. And it seemed, from what he had just said, that he might let her off the hook, for the sake of his friendship with Rick.

'Very well,' she said, lifting her chin defiantly. 'I shall be ready.'

Rick looked at her quizzically while he escorted her down the stairs to the exit. 'Is something wrong, Midge? Did you not hit it off with Monty? I must say, he seemed quite taken with you.'

Yes, the viscount was a consummate actor! She knew what he thought of her. He had made it quite plain. And yet tonight, with Rick watching, he had behaved like a perfect gentleman, according her consideration and courtesy. Even the way he had occasionally looked at her, with an intensity that made her feel like a specimen under a microscope, could be interpreted by others as genuine interest in her as a woman.

'Did he?' she managed airily. 'I cannot think why. When he is so handsome I dare swear he could have any female for the crooking of his finger.' She dived into the waiting coach with more haste than grace, and flung herself into the seat corner.

Rick poked his head through the open door. 'But he is calling on you tomorrow…'

'I am sure it is out of courtesy to you, Rick,' she muttered, tossing her reticule onto the seat next to her, and bending to extricate the flounce of her skirt, which had caught in the heel of her shoe. 'There is nothing about me that would attract a man like him.'

'Oh, I would not be so sure,' said Rick thoughtfully. 'He said a lot of very complimentary things about you when I met him in Limmer's last night. Said he felt as though he knew you well, through the letters you used to write me. Said any man would be lucky to get a girl like you for a wife. A girl with integrity and loyalty and…'

That had been before he found out her name was Hebden, though. She shook her head, saying firmly, 'I am not at all the kind of girl a future earl ought to marry.' As if to prove her point, the flounce parted from both her heel and the body of her skirt simultaneously.

'Well, that was what I thought at first,' Rick mused. 'For he only said he was going to help you find a husband. But once he clapped eyes on you, he did not let any of the other fellows come near you!'

No, he had not. But it was not because he felt anything like admiration for her! With fingers that were shaking with chagrin, she tied the trailing length of lace into a knot so that it would not trip her up when she got out of the coach later.

'You know, Midge,' Rick persisted, 'since your aunt has had the dressing of you—' he ran his eyes down her slender frame '—you look far prettier than you used to.'

Imogen managed to raise a wan smile. In truth, his

blind refusal to look at her as other men did warmed her to the core. 'When I was running about the fields in your cast-off breeches, with my hair in plaits, you mean?'

Rick grinned. 'With your front tooth missing and a black eye from falling out of a tree. Monty should have seen you then!' He laughed.

Imogen laughed too, but she could not think how Rick did not hear how false it sounded.

He would be so disappointed if he ever found out what his friend really thought of her.

But then, she sighed, slumping into the corner, Rick was only the latest in a long line of people she had disappointed, one way or another. Before she had become such a trial to her aunt and uncle, she had proved unworthy of inclusion in Hugh Bredon's will. But worst of all, the deepest hurt she had to live with was knowing that she had not even been of any great comfort to her own mother.

Amanda had spent all her life in mourning. She had found some compensation in nurturing Hugh's boys, but now it dawned on Imogen, on a fresh wave of pain: Imogen had survived babyhood, grown and thrived, yet had never been any consolation at all. Having a mere daughter had never made up for Amanda's loss of her sons.

Imogen rubbed at a tension spot forming between her brows. Seeing how much her mother had loved Hugh's sons, had she tried to be just like them, so that her mother would love her too? Not that it had done her any good. Her mother had focussed all her attention on them, even making Imogen promise, while she had nursed her during her final illness, that she would take care of them in her stead.

And now here she was, dressed by her aunt to resemble a young lady of fashion. With everyone expecting her to marry well. While inside she was still that girl Rick had just described. A scruffy, grubby, unwanted by-product of a loveless marriage. Desperately hoping somebody might take to her just as she was.

She almost groaned aloud. She had spent so long trying to prove she was just as good as a boy, that she had never learned properly how to be a girl. It was not just the viscount she repelled. She had already learned, from the year she had spent observing the interaction between the sexes in polite Society, that no man would want to marry such an awkward female. She may as well accept it. She had always been a misfit, and now it looked as though she always would be.

Her aunt bustled up to the carriage then, so Rick was obliged to stand aside.

'What a stroke of luck!' her aunt beamed as soon as the door closed and they were on their way. 'That Viscount Mildenhall should turn out to be a friend of Captain Bredon's. And that he is prepared to take you out for a drive tomorrow. Only think what this will mean!'

'Aunt, please, do not get your hopes up too high. It is just a drive in the park—'

'Yes, but with Viscount Mildenhall! Everyone will know he has forgiven you for the Champagne Incident. If he could, perhaps, be persuaded to stand up with you, for a dance or two, as well—which he might since he seems on such good terms with Captain Bredon—well, it will do wonders for your social standing!'

Imogen sucked in a sharp breath. This was an aspect to the case she had not considered. Just being seen driven about the park by the viscount would indeed be something of a coup. Her aunt would make sure everyone knew about his friendship with her stepbrother. Perhaps being considered a connection of his would outweigh the handicap of her heritage.

For once, she entered wholeheartedly into her aunt's enthusiastic preparations for the drive the next day. So much hinged on persuading Viscount Mildenhall to put aside his animosity towards her.

They had both noticed that the viscount seemed to favour the colour green; determined to curry favour with him, Lady Callandar dressed Imogen in a carriage dress and topcoat in that colour.

Her aunt regarded the finished effect with pursed lips.

'My chinchilla furs,' she said, snapping her fingers at Pansy, who ran to fetch them. 'You want to look as though you have every right to be riding next to a man renowned for the elegance of his attire,' she finished, draping the luxurious furs round Imogen's shoulders.

Of course, when Viscount Mildenhall arrived, he completely eclipsed her, in his voluminous driving coat, fastened with enormous mother-of-pearl buttons, and a curly brimmed beaver hat set at a rakish angle on his golden locks. But at least she knew she looked remarkably elegant, for once, rather than the hoyden he thought her!

He had come to fetch her in the very same curricle he had lent to Rick. The same wizened groom stood holding the horses' heads while they mounted up to the seat. As

Viscount Mildenhall tucked the rug round her knees, she whispered, 'Before you say whatever you have to say, I just wanted you to know that I am truly grateful for your not saying or doing anything last night to expose my dreadful conduct at Lady Carteret's.'

He straightened up swiftly and shot her an inimical glance. 'Do you think *I* wish people to know what happened on the terrace?'

Her spirits sank. Though he obviously felt some remorse for his part in that disgraceful episode, the way he looked at her told her that he was not about to shoulder any of the blame himself.

The brisk way he told the groom to stand clear of the horses and the stern set of his mouth as he pulled out into the busy street, told her that he was not yet ready to listen to her explanations for everything that had so far gone wrong between them.

He negotiated the remaining length of Mount Street, crossed Park Lane, then pulled into the park before speaking again.

'You are extremely fond of your brother, are you not?'

'Yes.'

'You would do nothing to hurt him, I trust?'

'Of course not!'

'Then—' the muscles of his jaw clenched as though he was steeling himself to proceed '—having given the matter careful consideration, I believe the best solution for all concerned, is for us to marry.'

There! He had said it. He had already written to arrange an appointment to speak to her maternal uncle, Lord Callandar, before he had discovered she was not only the wanton Miss Hebden, but also Rick's sister.

Not that it made one jot of difference in the long run. He glanced at her out of the corner of his eye. It had almost floored him to discover that the temptress whose charms he had sampled under the frosty moonlight, was the same woman one of his closest friends had always described as a paragon. A woman he had decided to help out of the difficulties she was experiencing.

He had been sure he was doomed to a miserable marriage with a scheming hussy. And as he got progressively more drunk as he saw a long, miserable future pan out before him, married to a woman he could feel no respect for, he began to wish he had not been so picky with Rick, when he had told him Midge needed a husband. He had always thought she had sounded like a really nice girl. Once upon a time, he had thought that if he ever married, he would want it to be to a girl like her. Someone who would be a loyal companion to him, even when they both grew old.

And though he had believed such happiness could now never be his, since he was committed to marrying Miss Hebden, he had decided to do what he could for Rick's little sister. Life had been hard on her. She deserved a shot at happiness. And so he had spent the day scouring town for men he knew would appreciate what she had to bring to a marriage. When by rights, he should have gone straight to Lord Callandar's house and sealed his own fate.

Not that it made any difference now. Miss Hebden was Midge. The girl Rick had said would enjoy romping about the estates with his neglected little brothers. The girl who would be well able to cope with his difficult father, having nursed her own cantankerous stepfather through his final illness.

The girl who, he saw out of the corner of his eye, was looking at him as though he had lost his mind.

'What, me and you?' She was now saying it as though the idea had never occurred to her. 'M-marry?'

He gave her the benefit of a cynical smile. 'Why not?' The more he thought about it, the more sense it made. He had been attracted to her from the first moment he had seen her. Even though he had known her only as the scandalous Miss Hebden. Now that he had learned more about her background, he could perhaps understand what had driven her to employ such desperate measures to get herself a husband. And there was no denying that she would cope with the situation at Shevington far better than most women.

'Why not?' she glanced over her shoulder at the groom, who bore the wooden expression of a servant pretending not to eavesdrop, and lowered her voice. 'Well, to start with, there is my reputation!'

He blinked. He had not expected her to argue. Leap up and down, and shout with triumph, perhaps. But not to argue.

'Explain,' he bit out curtly.

'Oh, come! You know all about my mother and father. And I noticed that you took good care not to introduce me as Miss Hebden last night. It is quite obvious that you cannot want the daughter of such a notorious couple in your family!'

'Don't be absurd!' Nothing had been further from his mind. In fact, his mind had not been engaged at all when he had first realized that Midge and Miss Hebden were one and the same person. He had just acted from some deep, visceral objection to permitting any other man to make any kind of overture towards his woman.

Not that he was about to admit to the wave of possessiveness that had overwhelmed him, the moment she had removed that cloak, and revealed the lush figure he had held in his arms the night before. It would be a grave error at this stage, to let her know what a hold she had over him. She was the kind of woman who would use it to her advantage! So, in a voice that even he felt was verging on the pious, he said, 'I was considering Rick's feelings last night. I did not want him to be hurt. And he would be, if he knew men were making wagers about which of them—' He stopped short.

But Imogen knew the nature of the speculation rife about her.

He allowed the horses to trot for several yards, before saying in a more conciliatory tone, 'No family is ever free from scandal, in one form or another. My own father's third marriage, for instance, was most unfortunate. His wife was far too young to marry a man already twice widowed, who wished to live in rural seclusion. She had—' he paused, settling his face into a determinedly blank expression '—a series of very well-documented affairs. My father is still haunted by doubts about the legitimacy of my young twin brothers, though naturally, he acknowledges them as his.'

Imogen gasped, and half turned to him on her seat. 'I do not know what to say.'

'Just agree to marry me, that is all I want to hear you say,' he said grimly.

'But you surely cannot want to—'

He cut her off impatiently. 'Rick must surely have told you how things stand for me. The earl is desperate to see me married. He cannot bear the thought I might die childless. And now you know why. He wants his *own* offspring to inherit his lands. Besides which, the longer I dally in town, the less chance I will have… Matters at Shevington are not…' He shook his head. 'I should be there.'

Imogen remembered her aunt telling her that the old man was at death's door, and laid a hand on his sleeve. 'I am so sorry. I forgot how unwell he is. Of course, I understand how important it is you get your future settled. But it cannot be with me…'

'I fail to see why. Rick knows us both well, and assures me we would suit.'

Why on earth was she persisting in saying she did not want to marry him, when she had been doing her utmost to entrap him for weeks? Unless, it suddenly occurred to him, his behaviour on the terrace outside Lady Carteret's ballroom had frightened her. He probed the inside of his bruised lower lip with the tip of his tongue. The first slap had been delivered in a spurt of temper, but those punches…

Had he really scared her so much she could no longer bear the thought of marrying him? He felt a frisson of guilt in regard to his conduct towards her. He had insulted her, manhandled her and torn her gown. He shifted uneasily in his seat. At Limmer's, later on, Rick had told him, his face grim, that his sister had been taken suddenly ill and begged him to take her home. He had been too sunk in his own gloomy reflections to bother questioning him, particularly when Rick proved reluctant to talk. But now he saw she must have been in quite a state for Rick to have felt it was more important to take her home, than storm straight outside and demand satisfaction.

He glanced down at her, sitting rigid on the seat

beside him, her hands clenched into fists in her lap as though she still wanted to hit him.

Well, it made no difference. He had made up his mind to marry her, and that was all there was to it.

'Miss Hebden,' he said sternly, 'I have promised Rick I will look after you. The only effective way to do that is to marry you. He feels guilty for the way his father mismanaged your affairs, and is concerned about how unhappy your maternal relatives are making you. Surely you do not want him to go back to France with worry over your future hanging over his head? A man in his situation needs all his wits about him.'

'His situation? You talk as though he is going straight back into battle. France is at peace now! From his letters, it sounds as though all he has done for months is attend balls and picnics and cricket matches!'

'That is beside the point. A military man needs to be prepared for any eventuality. There has been much unrest in the capital. The Bourbons are not popular. Plenty of people are agitating for Bonaparte to return. If that should happen, Europe will be plunged back into war.'

'That,' she said coldly, 'is all a matter of conjecture.'

'What is not a matter of conjecture though, Miss Hebden,' he said, drawing unfairly upon the most devastating weapon in his arsenal, 'is your conduct.'

'My conduct?'

'Yes. It is obvious to all who know you that it can only be a matter of time before you get embroiled in some real scandal—'

'I will do no such thing!'

'It will be unavoidable, if you will go about kissing men on moonlit terraces.'

'That's a despicable thing to say! *You* were the one who grabbed a defenceless female and mauled her about—'

'Hardly defenceless…' he indicated his bruised lip with one gloved finger '…reckless, unscrupulous, wild to a fault…' He ignored her outraged gasp. 'In fact, it is past time somebody took you in hand.'

'I do not need anyone to take me in hand as you put it…'

'On the contrary. You need a very strong man to keep you in line. I know only too well what you are capable of, and I will make damn sure that Rick never has to so much as blush for your conduct in future.'

'You vile worm!' she gasped. 'You are the very last man I would *ever* marry!'

'Coming it a little too strong, Miss Hebden,' he drawled cynically. 'Considering how very much you enjoyed kissing me.'

'A few fleeting kisses are one thing, marriage is quite another!'

'You will not be going about kissing any more men, Miss Hebden. Consider the feelings of your aunt and uncle, if you will not embrace respectability for Rick's sake. They must have spent a fortune on you, considering every time I have seen you, you have been dressed up to the nines. And I know you have not a penny to your name.'

'You can talk! Every time I have seen you, the extravagance of your attire has taken my breath away! A more vain, shallow, selfish…*peacock* of a man I have never met.'

'I am a catch, though. What do you think your uncle and aunt will say when they hear that after all they have done for you, you have turned your nose up at making such a brilliant match?'

'Why should they hear anything of the sort?'

'They will know. Because I have already arranged to call upon your uncle this evening. At which time, I intend to ask his permission for your hand.' He turned and smiled at her grimly. 'I give you fair warning, Miss Hebden. Do you think you will be able to come up with a reason for refusing my suit that will satisfy your guardians?'

She went very still.

'Quite so. They know, as I know, that marrying me is the best solution all round. And I think that, upon reflection, you will have to agree.'

Chapter Five

Imogen was speechless.

Viscount Mildenhall sounded determined to make her his wife.

But she could not believe he *wanted* to marry her! Any more than she wanted to…wanted to… She bit down on her lower lip and averted her face.

She could not deny there would be all kinds of advantages for her, if she accepted his proposal.

She wanted to leave town before she embroiled her poor dear aunt in some scandal. And marrying would be preferable to seeking employment. Mainly because her uncle and aunt would be so hurt if she demonstrated she would rather work as a governess than live indefinitely under their care. But also because every time she had thought about approaching Lord Keddinton, she'd had the sinking feeling that if she accepted a job he arranged for her, it would place her more deeply in his debt than she would like. This feeling was usually accompanied by a vision of a large sleek cat with a live bird struggling under its claws.

No, she would not be sorry not to have to go cap in hand to Lord Keddinton.

But then, what would it be like to marry a man who held her in such contempt?

Viscount Mildenhall was mercifully silent all the way back from the park. Nor had she, in the end, voiced one more objection to his threat to make a formal offer for her hand.

'Well?' her aunt asked her the minute Imogen trudged in through the front door. 'Is the matter resolved? What did he say?'

Imogen drooped into the drawing room and sank onto a chair. 'He asked me to marry him,' she admitted.

Her aunt shrieked, clapped her hands to her cheeks and collapsed into another chair.

'I know,' said Imogen, shaking her head. 'It's unbelievable.'

But her aunt had recovered from the initial shock, and had leapt to her feet, beaming with pleasure. 'Oh, Imogen. Congratulations! Well done!'

It did not occur to her aunt, thought Imogen with resentment, that she might have turned down such a flattering offer. Nor her uncle, who breezed into the dining room that evening, positively gleeful over what he termed 'Imogen's conquest.' The atmosphere at the table was more convivial than Imogen could ever remember it being since she had gone to live there. She had finally, she observed with a sinking heart, managed to do something they approved of.

Drat the viscount for being right about this! She did not have the heart to disappoint them. In the end, with what her aunt declared was a becoming show of modesty, Imogen had bowed her head and accepted her uncle's congratulations in a muted voice.

'His Lordship will be coming to dine tomorrow night, so that we may all discuss arrangements,' her uncle informed them both as he sawed off a generous portion of game pie and tipped it onto his plate. 'Captain Bredon will accompany him.'

'Captain Bredon?' Lady Callandar echoed in astonishment. 'You have invited him to dine?'

Imogen felt as surprised as her aunt looked. But Lord Callandar quashed any further objections by stating, 'His Lordship is bringing him, as his guest.'

'Oh, well, in that case, of course…' her aunt trailed off, bowing her head over her plate in dutiful submission.

Imogen was sure her aunt would never have raised any objections to having her stepbrother to dine, had she ever plucked up the courage to risk rousing her uncle's displeasure by inviting him. It had only been surprise that had made her seem to question her husband's choice of dinner guest. But apparently, the fact that Rick numbered a viscount among his closest friends now outweighed the ignominy of his humble birth.

Lady Callandar did look somewhat anxious when Rick breached all codes of etiquette the minute he entered the house—striding into the drawing room and enveloping Imogen in an enthusiastic hug. Fortunately, her uncle was too busy fussing around the viscount to even notice.

'I am so pleased for you, Midge,' Rick grinned. Then he leaned and whispered in her ear, 'You will like being married to Monty. Always thought the pair of you would suit.'

Imogen guiltily disentangled herself from his embrace. It was hard to know which was making her more uncomfortable; deceiving her brother or exposing her aunt to one of her uncle's tirades, by indulging in what he would term unacceptable behaviour in his drawing room.

Her aunt, seeing how uncomfortable she was, gamely tried to make light of the situation by swatting Rick playfully with her fan, and saying, 'You are not in France now, Captain Bredon. We cannot have these continental habits creeping into our drawing rooms.'

Rick backed off, muttering apologies, a dull flush on his cheeks.

Imogen wished there was something she could say to smooth things over. It was not Rick's behaviour she found difficult. It was the situation with the viscount.

She schooled her features into an expression of polite welcome as she made her curtsy to Viscount Mildenhall.

He bowed over her hand, the epitome of a courteous suitor, but there was a look of such cynical amusement in his eyes as he straightened up that Imogen wished she dared swat him with her own fan.

She mastered the impulse, out of consideration for her aunt's feelings, and the evening proceeded along utterly conventional lines.

'Do you have a date in mind for the wedding, my lord?' asked her aunt, as they took their places at the table.

'Before the week is out,' replied Viscount Mildenhall

tersely. 'When Captain Bredon will be rejoining his regiment.'

'Oh, but that will leave no time to purchase bride clothes!' wailed Lady Callandar.

'But you have bought me so many pretty clothes already,' Imogen pointed out.

'Indeed,' Viscount Mildenhall put in smoothly. 'Miss Hebden is a credit to your good taste. She always looks quite…lovely.'

The telling pause as he sought for a suitable epithet to describe her appearance had Imogen grinding her teeth. He did not think she was lovely at all. Though she might be the only one who noticed, he had as good as said that anything praiseworthy about her appearance was due to her aunt's good taste, not the raw material she had to work with!

However, on one thing they were in agreement. 'I do want to marry before Rick's furlough is over,' she put in, though it almost killed her to appear to side with the viscount. 'It will mean so much to have him to walk me down the aisle.'

'Don't be ridiculous, niece!' blustered Lord Callandar. '*I* shall be giving you away. You are living under my roof and I am supporting you. Captain Bredon is not even a blood relative!'

'Forgive me, Miss Hebden,' put in Viscount Mildenhall in a voice that, though quiet, managed to cut straight through her uncle's hectoring tones, 'but I have already appropriated Rick for my groomsman.' He turned then to her aunt. 'And I am sorry to rob you of your shopping expedition, too, but I have promised my father to return to Shevington as soon as is humanly possible. However—' and he turned on his most dazzling smile

'—we will be returning to town after a suitable interlude, and at that time my bride will require a whole new wardrobe to befit her new station in life. I am sure she will wish to involve you in carrying out the requisite purchases.'

Both her aunt and uncle subsided, vastly pleased with the viscount's suggestions.

Only Imogen still felt disgruntled. Nobody was making any concessions to what *she* wanted. It felt as though everyone she loved was ranged against her, on the viscount's side.

But worst of all, it had just hit her that she was going to become a viscountess. The notion was so absurd, she did not know whether to laugh or cry.

Since she was at the dinner table, she naturally did neither, but let the conversation flow round her without any further input.

When the ladies withdrew, her aunt wasted no time in letting her know she had erred, yet again.

'I know I have told you, time and time again, that it is not proper to display too much emotion in public, but I really think, on this occasion, that it would be permissible to look just a little pleased at your great good fortune. Your demeanour at table could have been interpreted as positively lukewarm.'

Imogen obediently mustered up a wan smile and, when the gentlemen joined them, set herself to being as pleasant as she could force herself to be. Viscount Mildenhall let no trace of the antipathy he felt towards her show at all; he was so charming towards her aunt and uncle, and on such very easy terms with Rick, that before long, she even began to wonder wistfully if, somewhere underneath all the finery and sarcasm she associated with Viscount Mildenhall, the Monty she had once admired so much might still survive.

How differently she would feel towards this match, if he had approached her first as Monty, the hero of her girlhood dreams. If she could believe he was spiriting her away from London because he understood how badly she wanted rescuing!

Instead of being determined to bury her in the countryside, and 'keep her in line.'

The next morning, Lady Callandar came bustling into the drawing room with her hands full of lists she must have sat up well into the night compiling.

She wore a very smug smile as she offered the first one for Imogen's inspection.

'The guest list,' she explained.

'It is rather short,' Imogen observed.

'Yes,' replied her aunt with relish. 'It is going to be a *very select gathering*. Only family, and those who have shown themselves to be your friends. Oh,' she breathed, 'how I am going to enjoy withholding invitations from all those nasty-minded tattle-mongers who have snubbed you!'

Imogen could not help smiling. She could just see her aunt dropping Viscount Mildenhall's name into future conversations. And dispersing tidbits of information about the massively wealthy but reclusive Earl of Corfe's country seat of Shevington, where, she would boast, her dear, dear niece now resided!

'I include Mrs Leeming, and Lady Carteret, you see,' she pointed out their names on the sheet of paper Imogen now held. Rick's name had been included, as had that of Nicodemus Bredon, though he was but a humble lawyer's clerk.

'Lord Keddinton, it goes without saying, and his dear daughters, who have taken such pains on your behalf.'

'And Lady Verity Carlow,' Imogen nodded. 'Yes, I should like to include her. She has always been truly kind to me.'

'And she is Lord Keddinton's goddaughter too. It would not do to offend a man like him by omitting a connection of his.'

'Did you know her brother, that is Captain Carlow, is in town at the moment? He is a friend of Rick's.'

Her aunt pursed her lips. 'That could lead to some awkwardness. If we invite the younger Carlow merely because he is in town, we shall have no option but to invite the oldest one too. You are aware that he has married,' she swallowed, 'Helena Wardale. The daughter of your mother's…that is, your father's—'

'I know there may a little awkwardness,' Imogen hastily put in, to spare her aunt from having to speak of her father's gruesome murder or the part Helena's father had played in it, 'if she accepts the invitation to my wedding, but I truly hope she will come. She has done nothing for which she need be ashamed. It is not her fault that her father—'

'Well,' her aunt interrupted with false brightness before words like *adultery, murder* or *execution* could be uttered in her drawing room, 'it is most commendable of you to take such a forgiving attitude. I am sure I would not like to be at odds with any of the Carlows—' she lowered her voice and muttered '—no matter who they are married to.

'There!' she declared, adding the names to the list. 'We shall invite them all.'

Imogen did not think there was anything particularly

commendable about her attitude. She just felt a strong sense of kinship with the daughter of the man who had been hanged for killing Kit Hebden. Though neither girl had anything to do with the crime, they had both lived under the shadow of scandal all their lives. True, Helena now had a place in Society again, but it was only as the wife of Marcus Carlow, Viscount Stanegate. Imogen had no idea what terrible fate might have befallen Helena's older brother and sister who, to all intents and purposes, seemed to have dropped off the face of the earth.

And far from believing she had any forgiving to do, Imogen often wondered if Helena was the one who might bear a grudge against Amanda Herriard's daughter. Helena had lost her father, her home and her position, because of that doomed love affair.

The days until Imogen's wedding flew by in a frenzy of organization. A Society wedding held at St George's in Hanover Square, followed by a sumptuous reception for the select portion of Society who had merited an invitation, required a good deal of planning.

And though there was not time to shop for a complete trousseau, Lady Callandar insisted she have just one new gown. She managed to get her modiste to conjure up a wedding dress that was a dreamy confection of soft creamy lace over an ivory satin underdress. Some poor seamstress must have sat up until all hours stitching on all the tiny seed pearls that decorated the snugly fitting bodice. The full-length, narrow sleeves ended in points, which came down over the backs of her hands, were also studded with seed pearls in a swirling design.

'It is so lovely,' Imogen said, wishing she could give her aunt a hug when she came into her room on the eve of her wedding, to check over all her lists one last time.

'You really have worked miracles over these last few days, Aunt.'

Lady Callandar signalled the maid who had come in behind her to deposit the tray on a console table by the door, before saying, with some satisfaction, 'Yes. I have every confidence that even though we threw this whole thing together at the last minute, it will pass off smoothly.' She dismissed the maid, took the glasses of rich ruby port from the tray, and carried them over to the bed, where Imogen was reclining.

'I do not know how much your mother may have told you,' she said, handing Imogen one of the glasses and perching on the edge of the bed, 'about the Duties of a Wife.'

Most people would think Amanda had told her young daughter far too much about what it was like to be married to a hell-raising rake. Imogen saw her mother as she had been during the last days of her life, her eyes glittering with pain as she catalogued every detail of her own disastrous marriage and begged her not to make the same mistakes.

But she very much feared that was exactly what she had done. From the very first moment she had clapped eyes on him, she had thought Viscount Mildenhall the most compellingly handsome man she had ever seen. Even discovering what an unpleasant nature he had, had done nothing to quench the fizz that a mere glimpse of him could start running through her.

And then he had kissed her.

To such devastating effect, she had agreed to marry him. Oh, she might have told herself she was merely falling in with what everyone expected of her. But she had a niggling suspicion that there were plenty of selfish reasons for marrying him, too. She had been guilty, when he had dined with the family, of sneaking peeks at his handsome profile when she was sure nobody else was watching her. Letting her eyes linger on those full, red lips. Recalling the episode on the terrace. And experiencing a very strong wish to soothe the mark her teeth had put there. And when he had looked up from his plate, and their eyes had met, a thrill had shot right through her, rendering her breathless for several seconds.

She could not even summon up the will power to dislike him any more. Even his arrogant assertion that he was a catch now only seemed like a bald statement of the truth. He *could* have married anyone he wanted! Yet he had, as a gesture of friendship to Rick, made the truly noble sacrifice of marrying a girl he did not like one bit.

Seeing the downcast expression on her niece's face, Lady Callandar took a fortifying sip from her own glass.

'Well, I am sure it will not be so bad for you, my dear, as it evidently was for your mother. I am sure Viscount Mildenhall will be able to set your pulses racing when he kisses you.'

To hear her aunt speaking aloud of kissing Viscount Mildenhall, when that was exactly what she had been thinking about, made Imogen's face flood with heat.

'Ah!' cried her eagle-eyed aunt. 'So he had kissed you already, has he, the young rogue!'

'Y-yes, Aunt,' Imogen confessed. 'I am so sorry…'

'Well, never mind,' she said magnanimously. 'You

are to be married, after all, and I can see that the prospect of becoming more intimate with him is not repugnant to you. Which is a good start. I should think that the first few weeks of your marriage, at least, should prove most enjoyable.' She sighed, and a faraway look came into her eyes. 'Ah, what it is to be a young bride, married to an energetic, well-put-together young man like that! Although—' she gave herself a little shake '—you must not make the mistake of thinking, because of the amount of time he spends with you, and the level of intimacy you will share, that he may be doing anything so vulgar as falling in love with you.'

From the way her aunt's shoulders drooped, Imogen wondered whether the older woman was talking about her own experience of marriage. There were still traces of the handsome man her uncle had once been, beneath the layers of flab that years of self-indulgence had added to his frame. She could just imagine her aunt as a young bride, marrying with high hopes, then having them dashed by her uncle's selfish, tyrannical attitude towards her.

'We all know,' her aunt continued in a rallying tone, 'that Viscount Mildenhall has chosen you primarily because you are the sister of one of his closest friends. And because you are a healthy, energetic young woman who is likely to give him the heirs his father is so keen to see him produce. For those reasons, he is prepared to overlook your lack of dowry. Or so he told your uncle.'

Ah. No wonder Lord Callandar had looked so pleased. He had managed to get his troublesome niece off his hands without having to dip into his pockets to induce somebody to marry her.

She sighed. She had long since accepted she was nothing like her mother, who had been so beautiful that she inspired men to the heights of passion. Not, she shuddered, that she wanted to cause men to fight over her. Or kill one another for love of her. But it would be nice to think she might stir just a little bit of admiration in her groom's breast.

Her aunt, misinterpreting that shudder, was instantly full of sympathy. 'It is the main duty of a wife to provide her husband with sons. It is a compliment to you, my dear, that out of all the women he might have chosen, Viscount Mildenhall picked you.'

He did not pick her, so much as give in to Rick's pleading to find a home for poor little Midge, she thought, slumping down into her pillows.

'Oh, Imogen,' Lady Callandar sighed tearily, 'I know you are a very affectionate girl, but you must not look for that sort of love within marriage. Especially not from Viscount Mildenhall. From what I have observed of him since he came into the title, he takes after his mother, the Earl of Corfe's second wife. She was a cold, proud woman.' Her aunt grimaced. 'Though that match was arranged by his parents, so it was hardly surprising they barely spoke to one another once she had presented him with a son. No, what you must hope for is that, in time, you will come to an easy understanding which will lead to a lifelong friendship.'

Perhaps that might be possible. Once he had a chance to get to know her, he would see she was nothing like he had so far imagined! And once he stopped being so suspicious of her…

Lady Callandar reached out and stroked a stray curl from her forehead. 'Knowing you, the first time he strays you will experience agonizing jealousy. But on no account, my dear, must you create the kind of scene that will make your husband uncomfortable. No matter how many little affairs he may have, what you must remember is that you will always be his wife. His viscountess. It is equally important,' she ploughed on, in spite of Imogen's shocked gasp, 'that you do not indulge your craving for affection until you have presented your husband with an heir. Even your mother, silly creature that she was, managed to wait until she had given birth to a healthy boy.'

'It was not like that! She did not mean to have an affair with Lord Leybourne. It just happened!'

Lady Callandar pursed her lips. 'These things never *just happen*, Imogen.'

Imogen flung herself back against the pillows, a scowl on her face. Her aunt did not understand what it had been like for her mother; that was the trouble.

'It was madness, Imo,' Amanda had sighed, though her eyes had been alight with an emotion Imogen had not been able to decipher. 'We knew what we were doing was wrong, but, oh, we could not deny ourselves just a few snatched hours of happiness out of the wasteland Kit had made of my life.' She had sighed and plucked at the coverlet with her emaciated, yellowed hand. 'Not that your father cared one whit,' she had pouted. 'He thought it was a huge joke. He mocked William for being able to stomach touching me when I was pregnant. He taunted me with accounts of his current mistress. About her taut stomach and firm breasts. But William defended me.' She sighed wistfully. 'I remember Kit sitting at my dressing table, mopping at a cut over his eye with one of my handkerchiefs and laughing about the impressive physical prowess of the lover I had taken, and—' she had shuddered disgustedly '—saying he was quite looking forward to discovering whether William had managed to teach me any new tricks. He said that if I had learned to be a little more enterprising, then he might not find it such a chore to resume his marital duties once I had delivered his child. That I might look forward to receiving more of his attention—' The feverish confession had ended in a fit of coughing, as it so often did.

Imogen tried to shut out the image of her mother's wasted frame, but she could not silence her words. Not when they chimed so exactly with what her aunt was warning her marrying into the nobility would entail.

'I do concede,' her aunt admitted, 'that there were extenuating circumstances. I remember that the Earl of Leybourne was your mother's most ardent admirer, until Baron Framlingham came onto the scene. The woman he married was nowhere near so beautiful as your mother, and I suppose, when they were all thrown together by that Home Office business—'

'Yes!' Imogen sat up and grasped her aunt's hand. 'He told her that although he had tried to be a good husband, the feelings he had for his first love had never completely died. And she said the moment she saw him again, she was filled with regret for the choices she had made, and wished she could somehow wipe away all the years of misery she had suffered with Kit. They went outside into the garden, and she wept all over him, and he tried to comfort her, and...'

'I suppose she told you one thing led to another,' said her aunt dryly. 'But I have to inform you that nobody just falls into an affair. They choose it. For whatever reason. Boredom or revenge, or as in your mother's case,' she added wistfully, 'perhaps for comfort.' She visibly took herself in hand, before saying bracingly, 'Imogen I do hope you will take your mother's fate as a warning. You must not yearn for the unobtainable in your marriage. Strive instead to be content with what you have.'

On these words, her aunt left the room, leaving Imogen sickened at the prospect of enduring the kind of marriage her aunt had just outlined. Where she was expected to turn a blind eye to her husband's infidelity, as her aunt clearly had to whenever her uncle strayed, and count herself lucky anybody had deigned to marry her in the first place!

She was the very last person in the world who ought to become a viscountess!

Although, realistically, she supposed it was too much to hope that a man as attractive as Viscount Mildenhall would stay faithful to any one woman for very long. Especially one as plain as her. She sank back into her pillows and glared up at the canopy.

And her aunt, who she had always thought of as being the arbiter of etiquette, seemed to think there would be nothing wrong with her having adulterous affairs as some sort of…compensation! So long as she had got the main duty of being a wife over with first.

She sat up, blew out her candle with a vengeance and thumped her pillow before flinging herself back into it.

She supposed at least she was going into her loveless marriage with her eyes open. Whereas her poor mother had believed Kit loved her.

Her aunt seemed to think Viscount Mildenhall would restrict himself to her, until he had got her pregnant, too, whereas her father…

She rolled onto her side, drawing her legs up to her chest. Kit had never had any intention of so much as nodding towards the conventions of marriage. As soon as he had got his hands on the inheritance he had married Amanda to secure, he had gone out and celebrated in the wildest fashion imaginable. He had flaunted a succession of mistresses in public. And then, when Amanda did not immediately fall pregnant, set out to prove that the fault was not his. He had eventually brought home a baby boy that he had fathered on a Gypsy woman, informing Amanda that since she could not give him a son, she would have to see a bastard filling the empty crib in the nursery.

Kit had intended to humiliate her by forcing her to care for his illegitimate son. But he had overlooked the fact that Amanda adored babies. And that by this time, she had given up all hope of ever having any children of her own. He had told her so often she must be barren, that she had come to believe it.

'Imo,' she had sighed, her eyes filling up with tears, 'he was such a beautiful baby. With a shock of dark hair and your father's smile. I might not have been his real mother, but I felt just as though he was my firstborn. He was not responsible for his parents' actions. Poor, helpless little mite! It was cruel of Kit to bring him into our home and try to use him as a weapon. I never forgave him for that!'

Kit had been disappointed to see Amanda finding consolation in caring for the boy as if he was her own, and quickly tired of having a squalling brat in the house. So he began to torment her by threatening to send the boy back to his real mother. What had sealed little Stephen's fate, though, had been Grandpapa Herriard storming into

the house and demanding that Kit house his by-blow elsewhere. Amanda had, she told Imogen, gone up to the nursery and held the little boy in her arms, fearing it might be
the very last time she held any child she could call her own.
But her father's attempt to browbeat him into 'doing the
right thing' made Kit dig in his heels. For if there was one
thing Kit Hebden relished, it was behaving badly. Having
a Gypsy brat openly living in his house, forcing his wife
into what everyone interpreted as a humiliating position,
suited his warped sense of humour down to the ground.
And so Stephen had stayed.

And Society had been duly shocked.

Imogen frowned. Viscount Mildenhall had told her he
was no stranger to scandal, on account of his stepmother's actions, but he had not said he would ever actively
court it. On the contrary, he had not even wanted anyone
to know what had happened out on Lady Carteret's terrace. He also said he was willing to take her in hand,
to spare Rick's blushes for her future conduct. If he
had an affair—no, when he had an affair, she corrected
herself—he was the kind of man who would conduct
it with discretion. And if there were any by-blows, he
would certainly not bring them home and force her to
raise them!

Viscount Mildenhall might be a handsome charmer,
but he was *not* cast in the same mould as her father. In
his own fashion, he would probably attempt to be a good
sort of husband.

Anyway—she huffed, turning over—*if he wasn't, he
would have Rick to answer to!*

Imogen woke the next morning, feeling a sense of
hope rising unbidden within her. It was the culmination

of every girl's ambition to marry well. And in Society's eyes, she had succeeded.

Viscount Mildenhall was handsome and wealthy, and his kiss had been so potent she still felt a little thrill every time she thought of it. She had no reason to feel cheated. Persons of her class very rarely found love within marriage. Her aunt may have had hopes at one point, but now she seemed heartily thankful that Lord Callandar scarcely set foot in his own house. She had her own social circle and her own interests which kept her cheerfully occupied.

And very few endured such misery as Kit Hebden had put her mother through, either.

No, it was far better not to marry for that sort of love. For, after the fires of passion had burned out, her mother had warned her, all that was left were the ashes of cold despair.

She flung the covers aside and swung her legs out of the bed. There was no way of knowing what marriage with Viscount Mildenhall would bring her, but today she was going to cling to the hope that perhaps, given time, they might achieve that state of easy companionship she had observed her mother enjoying with Hugh Bredon.

And at least she had the satisfaction of knowing she was repaying all the kindness her aunt had shown her, by entering into a marriage of which she thoroughly approved.

Imogen smiled wryly to her reflection in the mirror as her maid fixed her bonnet in place. It had felt like a crime to hide her gorgeous gown under her coat, but the day was too chilly to drive to the church without one.

As she climbed into the carriage, it struck Imogen that there was another aspect to her wedding day that pleased her. Gathered in St George's chapel that morning would be representatives of all the families that had been torn apart by the murder of her father. Lords Framlingham, Leybourne and Narborough had once been friends, working together to solve a crime that was taking place in some high office.

Until the night Lord Narborough had found Lord Framlingham bleeding to death in his garden, with Lord Leybourne bending over him, a bloodied dagger in his hand.

Narborough had refused to believe his friend's protestations of innocence, and had given evidence against him that resulted in him being hanged for treason, as well as murder.

Shattering the bonds of friendship.

Yet today, their children would stand together in St George's chapel, each, she fervently hoped, demonstrating by their attendance that they were putting past enmities aside. The fact that a Wardale had already married a Carlow had been a good start.

Now she fervently hoped that a Wardale could look a Hebden in the eye in a spirit of forgiveness and reconciliation.

When the carriage drew up outside the chapel, Imogen, determined to look her best for the viscount, waited for the footman to let down the steps and hold out his arm to steady her, rather than jumping down carelessly, scarcely looking where she put her feet, as she usually did. She had no intention of beginning her marriage to a man who set such store by appearances by walking up the aisle with muddy shoes or a dripping flounce from landing in a puddle.

She waited patiently while her maid smoothed down

her skirts, adjusted the set of her bonnet and brushed a piece of fluff from the shoulder of her coat, while her uncle distanced himself from the feminine flutter by strolling up and down.

Pansy was just leaning back into the carriage for Imogen's bouquet, when a man who had been lounging against one of the pillars called out, 'Imo?'

Imogen looked up with a slight frown on her brow to see who was calling to her. Nobody called her Imo these days. She was either Miss Hebden, or Imogen or Midge. So the voice felt like a dark hand, reaching out to her from her very distant past. A past that she had hoped was going to be laid to rest today. And so her voice, when she replied, 'Yes?' quivered with trepidation.

The man stepped out of the shadows into the light, and Imogen gasped.

It was the first time she had seen a Gypsy up this close. But there was no mistaking his origins, with the flamboyance of his clothing, his long, black hair and the swarthy complexion set off by the gold hoop in one ear.

He came a step closer.

'For you,' he said, holding out a small packet tied up with string. The silver bangle he wore round his wrist glinted like a knife blade in the sunlight. 'A reminder.'

Though the gift and his words made him appear to be a well-wisher, something about his stance and the tone of his voice were vaguely menacing.

But even though her instinct was to draw back, she thought it would be unwise to offend a Gypsy, especially on her wedding day. The woman who had borne Stephen had tracked Amanda down after Kit died, and cursed her for robbing her of her son, swearing she would never see a son of her own reach adulthood. Amanda had only just had a miscarriage and then she promptly lost little Thomas to a fever. After that, Amanda had been convinced that if she had any more sons, they would die, too. The Gypsy woman's curse had haunted her for the rest of her life.

So Imogen steeled herself to reach out her hand and accept the man's gift.

But just before she could do so, her uncle, who had finally noticed what was going on, let out a bellow of rage.

'Get away from my niece, you filthy cur!' His walking cane made a swishing noise as he lashed out at the Gypsy's extended arm.

But the Gypsy's reactions were swift. The cane clattered down upon the flags without striking his arm.

Her uncle then rounded on her, growling, 'Who have you been tattling to, you stupid girl? The one thing, above all else, you should have kept quiet about…and now somebody is using it to make trouble.'

Imogen gazed at her uncle in stupefaction. Then turned her bewildered gaze on the stranger, who was regarding her uncle with a smile of what looked like grim satisfaction. Her heart began to pound in her chest. It was the most incredible coincidence that a Gypsy should turn up at her wedding, with a gift and an admonition to remember, after she had spent so much time the night before, lying in bed, thinking about her illegitimate Gypsy half brother.

She saw what her uncle meant. The man who stood before them, a mocking smile on his face, was a visible reminder of her family's deepest, darkest shame.

'Go on!' Her uncle blustered, waving his stick ineffectually at the Gypsy, who dodged each blow with ease. 'Be off with you!'

'Nothing to say, Imo?' The man rounded on her, his eyes burning with blatant hostility. 'Don't *you* want me to leave?'

Imogen's mouth opened, but no sound came out. She was so shocked, she did not know what to say. It seemed incredibly cruel of someone to have sent a Gypsy to her wedding, to remind everyone that she had once had a half brother with Romany blood in his veins.

Her uncle seized her by the arm and began to drag her across the portico, towards the door of the chapel.

'Come away,' he huffed. His face was red and shiny from unaccustomed exertion and thwarted rage. 'The impudent fellow won't dare to follow us in there!'

'You may have forgotten me, Imo,' the Gypsy snarled as her uncle dragged her away. 'But I, Stephen, have never forgotten you!'

From somewhere she managed to find the strength to tear herself from her uncle's grasp, and turn back. Surely, hardly anybody alive today could know the name of her Gypsy half brother.

'How could you know his name was Stephen?' she grated. 'Are you from his tribe? Is that how you know about me?'

The man who claimed to be Stephen smiled in a way that was totally without mirth. And she felt a jolt of recognition. She had seen that very smile in the mirror, not an hour since! It was the way she always smiled, when she recognized some absurdity. *A shock of dark hair...* she seemed to hear her mother saying '*...and his father's smile...*'

Everyone said how very like her father she was, too! She took another step towards him, her eyes searching his features, her breathing ragged. His lips were the same shape as hers. He had the same slant to his eyebrows, the same prominent cheekbones.

'Stephen?' she whispered, stretching her hands out towards him. 'Can it really be you?'

'Don't be so foolish, niece!' her uncle snapped. 'This is just some miscreant, out to make trouble for you. Come away, girl, before it is too late.'

But she could not tear her eyes from the Gypsy's face.

'Are you really my brother?' she demanded.

The Gypsy held her gaze boldly, proudly, unashamedly.

And then he nodded.

'Uncle,' she declared, whirling round to face him, 'I have not raised one single protest about any arrangement you and my aunt have made regarding this day. In fact, I have had no say in any of it! But I will stand firm in this matter. If he really is my brother, then I want him at my wedding!'

Snatches of Imogen's protests echoed all the way to the front of the church, where Viscount Mildenhall was standing waiting for her.

'…not raised one single protest…arrangement you and my aunt…will stand firm…'

The guests were turning in their seats, peering over the tops of the box pews, curious to see what all the commotion was about.

Something like a cold fist clutched hard inside the viscount's chest. Miss Hebden had told him she did not want to marry him, but he had not believed her. He had trampled on all her objections, then approached her uncle, having uttered dire warnings of what the consequences would be if she refused him.

Yet Rick had told him his sister was straight as a die. That she would always be honest.

Right from the first, she had said she was not interested in him. That very first night, when she had thrown her drink over him…

There had been a group of girls standing behind her, laughing behind their fans as she had tried to apologize for what she claimed was an accident.

He had not believed her then. He had bracketed her with all the other females who had attempted such encounters to gain his attention. Especially once he had learned she was Miss Hebden, daughter of a notorious rake and a shameless adulteress.

He cast his mind back to the stories Rick had told of her growing up and how difficult she was finding it to behave with the decorum expected of young ladies in Society. And replayed the scene in his mind with her as Midge, Rick's tomboyish little sister, chatting away to her companions, waving her hands about exuberantly… with her back to the door.

She had not, he realized with cold certainty, known he was there at all.

Though her so-called friends had.

They had set her up!

His head snapped round to where the Misses Veryan were sitting, craning their necks to see what was going on in the porch. Their faces were alight with the same malice they had exhibited that night.

And as for the terrace outside Lady Carteret's

ballroom… He almost groaned aloud. She had strenuously insisted she had only gone out onto that terrace for some fresh air. Now he fully understood why she had bitten him and punched him in the face. His behaviour had been unforgivable!

But she had looked so alluring in that silver gown, that wistful expression on her face…he almost doubled over as hurt pierced him through. She had claimed she had been thinking of some other man. If that was the truth, as he now accepted all her other protestations were the truth, then Midge's affections were engaged elsewhere! She had never intentionally pursued him, let alone wanted to marry him. That notion had sprung entirely from his own vanity.

The girl who had written all those loving letters to Rick had such a giving nature, she was bound to yield to her family's wishes. Yes, he could see it all now. She had tried valiantly to give up all hope of this other man, but he had seen the night he had dined in their home what it was costing her. Her sense of family duty had got her as far as the church door. But the thought of actually tying the knot with a man she had not hesitated to call a vile worm was just too much.

'Rick,' he grated, feeling as though something inside him was dying. 'Go and find out what she wants. And make sure she gets it.'

With a puzzled frown, Rick got to his feet and strode out of the chapel.

Funny, but when he had decided to marry Miss Hebden, he had thought she was the victor and he was her prize. Yet now it felt as though if Midge would not have him he would be losing something that would have enriched his life immeasurably.

At the chapel door, far from the quarrel quieting down, the voices grew even more agitated. Rick's reasoning tone mingled with Midge's cries of protest and her uncle's bombastic hectoring.

Finally, he could take it no longer.

Midge could not possibly hate him more than he hated himself for the way he had misjudged and maltreated her. If the only way he could make amends was to set her free, then he must do so.

As he stalked down the length of the aisle, the eyes of all the assembled guests followed his progress avidly. He reflected how he had once foolishly thought that marrying her would be the price he would have to pay for his ungentlemanly conduct on Lady Carteret's terrace. Now he knew better. The price he must pay for alienating Midge would be letting her go.

Chapter Six

'Midge, the fellow is an impostor!' Rick was saying. 'You know he is. My father left no stone unturned in his search for the little boy your mother wanted to adopt. He found the orphanage where your grandfather had tried to conceal him.' He took hold of her shoulders, forcing her to look into his face. 'And the records that proved he was killed in a great fire that destroyed a whole wing of the place.'

'But look at him!' Imogen protested. 'The records must have been wrong. Or your father...' A dreadful doubt shook her. 'He didn't want to have him in the house!' She gasped. 'Just like my grandfather!'

'Do not say one word against your grandfather,' her uncle weighed in. 'He was doing his best to put things right. Utter disgrace to foist the brat on your poor mother in the first place! Should never have been brought into the marital home!'

Rick shot him a look of annoyance. 'Begging your pardon, sir, but tearing a boy she thought of as her son away from her was not the best thing for my stepmother at all. Nearly broke her heart to lose the boy, wherever he might have come from. Mourned his loss to her dying day. Midge,' he sighed, 'for heaven's sake, my father may have had his faults, but he would not have broken his word. Amanda only agreed to marry him on condition he promised to search for that boy.'

But Imogen no longer shared Rick's faith in his father's notion of honour. He had not been unduly worried about leaving her penniless, when he had helped himself to the inheritance her mother had tried to bequeath her. With hindsight, she could see that he had only tolerated having her about, for Amanda's sake. She did not think he had ever quite managed to forget she was Kit Hebden's child too. And Stephen had not one single drop of Amanda's blood running through his veins. Would he really have welcomed Kit's bastard into his home and allowed him to be brought up alongside his own sons?

Catching a movement out of the corner of her eye, she turned and saw Stephen push himself off the pillar, against which he had been lounging, to stare at her as though he could not believe what he was hearing.

'Hugh Bredon was not lying, and the records were not wrong!' Lord Callandar shouted. 'He did manage to locate the foundling home where my father sent the boy. And there was no question the brat died in a fire. I saw the records myself.'

'Then who is he?' Imogen's bouquet swooshed through the air as she waved in the direction of the Gypsy. 'Why does he know so much about what every-one tried to hush up? Why does he look like me?'

'Stop talking such nonsense, girl! He looks nothing like you.'

'But his smile, Uncle! And the shape of his brows when he frowns. They are straight. Just like mine. Like my father's.'

'What is going on?'

At the sound of Viscount Mildenhall's calm authoritative voice, everyone involved in the altercation turned to where he was standing in the church doorway.

Imogen ran to him and grabbed hold of his forearms.

'Oh, please, Monty, help me! I have done everything you have asked of me, haven't I? Won't you let me have my way in just this one thing? It is our wedding. Yours and mine. Surely I may have just one guest of my own choosing? If you say he may come in, then nobody else has the right to refuse him. He can sit right at the back, if you like, right out of sight!'

He tensed as she specified that it was a 'he' they were all arguing about.

'Perhaps,' he said coldly, 'it would help if you were to explain exactly who *he* is you are so keen to attend our wedding despite your uncle's objections?'

'Stephen,' she said, stepping back and releasing his arms as though they burnt her. 'My brother.'

'Your *brother*?' It felt as though the sun had come out. 'I see no reason why your brother should not attend if he wishes. Why all this fuss?'

'Because he is not her brother, that's why!' bellowed her uncle. 'The impudent rogue who claims kinship with her is just some filthy Gypsy, trying to cause trouble!'

'It's true, Monty,' put in Rick, stepping forward. 'The Gypsy boy in question died years ago.'

'A Gypsy?' He was so relieved it was not the marriage itself she was objecting to he would have cheerfully given permission for a whole tribe of Gypsies to dance right down the aisle banging tambourines if that was what she wanted.

But before he could tell her so, she had lifted her chin, and said, 'Yes! My father took a Gypsy woman as a lover…'

Her uncle groaned and covered his face in his hands. She flung her shoulders back, her whole posture now screaming defiance as she continued, 'And she had his son. And my father brought him to live with us until my grandfather sent him away while my mother was too ill to know what was happening. And his name is Stephen, and he brought me a gift!' She waved her bouquet towards one of the pillars where he had noticed a swarthy individual lurking before. But there was no one there now.

'Oh!' she shrieked, darting to the edge of the portico. 'He has gone! I must find him!'

Her uncle, surprisingly swift for such a portly man, darted after her, grabbed her arm and pulled her back as she would have run down the steps.

'Oh, no, you don't! We have a church full of guests waiting!'

Viscount Mildenhall strode across to the top of the steps, where she was still struggling with her uncle. 'Midge,' he said firmly. 'Your uncle is right.' For a second, a look of utter loathing blazed across her face. He gritted his teeth and went on, 'You cannot go running all over town, today of all days. Let Rick find him for you. Captain Bredon!' he barked.

To his relief, years of military discipline had Rick snapping instantly to attention. 'Sir!'

'Find out where the fellow went, and see if you can make some sense out of all this.'

'Right away, sir!'

Imogen's eyes widened as Rick ran obediently down the steps, crossed the street and approached a group of people who had been avidly watching the altercation on the church steps. One of them raised his arm and pointed. Rick promptly trotted off in that direction, and was soon lost to sight.

'Rick will get to the bottom of this,' he vowed. 'You know you can trust him.'

He saw the fight go out of her.

'Y-yes,' she said in a muted voice, hanging her head. Viscount Mildenhall looked pointedly at where her uncle's hand still held her arm in a vice-like grip and Lord Callandar finally released her, but she just stood there, looking so lost and alone that the viscount could not help himself. He drew her into his arms and held her close, rubbing his hands up and down her back. After an initial start of surprise, she leaned into him. He felt a flare of triumph at the way she was drawing comfort from him, even if it was only because nobody else was offering it.

Her uncle made a disparaging noise at the back of his throat and stalked off towards a knot of people who'd had the temerity to creep up the steps at the far end of the portico.

'Better now?' said Viscount Mildenhall presently, slackening his hold.

She nodded, stepping back and glancing around her guiltily, as though just becoming aware of their breach of etiquette.

Until her eyes snagged on the pillar where the man who claimed to be her brother had been standing. And gasped.

Lying on the ground was a small brown-paper packet.

She swooped on it like a hawk to the prey.

'Imogen! Put that down this instant!' her uncle bellowed.

She rounded on him, cheeks flushed, the gift clasped between both her hands as though she would fight anyone who attempted to take it from her. Then, without taking her eyes off her uncle, she began to sidle towards Viscount Mildenhall as though seeking sanctuary.

Viscount Mildenhall's heart missed a beat. There was a damp patch on her gown where she had knelt on the flags to pick up the packet she was convinced came from her brother. Her glove had a green smear of moss on it, and petals from her bouquet were scattered all over the flagstones. Her bonnet had been knocked askew in the tussle with her uncle and her curls were falling into her eyes.

Now she looked like Midge! The girl who was more at home climbing trees after birds nests than flitting about drawing rooms. Midge, who had written such amazingly warm and witty letters to Rick, though he was not even her real brother. Who had cast her mantle of goodwill over him, too, congratulating him on his promotions, commiserating with him on his injuries and convincing him that somewhere out there, away from the hellish brutality of the battlefields that comprised his life, warmth and decency still existed.

He did not think he had ever seen a woman look more appealing. He felt a strong rush of affection for the impulsive, honest, direct woman he was about to take to wife.

Swiftly followed by a vision of spending a lifetime pulling her out of the scrapes her impulsive nature was bound to catapult her into.

'I'd better take that,' he said firmly, stepping in between her and her uncle. He placed his hands over hers, and lowered his voice, so that only she could hear him. 'I will keep it safe for you. No need to provoke your uncle any further.'

She looked deep into his eyes, and though he could see a brief struggle taking place there, eventually she relented, relaxing her hold on the package and letting him take it from her.

'We must have a long talk about all of this, later,' he continued, slipping the package into an inside pocket, 'and decide what is to be done. But for now...' He held out his arm, and jerked his head in the direction of the church.

'I...' She straightened up, pushed her hair off her face and gripped her battered bouquet with renewed resolve. 'I...' She looked over her shoulder one more time, in the direction the Gypsy and then Rick had gone, and he saw a brief look of anguish flash across her face.

But then she took his arm. She did not merely lay her hand upon it, but linked her own arm through it, as though she needed something solid to cling to as he steered her away from her uncle, who had begun to harangue the crowd. He could feel tremors running through her whole body, but she kept her head held high even when the buzz of conversation within the church hushed into an expectant silence the moment they stepped over the threshold.

He bit back an oath. Everyone was looking at them as though he owed them an account of what had just taken place in the portico. Well, he was certainly not going to dither about in the doorway, answering a lot of questions about a business that was nobody's concern but Midge's! The best thing to do would be to get on with the ceremony as though nothing untoward had occurred.

Squaring his shoulders, he marched briskly down the aisle. So briskly in fact, that Midge had almost to trot to keep up with him.

Then he barked, 'You may commence!' to the rather startled clergyman.

Shocked gasps rippled through the congregation, which doubled when Lord Callandar came striding down the aisle on his own and took up his position behind the bridal couple, audibly muttering imprecations.

'Are you sure you wish to proceed?' the minister asked Midge, pointedly ignoring Viscount Mildenhall.

Her cheeks went pink, but her voice was firm as she declared, 'I am!' The minister looked at the way she was clinging to Viscount Mildenhall's arm, appeared satisfied, and after clearing his throat loudly, opened his prayer book and intoned the opening words.

All went well until he asked who was giving the woman away. Lord Callandar prized Midge's fingers from Monty's arm and practically flung her hand into Monty's extended palm. Then strode away, still muttering under his breath to take his place beside his own wife, who had such a frozen expression on her face she might have been modelling to be a waxwork dummy.

And from somewhere behind him Viscount Mildenhall heard a sound a bit like muffled coughing. A grin began to tug at his lips. It sounded suspiciously like that ne'er-do-well Hal Carlow trying desperately not to fall about laughing.

His stance eased. He would not mind letting just Hal know what had sparked off the whole episode. He didn't think Midge would object, since Hal was a close friend of her brother, too. Actually, he reflected, she had not seemed to care if the world knew her brother was a Gypsy. She would have had him in the church, and probably introduced him to all and sundry, had he not slunk off into whatever back alley he had crawled from.

Lord, he grinned, that would have set the cat among the pigeons!

As he turned to leave the church—vows made— with Midge still clinging to his side like a limpet, he made a point of looking Hal straight in the eye. The scoundrel was still holding a large handkerchief to his face, and his eyes were watering. The only thing the irrepressible joker would have found more entertaining would have been for the argument in the porch to erupt into a full-blown brawl which spilled into the church. For a moment, his mind filled with a vision of Midge setting about all and sundry with her bouquet, raining petals and broken foliage all over the nave. With a completely straight face, Viscount Mildenhall lowered one eyelid in a surreptitious wink.

There was a decided spring to his step as he led Midge

out into the sunshine, towards the carriage that waited to take them back to Mount Street. He felt more like himself than he had since setting foot back in England.

London Society was foreign territory to him; that was the trouble.

Until his older brother had died, he had existed almost exclusively in what was very much a man's world. First school, then army barracks and the officer's mess, where he had earned the respect of his subordinates and made friends where he felt some connection.

He had not wanted to leave the Army any more than his father had wanted to see him step into his brother's shoes. He had left Shevington as much to escape the feeling he would never measure up to the earl's favoured firstborn, as to appear to be obeying his edict to find a wife.

But the husband hunters had come out in droves the moment he had arrived in town, anyway. He had been appalled by all the posturing and simpering, the sly yet cutthroat competition between girls who pretended to be friends with each other.

Nothing he did ever managed to shake them off. The more obnoxious he made himself, the more obsequious everyone became.

Except Midge. She had detested that fop, the version of Viscount Mildenhall he had created, almost as much as he did.

Well, everyone would call her Viscountess Mildenhall from now on, but he could not see the acquisition of a title changing her one little bit. Just as, he suddenly saw, nothing had ever managed to dent Hal Carlow's sense of the ridiculous, not even his recent promotion to major.

Just because he had suddenly acquired a title, it did

not mean he had to strive to be something he was not. Today she had called him Monty. No, she called Monty back to life. He had barked out orders, Rick had snapped to attention, and he and Hal had experienced a moment of perfect camaraderie.

Gaining a title was only like getting a promotion of sorts. He was the same man inside that he had always been.

It felt as though a weight rolled off his shoulders as he made the decision to take a leaf out of Midge's book. He was going to stay true to himself, and to hell with everyone else's expectations!

Thank God he had run into Rick Bredon! And that he had, against all the odds, managed to get Midge to the altar.

It was only as he handed her into his carriage and he noted the dejected slump to her shoulders, that the massive discrepancy between their attitudes towards this marriage hit him all over again.

'This has not been the wedding day you must have wanted,' he acknowledged, climbing in and sitting next to her. 'But it can only get better from here on in, I promise.'

She had not wanted to marry him; he accepted that now. She had gone through with what she saw as her duty to her family. And she had done so with her head held high.

Damn, but he was going to make sure she never regretted marrying him! And he was going to start by wiping all thought of that other man right out of her head. He took her chin in his hand, put his arm round her shoulder, and declared, 'I am going to kiss you now. And this time, you will not slap my face. Or bite me.

Unless,' he mused, 'it is like this.' And he sucked her lower lip into his mouth and nibbled at it.

She gave a shocked gasp, giving him the opportunity to thrust his tongue into her mouth.

She did not struggle. On the contrary, after only a brief moment of tension, she melted under his determined seduction like butter on a summer's day.

He knew he had not imagined her response to his kisses out on Lady Carteret's terrace! If he had not been in such a foul mood, if he had not insulted her...

He groaned, and tugged her onto his lap. There was a loud ripping noise. He glanced down to see that his boot was still firmly planted on a portion of material that had come away from the hem of her gown. He tensed.

Most women, he knew, would have berated him for his clumsiness. Midge only sighed as she assessed the damage, before tilting her face towards him again.

'I will buy you another,' he vowed swiftly, taking ruthless advantage of the last interlude of privacy they were likely to get before nightfall.

Midge sank down onto the chair before the dressing table and stared in shock at her reflection. No wonder Monty had suggested she ought to go upstairs and freshen up before greeting their guests. She looked the complete antithesis of what a Society bride should be. Her hair was all over the place, her gloves were beyond redemption, and she was going to have to take off the beautiful dress her aunt had somehow managed to conjure up for this day. As for her bouquet: it was no more than a memory. It had already been coming apart before it got crushed between them as he had pulled her onto his lap. And when he had lifted her out of the carriage

and set her on her feet, she had been too stunned from
those few minutes of untrammelled passion to do more
than blink up at him as the broken stems and crushed
blooms rained down to the pavement.

Pansy had taken one look at her and run straight to
the pile of trunks at the foot of her bed, bless her.

'It was not all my fault,' she began to explain, but
Pansy was too busy pulling out dresses to determine
which was the least creased, to pay attention.

The maid probably would not believe that a man
as fastidious about his own appearance would have so
casually reduced her to this state anyway, not when she
had come home with her things in like condition so
many times before.

Though he had looked far less flamboyant than usual,
today, now she came to think of it. Even more soberly
dressed than he had been on the night they had met at
the theatre.

Pansy, having made her selection, bustled up to her
and unbuttoned the back of her gown, while Midge
pulled off her soiled gloves.

Changing into a clean gown was the least of her wor-
ries. Once Pansy had made her look respectable again,
she was going to have to go downstairs and face all
those guests, having just turned what should have been
a solemn and sacred occasion into something resembling
a farce.

She disappeared under layers of satin and lace
as Pansy pulled the ruined gown over her head, and
emerged with scarlet cheeks. When she thought of the
way Viscount Mildenhall had practically frog-marched
her down the aisle!

Though, to give him credit, he had hung on to his

temper until then. In fact, he had been surprisingly sympathetic to her, all things considered. He had not automatically sided with her uncle over the question of Stephen. He had even sent Rick to investigate. And he had promised they would discuss it all later.

Once the wedding breakfast was over.

Her stomach did a little somersault at the prospect of being alone with him again. The episode in the coach had been such a staggering surprise. She had never experienced anything like it!

Except—she frowned as Pansy stood her up to lace her into her fresh gown—for a few fleeting moments during their tussle on Lady Carteret's terrace.

As Pansy pushed her down onto the stool again and set about her rioting curls with a hairbrush, she wondered if he had been attempting to...not punish her. Discipline her, perhaps? He had given her some kind of warning about her behaviour before he had begun to ravish her mouth, but for the life of her she could not remember exactly what he had said.

Though he had definitely been trying to punish and humiliate her at Lady Carteret's. It was only some perversity in her nature that had made her revel in such rough treatment.

In far less time than Midge would have liked, Pansy was pushing her out of her bedroom. She dawdled down the stairs and paused on the threshold of the ballroom, where the guests were already milling about.

Bedworth took a breath, as though to announce her. She grabbed his arm, saying, 'Oh, please don't!' Everyone would turn and stare at her again, and she would have to walk in alone, when she knew she ought to have been there, at her husband's side, to receive them correctly when they had first arrived.

Her uncle was pacing up and down the end of the room where the tables were laid out, his expression thunderous as he glanced down at the pocket watch he held in his hand.

Frantically, she searched the room for a friendly face.

She saw Nick by the fireplace, talking to Lord Keddinton. As she had been leaving the church earlier, Lord Keddinton had managed to express, with one supercilious lift of an eyebrow, that he had expected nothing else from such a hoyden. It was just as well she had never got round to asking him to help her find employment. She would always have reflected badly upon his judgement of character.

Though she could not blame Nick for making the most of the opportunity to approach the great man. Everyone knew the vast extent of Lord Keddinton's influence. And Nick had no chance of ever securing a more powerful patron.

No, she would keep well away from them both for now.

The Veryan girls were standing in a corner, heads together, looking very pleased with themselves. They were probably discussing the way she had managed to make even her triumph in snaring the most eligible bachelor in town into a spectacle that would be gossiped and sniggered about for days.

There was no sign of Viscount Stanegate or his wife, she noted with disappointment. She had particularly wanted to speak to William Wardale's daughter. She had meant to make a point of smiling at her during the ceremony, but of course she had been in no fit state to smile about anything by the time Monty dragged her down the aisle.

At last, her eyes came to rest on Rick, who was standing talking to Lady Verity's other brother, Hal Carlow, and her heart gave a little lurch. The one person, above all others, she had wished to attend her wedding ceremony had not been there!

'Rick,' she said, the other occupants of the room fading into insignificance.

He had been deep in conversation with Major Carlow, but at the sound of his name on her lips he raised his head and came striding towards her, his face creased with concern.

'I am sorry, Midge,' he said, taking both her hands in his. 'The fellow disappeared completely. Crawled back under whatever stone he had been hiding under, I expect.'

'Rick! How can you be so unkind? If that man is Stephen…'

'Ah, yes, *if*,' he said sharply. 'Look, Midge, don't you think it more likely that somebody just wanted to spoil your wedding day? And paid some passing stranger to pose as…well…Stephen Hebden? You snatching Monty out from under them all will have put quite a few noses out of joint, I daresay…'

Midge's mind flew back to the malicious smiles upon the faces of the Veryan girls. And the way they had always managed to make her look ridiculous. And she wondered if Rick could be right.

'I thought…' She shook her head. 'He knew so many things…I couldn't see how he could have known them if he wasn't…'

But Major Carlow, who had sauntered over, was look-ing at her with an expression it was hard to fathom.

'Did I hear a'right? It was Stephen Hebden trying to gain entry to the church just now?'

'Yes,' said Midge, at exactly the same moment Rick said, 'No! Fellow claiming to be Stephen Hebden. But Stephen died years ago—'

'Only wish to God he had!' rapped Major Carlow. Then, pulling himself up short, 'Beg pardon, my lady, but I have had some experience of his tactics, and I think it only fair to warn you…' He petered out, just a second before she became aware Monty had joined them in the doorway.

'Having to beg my lady's pardon already, Hal? And you not five minutes in the house, you unmitigated scoundrel!'

Major Carlow smiled, but not with the same insou-ciance she had seen in him earlier.

The three men then indulged in a few moments of jovially insulting one another, the way her three step-brothers had used to do. As she listened, she felt Monty's arm slide round her waist. She knew she ought to have made some protest, but she couldn't summon the will power to pretend she was not downright glad of his physical support. She had never felt so plain and gauche as she did standing there in the first gown to come out of her trunk, in the shadow of two officers in dress uniform and the most handsome man in the world.

She wondered, with a little pang of hurt, if this was why Viscount Mildenhall had dressed so plainly today. Because he did not want to outshine his fubsy little bride.

It was kind of him, if so. For she was sure he would

much rather be wearing something that showed off his physique, like the major's snugly fitting uniform.

As though Monty had sensed she was feeling left out, he squeezed her waist a little more firmly, before saying, 'Come, then. Let us put on our Society faces, and go and greet our other guests properly.'

'Before we do,' she said, 'may I ask, that is,' she could feel her cheeks going red as she looked up into Major Carlow's face. 'I notice that Viscount Stanegate and his wife have not arrived. I do hope…'

'Nell's not feeling quite the thing, so Marcus took her home, thank God,' he said. 'Hate to think how upset she would have been had she heard that Gypsy troublemaker was hanging about the church.'

Midge blinked up at him in surprise, but before she could ask exactly what he had meant by that cryptic statement, Monty was dragging her away.

'No more of that now, please,' he murmured into her ear as he steered her towards the first knot of wedding guests. 'I will find out what he meant, discreetly, and we can discuss it later. For now, we have a job to do.'

He startled her by dropping a swift kiss on her cheek. 'Pretending to be respectable pillars of Society.'

She felt both the words and the deed like a blow, an unnecessary reminder that he thought her very far from respectable!

Later, she vowed, when he discussed all the items on his agenda, she was going to bring up the matter of his erroneous opinion of her!

He seemed unaware of her simmering resentment as he guided her through the room, charming one group of guests after another. He kept his arm round her waist, holding her close to his side as though he could not bear to be parted from her by so much as an inch!

But by the time they sat down to dine, the whole atmosphere had lightened considerably. The banquet her aunt had arranged was truly magnificent, the waiting staff smoothly efficient, and conversation around the table was soon flowing as freely as the copious quantities of champagne her uncle had supplied.

It could not have gone off better.

Even Midge managed not to knock anything over or spill anything down her gown.

When it was time to leave, her aunt, who was looking much less fraught after the amount of champagne she had imbibed, came to bid her farewell.

'Well, I must say, you have married a man with great presence of mind. The way he handled our guests, as though he saw nothing untoward in that Disgraceful Scene outside the church…'

She reached out and patted Midge on the cheek. 'And, after all, you will be a countess one day. Then—' she drew herself up to her full height '—they will all have to keep their tongues between their teeth!'

Midge gathered that her aunt must have spent a great portion of the afternoon fielding spiteful comments about her conduct, but rather than looking harassed, Lady Callandar was positively vibrating with triumph.

'Next time you make an exhibition of yourself,' she said, with an almost mischievous twinkle in her eye, 'and knowing you as I do, I am certain there *will* be a next time, you would do well to follow your husband's lead and brazen it out. Act as though you have nothing to be ashamed of. Never apologize.'

And then, to Midge's complete astonishment, her aunt

leaned forward and kissed her on the cheek. In spite of the fact that anybody might have seen her!

'I shall look forward to calling upon you when you return to town,' she finished, with a warm smile.

Imogen raised her hand to her face, stunned by her aunt's public demonstration of affection and approval. If only she could have unbent towards her sooner! The months living in Mount Street would not have been anything like as difficult.

Monty had been standing a few feet away, in what looked like deep conversation with Rick and Major Carlow. But the moment her aunt left her, he excused himself and came straight over.

'Is anything amiss?'

He could tell that Lady Callandar had said something that had rocked Midge to the core. Without caring about the impropriety of it, he put his arms round her and hugged her hard.

He could scarcely credit how fiercely protective he had grown towards her, in such a short space of time. When he had seen her hovering in the doorway earlier, her eyes wide with apprehension, he had wanted to simply whisk her away to somewhere where nobody would ever hurt her again. It had hurt when those misty grey eyes had swept straight past him, to come to rest on the form of her beloved stepbrother. But it made no difference to his resolve to protect her. Show them all that he did not disapprove of what she had done or the way she was. So he had crossed the room. Gone to stand beside her. Faced down the starchy matrons who had looked down their noses at her, and the girls who had sniggered at her. She had not objected to him putting his arm round her waist, so he had kept it there. At one point, she so far forgot herself as to lean her head on his shoulder for a few seconds. Yes, he was really pleased with the progress he had made with his reluctant bride.

'My aunt,' she said with an ironic twist to her mouth, 'has just informed me that now I am *your* wife, I can get away with all manner of social crimes, providing I never apologize for them.'

Monty frowned. That comment was tactless in the extreme. It was as though her aunt expected Midge to be a failure. What a dreadful way to send her into her married life!

Hoping to put a positive slant on things, he said ruefully, 'Whatever you do, now that you have a title, certain people will always toady to you, that is true.'

Midge glanced up at the cynical expression on his face, her heart sinking. He might have brazened things out, as her aunt put it, for the benefit of the wedding guests, but deep down, he knew she was destined to be a social failure. All the pleasure she had felt at finally winning her aunt round dissipated at the realization she still had a long way to go to earn her husband's respect.

Chapter Seven

Pansy put the finishing touches to Imogen's night attire, helped her up into the enormous bed, and withdrew from the room with a sentimental sigh.

Imogen slumped back against the pillows, chewing on her thumbnail.

She did not know what to make of her husband anymore. She had got so used to thinking he was a pompous ass. But there had been moments today when she had felt positively grateful to him. Just for being there!

Any minute now, though, she sighed, he would be walking through the door that connected her room to his, so they could have that 'long talk' he had threatened her with. When they would 'decide what was to be done.' And she had a nasty suspicion that, since nobody else would be watching, he would revert to his true colours.

She heard a floorboard creak and her eyes flew to the connecting door.

More than half expecting to receive a scolding, she

sat up straight, nervously pushing her hair off her fore-head with trembling fingers.

Just about everything she'd done since coming to London had resulted in a scold. She glanced round at the opulence of the room he had assigned to her, as his viscountess, and felt a little pang of yearning for the cosy little room up under the eaves of the Brambles. Nobody had ever gone up there to replay the catalogue of errors she had committed during the preceding day.

She lifted her chin, tamping down on the deceitful feeling of nostalgia. The reason Hugh had never scolded her been because he had not cared, one way or the other, what she did, so long as nothing interrupted his studies. Whereas her aunt's constant sniping stemmed from her concern as to what other people would make of her. And as for her husband…

Her breath hitched in her throat as the door opened and Monty, clad in a magnificent green silk brocade dressing gown, entered the room.

He was bound to have something to say about her conduct. It was only natural for him to want his wife to maintain certain standards in public.

She searched his handsome face anxiously. There was an intent expression in his eyes as he advanced towards the bed, but he did not look cross.

She smiled at him, relieved that he really did appear willing to discuss the incident in the portico with an open mind.

He sat on the edge of the bed and took her hand. Raised it to his lips and kissed it. Smiled back at her…

And it was only then she noticed the absence of what she had hoped they were going to discuss.

'Where is it?'

'Where is what?'

'The gift Stephen brought me. You said you would take care of it for me.'

There was a horrible sinking feeling in her stomach. Had he just said whatever he had felt would make her behave, without having any intention of truly listening to her opinions? She remembered the ruthless way he had bullied her into marrying him, and snatched her hand out of his.

'You have not…you have not disposed of it, have you?'

He shot to his feet, staggered at how much she could hurt him by harbouring such a suspicion!

He turned on his heel and stalked back into his room, flinging open the doors of his wardrobe to find the jacket that he had been wearing earlier. The packet must still be in the inside pocket. Damn that rogue of a brother of hers!

Damn Viscount Mildenhall too. He shut his eyes and leaned his forehead against the cool wood of the wardrobe door. What a coxcomb he was, to assume his new bride, a girl he had coerced into marriage, would now be so overwhelmed by the honour he had bestowed on her that she would by lying in bed, panting for him to come to her.

He sure as hell would not have taken getting a girl into his bed for granted when he had been merely Lieutenant Vernon Claremont. Oh, he had learned that his looks made him attractive to the fair sex. He had wooed and won his fair share.

But he had not wooed Midge.

Just assumed…he grimaced. 'Put yourself in her

shoes,' he growled to himself, shaking his head. If he had just endured the day she'd had, would he be feeling amorous?

No wonder she accused him of being arrogant.

Well, if he had been, marriage to her would soon cure him of that! She had quite a knack of puncturing the over-inflated opinion of himself he had acquired as a result of all the toadying that went on in London Society.

He whirled round on hearing the rustle of silk behind him. Midge stood in the doorway, her hands clasped at her waist, her grey eyes frosty.

Dear God, he hoped she had not heard him talking to himself!

'I apologize,' she said stiffly. 'I did not mean to imply that you are not completely trustworthy. You said you would take care of it, and I am sure you would not lie to me.'

The words might have been humble, but she had spoken them as though she was delivering a challenge.

She more than half expected him to lie to her, he realized. She really did think he was a… What was it she had called him? Oh, yes, a vile worm.

His lips pulled tight into a flat line, he turned his back on her and resumed the search of his jacket pockets.

'You must forgive me for forgetting all about this,' he said sarcastically, as his fingers closed round the elusive article. 'It is just that discussing your brother was the last thing I expected to be doing on my wedding night.'

Imogen's eyes snagged on the wedge of flesh that became exposed when his dressing gown gaped as he threw her brother's wedding gift to her. He was not wearing a nightshirt!

Her eyes swept the entire length of him, ending in a fascinated perusal of his bare calves and toes. She gulped. He did not appear to be wearing anything at all under that dressing gown.

She remembered the look on his face as he had approached her bed, the gleam in his eyes when she had smiled. The eager way he had grasped her hand.

And his bitter words as he riffled through his wardrobe at her behest.

'I do beg your pardon,' she said, hanging her head. She had been so busy thinking of things to resent about him, she had entirely forgotten what a poor bargain he was getting out of this marriage. That there was only one thing he considered her fit for.

'I c-could leave opening this until morning.' He had not attempted to deceive her, she could see that now. It was just that her concerns seemed trivial to him. Because she was a mere female. And he was a typically thoughtless, selfish male.

She returned to her room and laid the packet on her bedside table.

'Oh, no you don't,' he growled, stalking into the room after her. 'We will get this business out of the way, since it is so very much on your mind. I intend to have your undivided attention when I make love to you for the first time.'

His lips twisted into a sardonic smile as she snatched the packet up and went to sit on the ottoman at the foot of the bed. She would have permitted him to assert his marital rights over her, dutifully, but he would have to be blind not to see that her fingers were itching to untie the knot on that damned parcel, rather than the belt of his dressing gown.

He joined her on the ottoman, wondering if any other bridegroom had ever found himself coming so low down on the list of his bride's priorities on his wedding night.

She looked up at him warily when he sat down, a question in her eyes.

'Go on.' He sighed. 'Let us see what all the fuss was about.'

With a smile of relief, she tore open the wrapping paper.

Then went white.

He forgot all about his own fit of pique when he followed her appalled gaze and saw, lying in her lap, a replica of a hangman's noose. Fashioned from what looked like a lot of silk scarves plaited together.

'Dear God! What is the meaning of this? Is it some kind of threat?'

'Not a threat, no,' she said in a thin, reedy voice. 'He said, it was to remind me. I stupidly thought...' She raised one trembling hand to her brow to push back a hank of hair that had flopped into her eyes.

'You see, on the way to church, I had such high hopes...'

His heart leapt at her words. Had she, too, seen that they could forge something good together?

'...the children of all three families brought together, to celebrate a new start...the Carlows were there, and William Wardale's daughter, and me, Kit Hebden's daughter. And then *he* showed up too, and I hoped finally, we would all be able to move out of the shadow of what our parents did...'

Her fingers hovered over the glistening silken noose coiled in her lap, as though not quite daring to touch it. Lest it develop fangs and strike out at her like a venomous snake.

'Midge.' He took her chin in his hand and turned her face towards him. 'You are making no sense.' The only thing he knew for certain was that, once again, her mind was far from him.

She shivered, and the vague, troubled look crystallized into something like ice.

Her lips pressed firmly together, she pushed the torn edges of the packaging back into place, to conceal the silken rope. Then she got up, walked to the fireplace, and threw it into the flames.

'Rick was right all along,' she said bitterly. 'Someone did want to ruin my day. Only it was not some rival for your title.' She flicked angry eyes over him. 'But my own brother. Half brother,' she corrected herself, seizing the poker and holding down the package as the heat began to make the paper uncurl. 'The announcement was only in the *Gazette* yesterday, so he must have known where I was all along. And never once did he come forward. All those years, we thought he was dead. Mourned him. While he was out there, watching us, hating us, waiting for some chance to strike back at us…'

'Midge, you cannot possible deduce all that from a few silk scarves fashioned into a hangman's noose—'

'Oh, but I can!' She turned round to look at him. 'You don't understand. You don't know…'

She swayed on her feet. The poker fell into the hearth with a clatter. Monty swept her into his arms, drew her away from the fire and settled her on the edge of the bed.

'Then tell me,' he murmured.

She wrapped her own arms about her waist. 'How much do you already know?'

'I suppose, only what is generally known. The tittle-tattle about your mother's lover killing your father. And him being subsequently hanged for the murder. But until today I had never heard of the existence of…an illegitimate Gypsy boy. Nor do I understand why those three families in particular, gathering together, could have much significance.'

She nodded her head, just once, as though making up her mind about something.

'My father and Lord Leybourne and Lord Narborough were working together on some kind of state secret. My mother did not know exactly what. Except that one night, my father told her he knew who the spy was, and he was going to meet the other two and tell them how he had worked it out. Lord Narborough found Leybourne later, crouching over my father's body, with a dagger in his hand. And eventually Leybourne was hanged for murder and treason. They used a silken rope, since he was a peer of the realm.' She jerked her head towards the direction of the fireplace, without taking her eyes off her hands, which were now clasped together in her lap.

'The shock made my mother very ill. Grandpapa Herriard took the opportunity to get rid of Stephen, when he moved us all back to Mount Street. But Stephen's mother came looking for him. It seems my father had promised her he would raise her son like a little lord. She blamed my mother for the broken promise—and put a curse on her.'

Viscount Mildenhall could not help the derisive snort that emanated from his mouth.

Midge looked up at him coldly. 'It might sound like a joke to you, sir, but the words were so accurate they haunted my mother to the end of her life. The Gypsy woman said that because she had stolen her son, she would never see a single one of hers live to adulthood. My mother had just had a miscarriage. And not long after that, my younger brother, my only real, full brother, took ill and died too.'

'It was probably just a coincidence—'

'You have not heard the rest,' she broke in. 'After cursing my mother, she went to Wardale's execution, screamed curses at all three families involved in the loss of her son and her lover, and then hanged herself too. With a silk scarf. That—' She did glance at the fireplace then, appearing momentarily distracted from her narrative by the sight of the purple and blue flames licking along the charred edges of the symbolic noose. She shuddered again, saying, 'It is a reminder that my family, along with the Wardales and the Carlows, destroyed his mother. And that her curse will keep on eating us all alive until her form of justice has been satisfied.'

She turned and buried her face against his shoulder.

'I am sorry I seemed to scoff at the revelation of a Gypsy curse,' he said, hugging her tight. 'And I am not sure I believe in such things now. But one thing I do believe, and that is that man holds a grudge against you all. Hal Carlow warned me that he has already tried to cause trouble for his family, and the Wardales. Well, tomorrow,' he said, looking down into her troubled face, and smoothing the hair from her brow, 'I am taking you down to Shevington.' He had never thought of the place as a refuge before, but it could be for her. From the malicious gossip that painted her as something far different from her true nature, for one thing. And, 'The devil will not be able to get at you there.'

Though the thought that the Gypsy might do her some actual, physical harm alarmed him, there was a tiny part of him that welcomed having the opportunity to demonstrate his ability to protect her. So that she would come to rely on him.

'I don't suppose he will ever come near me again.' Her shoulders slumped. 'He only came to the wedding today to sow discord. The first time members of all three families have gathered together for a generation, and he ruined any chance there might have been for some kind of…reconciliation between us all.'

He wanted to tell her to forget the Gypsy. To put it all behind her. But he had seen her face when she thought she had regained a brother she had long thought dead. To have found him, only to discover he had only revealed himself in order to declare his enmity, was not something she would get over in a hurry.

'I won't *let* him come near you again,' he swore. 'The man is a menace!'

He thought there was a flare of something mutinous in her eyes, before she subsided and said in a subdued tone, 'I am sorry. I have caused you nothing but trouble today.'

'Nonsense!' he rapped. Nothing that had happened today had been her fault, yet here she was, sitting with drooping shoulders, apologizing to him! When he should be the one making her feel better. She had been pushed into a marriage she had not really wanted, to a man she had taken in dislike, only to please her family…and how had her family repaid her loyalty? Her uncle had been angry, her aunt distant, one of her stepbrothers had blatantly made use of the wedding breakfast to suck up to Lord Keddinton, and a half brother had emerged from his hiding place to openly declare his hatred.

'You cannot choose your family, more's the pity,' he said, dropping a kiss on to the top of her head. 'Just wait till you meet mine! Anyway, let us not talk about anyone else tonight. Let me tell you instead—' and he took both hands in hers, gazing straight into her eyes as he said '—you have done me a very great favour today.'

'By marrying you.'

'Well, yes. But more than that. You reminded me who I really am.'

The wounded look in her eyes turned to one of confusion.

'Viscount Mildenhall—' he pulled a face '—is a…is a…' He floundered, finding it was not so easy to explain the tangled emotions that had led him to mislead members of the Ton into betraying their shallowness. 'Well, to use your own words, a coxcomb.'

'I don't remember,' she said hesitantly, 'ever calling you a coxcomb.'

'You should have! I was…I don't know.' He ran his fingers through his short, blond hair, leaving it sticking up in spikes. 'I have been so used to being a soldier, dealing with life and death on a daily basis, that suddenly being thrust into a world that revolves around utterly trivial issues, I—' he sprang to his feet and paced away '—I was supposed to consider my position and not do anything to bring the title into disrepute. I got such a lecture, before coming to town, about the clubs my brother had belonged to and the style in which he lived that I…'

'You rebelled,' she breathed, her eyes growing round. She had wondered what on earth had happened to turn Monty, the epitome of all the manly virtues, into that dandified, rude…*angry* viscount. And he had been angry, she now perceived. All the time. Not just when she happened to cross his path.

'Yes—' he turned and looked down at her '—that is exactly what I did.'

She heaved a great sigh, looking up at him enviously. 'How I wish I could have had the courage to do that. I went the other way. I…squashed myself into the mould they tried to make for me…'

He strode back to the ottoman, grabbed her hands and tugged her to her feet.

'When Rick told me how miserable his sister was, I wanted to rescue her…' He paused, a frown on his face. 'Of course, I did not know she was you, but—' he squeezed her hands tightly '—earlier on, you said this marriage could be a new start. Oh, I know you were thinking about the mess your parents left behind them. But—' and his eyes took on an intensity that called to something deep inside her '—could it not be a fresh start for us?'

'Us?' Her eyes were wide and misty, the way he had seen them look after he had kissed her. Her lips were slightly parted, too. His heart thudded heavily against his rib cage.

'You and me,' he growled, scarcely resisting the urge to step forward and close the minute gap that still separated them. 'I will never try to mould you into some unattainable image, Midge. I shall not expect anything from you that you are not equipped to give.'

And then he traced the length of her lower lip with his forefinger.

She had the strangest urge to capture the finger between her lips and nibble at it. Her eyes flew to his. He was looking at her expectantly.

And then he smiled at her.

He was such a handsome man. Even when he was scowling, there was still something about the vitality of him that had made her body leap in response.

But to have the full force of that smile turned upon her...oh, it went straight to the very core of her, like a cup of hot chocolate on a bleak winter's day. Because his former words had been almost as devastating as they were heartening. Yes, he expected her to be a social disaster, but he would never hold her inability to behave decorously against her. He was prepared to accept her exactly as she was.

Just as, she suddenly perceived, he was hoping she would try to see the best in him. He wanted her to forget the vain, pompous ass who had paraded about town dripping with jewels. To look beneath the gaudy clothing and see the man he wished he still was.

'I will always think of you as Monty, then,' she vowed.

Afterwards, she was never quite sure who had moved first. She only knew that they were in each other's arms, kissing each other as though their lives depended on it.

She no longer felt the need to hold back from him. Or pretend that she objected to the way his hands were exploring her body.

He wanted her.

Just as she was.

And for the first time in her life, she was not a bit sorry she was female. Her body, which she had so often despised, now seemed like a treasure chest, which he was unlocking, revealing unimaginable riches within.

She felt a little shy when he finally laid her on the bed, having divested her of every stitch of clothing. Blushed when he tossed aside his dressing gown and joined her.

But the feel of his hard, naked body next to hers was so delicious, the sensations he roused as he kissed and caressed her softness so powerful, they soon swept modesty aside.

When he made them one flesh, she felt complete for the first time in her life. More fully herself than she had ever dreamed she could be.

But he did not stop there. He drove her on, into new realms of sensuality that almost began to frighten her. Finally being encouraged to behave exactly as she wanted was one thing. But now she was beginning to feel as though she was almost out of control.

'Monty!' She gasped, her eyes flying wide open. 'I can't…it's too much…'

'Let go,' he murmured breathily into her ear. 'Let it happen.'

Then he raised himself up so that he could look into her face.

'Trust me…it will be good…'

The lower half of his body ground harder against her, just where the exciting feelings were at their most intense.

That intensity swelled to a crescendo. The most

incredible pleasure she had ever known blasted through her, from the tips of her toes to the roots of her hair.

'It's happening!' she cried, in shock, clinging to his shoulders as she flew apart.

'Oh, yes,' he groaned. 'Yes, it is…'

Time stood still as everything shook and pulsed and throbbed.

And then they floated gently back down to earth, like the sparks after a rocket has exploded.

Together.

As the carriage swept through the park gates and Midge got her first glimpse of Shevington Court, her stomach tied itself into a knot. Not for the first time that day, she was glad Monty had elected to ride beside the carriage. For she would have felt obliged to find something positive to say about the imposing set of stone buildings sitting on top of a rise, dominating the entire landscape. The closer they drew, and the larger she realized the place was, the greater grew her sense of inadequacy. She had never even attended a house party in a home so grand. Now she was expected to live here!

By the time the carriage drew to a halt beneath the *port cochère* Monty had already dismounted, and it was he who came to hand her out. He did not, as a footman would have done, merely extend his arm for support, but took hold of her waist and bodily lifted her to the ground.

His hands seemed to burn through the material of her coat as she recalled, with a flush, how they had felt on her bare skin the night before. But as he set about deftly straightening her skewed bonnet she began to feel annoyed. How could he remain so calm, so unmoved by their proximity, when she was in a breathless state of arousal! It was galling to think that if he decided to kiss her, she would simply collapse backwards into the carriage, dragging him in after her, and never mind what the servants might think as she slammed the door in their faces. But of course, he did no such thing. Once he had assured himself that she was tidy, he tucked her hand in the crook of his arm and led her up the flight of shallow stone steps to the front door.

She had to cling to his arm for support, so weak were her knees by this time. The man was a menace to female kind!

'It's not what you would call a comfortable home,' he startled her by saying. 'Draughty barracks of a place, positioned as it is on top of a hill. My grandfather built it for show, more than convenience, I think. Good training for me, though,' he finished enigmatically, turning to eye the ranks of windows.

'Training?' she asked.

'Oh.' He seemed to snap back to her from far away. 'For school. Army barracks. Bivouacking in the Pyrenees…' His voice trailed away as the immense double doors swung open as if by magic and a stately butler materialized from the shadowy interior. 'Good day, Francis.' He nodded, then murmured into her ear, 'Indeed, you may find that the wearing of extra petticoats may prove beneficial. I shall have to inspect the efficacy of your underwear thoroughly, every day, I should think, to make sure you don't catch cold…'

The thought of him inspecting her underwear made her go hot all over. And so she entered the imposing main hall of Shevington scarlet-cheeked, thoroughly flustered and rather aggravated with him for not only having put her in such a state, but also for remaining completely unmoved as he did so.

A veritable army of staff, in smart black-and-gold livery, were all lined up in the hall to greet them.

She was momentarily grateful that Monty had lifted her out of the carriage and made sure she would pass muster. She would not have liked to run the gauntlet of all those curious eyes with a trailing hem or her bonnet askew.

But that brief spasm of gratitude soon passed. For rather than making any attempt to lighten the atmosphere, he stalked along at her side, his hands clasped behind his back, his face unsmiling as the housekeeper went through the roll call of names.

He looked, in fact, exactly like a stern major, inspecting the troops. She would not have been a bit surprised if he had straightened a footman's powdered wig or snapped at the lowly boot boy to shine up his rather tarnished buttons.

But at last, parade was over and the troops dismissed. And the housekeeper, Mrs Wadsworth, gestured towards the grand sweep of the staircase.

'Your rooms are on the west corridor,' she announced, leading the way.

'You will never get lost,' Monty murmured in her ear as they followed her, side by side. Then he held out his hands, spreading his fingers in an elongated rectangle. 'South front, east wing, west wing.'

'His lordship,' said Mrs Wadsworth, flinging open a set of double doors about halfway along the corridor, 'thought you would wish to have this set of apartments.'

'Did he, by God,' Monty murmured to Midge, out of

the corner of his mouth, 'you are honoured. Last time I was here, I only merited one of the guest rooms.'

'Her Ladyship's sitting room.' The housekeeper waved her arm round the room they had entered. It was a perfect square, and very green, was Midge's first impression. Pale green walls, dark green curtains and various shades of green upholstery on all the furniture. Then her eyes took in the ornately plastered ceiling, with generously proportioned picture rails below. And the almost paper-thin, floral porcelain ware that decorated every available surface. And the very expensive-looking carpet in the middle of the highly polished floor. And the low table positioned before the fireplace, with an immense vase, from the same source as the rest of the china, squatting on top.

It might have looked less hideous if somebody had thought to fill it with fresh flowers, but she supposed there were not many large enough, at this time of year, to do it justice.

'Viscount Mildenhall's chamber is through that door, and yours through this one,' Mrs Wadsworth explained, pointing to two doors on opposite sides of the green room.

'His Lordship will be along shortly to meet you and welcome you to your new home,' Mrs Wadsworth said to Midge. 'I shall have the tea things brought up.'

Midge's anxiety level soared to new heights. She had no wish to drag the poor old earl out of his sick bed. She turned to ask Monty if he thought it might be better if they were to go to him, only to see him stalking through the door that led to his own room. She could hear him muttering to his valet, flinging open doors and slamming drawers. He was clearly not in the best of moods, for some reason. And she did not know him well enough to know how to deal with him yet.

Not quite daring to tread on the luxurious carpeting, Midge kept to the bare boards round the edge as she made her way to the door that led to her own room.

She peeped in to see a footman depositing a trunk at the foot of the bed.

'Not there you great lummox,' Pansy was saying scathingly. 'Over there, by the cupboards!'

Midge's lips twitched at the sight of the brawny footman meekly doing the diminutive Pansy's bidding, and she backed away to the relative peace of the fussily feminine sitting room.

The door to Monty's room was now closed. Well, that answered the question of whether to go and talk to him or not!

Feeling rather at a loose end, Midge sidled along to a window and gasped with pleasure. She could see a river winding artistically down to a lake that filled the bottom of a thickly wooded valley. And, if she pressed her nose to the windowpane, the corner of a building that looked very much like stables. She hoped there would be a decent mount for her. Her spirits lifted as she regarded the short turf sweeping round the lake and a track leading into the woodland. Oh, how she would enjoy being able to go for a really good gallop again!

Somewhere, at the bottom of one of her trunks, she'd had Pansy pack the disreputable old riding habit she had brought with her from Staffordshire. She had ensured it survived every single one of her aunt's culls of her wardrobe, and now she could hardly wait to don it again!

She was just wondering if it was safe to enter her room yet, to get washed and changed in readiness for the earl's visit, when she heard a hesitant scratching noise at the main door.

When she opened it, she saw two identical small boys, dressed in nankeen breeches and rather shabby jackets.

'You must be Monty's brothers!' She beamed down at them. 'You look so much like him!' And they did, in spite of what he had said about them possibly having different parentage. Both of them had his thick, fair hair, startlingly green eyes and dimples in the centre of very determined chins.

One of them dug the other in the ribs with his elbow. 'She means Vern.'

The other nodded. 'Spec so.' Then added, 'We aren't supposed to be here.'

'But we wanted to take a look at you.'

'And show you Skip,' said the first, looking down at the front of his jacket which was filled out by a mass of something squirming. The corner of a dog's ear promptly flipped out over the edge of the boy's lapels.

'Oh, is it a terrier?' she asked, warmed by the first sign of anything approaching informal behaviour since setting foot in the house.

The twin with the bulging jacket nodded. 'Best ratter in the county,' he declared.

Midge bit back a grin. The boy was probably only allowed to use his dog under the strict supervision of a gamekeeper, within the bounds of his own park. But the fact remained he was immensely proud of his pet and wanted to show it off to his new big sister.

She pulled the door open wider to let the boys and their dog in. The twins scanned the corridor behind them rapidly, then exchanged a look with each other, before darting into the formal sitting room.

The minute the door closed behind them, the boy with the dog undid his jacket, and a very excited tan-and-white terrier dropped onto the rug. Tail up, nose down, it embarked on a rapid exploration of the room. Its little paws scrabbled frantically on the smooth surface of the floorboards when it left the safety of the carpet, but it had been running so fast it was unable to slow its skid by much, and landed against the wainscot under the window with an audible thud.

Midge stifled a giggle as, with a doggy attempt at nonchalance, Skip put his nose straight down and began to sniff determinedly along the wainscoting, as though this was exactly where he had decided to be.

'Looks like he's got the scent of a rat,' said his owner knowingly.

'I am sure there are no rats up here,' said Midge. There were so many staff, and the household appeared so strictly ordered, she was quite sure no rat would find a home behind the woodwork.

'Do you—' the second twin took a deep breath '—do you like animals?'

'Yes, I do.'

He brightened up immediately, reached into his own jacket, and extracted the sinuous body of a ferret. 'This is Tim. I use him for rabbitting.'

Skip's head shot up. He looked straight at Tim, pulled back his lips and snarled in the manner of one greeting an old adversary. The ferret shot out of the boy's grasp, the dog bounded back onto the carpet, and for a few seconds, the floor about Midge's feet was a blur of fur and teeth and tails.

The ferret emerged from the mêlée first, streaking across the rug and straight up the curtains where it found a precarious perch on the curtain rod.

The terrier started jumping up and down on the spot, yapping furiously for a few seconds, then, balked of its prey, sank its teeth into a fold of velvet and worried at the curtain as though killing a rat. The action made the curtain pole, on which the ferret was balancing, rattle in its moorings. Tim promptly abandoned it and ran along the picture rail, scattering items of pottery as he went.

Uttering a cry of alarm, Midge flew across the room in time to catch a bud vase, a cup and a plate in rapid succession while Skip, who seemed to have temporarily forgotten that it was the ferret he had been after, redoubled his ferocious attack on the curtains.

When the ferret reached the chimney breast, instead of swarming round its edges, it ran straight down the silk wallpaper, landing on the tea table, where it used the vase as a springboard to launch himself into his master's waiting arms. The vase wobbled, rocked, then pivoted towards the edge of the table. Midge dived to catch it, at the exact same moment that Skip's hind legs found purchase on the carpet and he finally managed to make some headway. Just as Midge's hands closed round the vase, the curtain pole parted company from its moorings, bringing yards of green velvet slithering down on her.

From within the smothering folds of the curtains, Midge heard the crash of breaking crockery, a yelp and the clang of the brass curtain pole landing on the floor.

It was hard to breathe. Even harder to find a way out of the heavy curtaining wrapped round her body. Eventually, she found a chink, through which she saw

Get 2 Books FREE!

Harlequin® Books,
publisher of women's fiction,
presents

 HARLEQUIN® HISTORICAL

GET 2 BOOKS

We'd like to send you two *Harlequin® Historical* novels absolutely free. Accepting them puts you under no obligation to purchase any more books.

HOW TO GET YOUR
2 FREE BOOKS AND 2 FREE GIFTS

1. Return the reply card today, and we'll send you two *Harlequin Historical* novels, absolutely free! We'll even pay the postage!

2. Accepting free books places you under no obligation to buy anything, ever. Whatever you decide, the free books and gifts are yours to keep, free!

3. We hope that after receiving your free books you'll want to remain a subscriber, but the choice is yours—to continue or cancel, any time at all!

EXTRA BONUS

You'll also get two free mystery gifts! (worth about $10)

FREE!

Return this card promptly to get
2 FREE BOOKS and 2 FREE GIFTS!

 HARLEQUIN® HISTORICAL

YES! Please send me 2 FREE *Harlequin® Historical* novels, and 2 free mystery gifts as well. I understand I am under no obligation to purchase anything, as explained on the back of this insert.

About how many NEW paperback fiction books have you purchased in the past 3 months?

❏ 0-2
E9P7

❏ 3-6
E9QK

❏ 7 or more
E9QV

246/349 HDL

FIRST NAME	LAST NAME

ADDRESS

APT.#   CITY

STATE/PROV.   ZIP/POSTAL CODE

Visit us at:
www.ReaderService.com

▲ DETACH AND MAIL CARD TODAY! ▼

(H-H-10/10)

If offer card is missing, write to The Reader Service, P.O. Box 1867, Buffalo, NY 14240-1867 or visit www.ReaderService.com

BUSINESS REPLY MAIL
FIRST-CLASS MAIL   PERMIT NO. 717   BUFFALO, NY

POSTAGE WILL BE PAID BY ADDRESSEE

THE READER SERVICE
PO BOX 1867
BUFFALO NY 14240-9952

NO POSTAGE
NECESSARY
IF MAILED
IN THE
UNITED STATES

that the sound of breaking crockery had come from the doorway, where a maid had dropped the promised tea tray. The vase, she noted with a feeling of triumph, was lying cushioned by a fold of velvet, the plate, cup and bud vase beside it. She pushed the curtain off her face and sat up.

'Not a single thing broken!' she crowed, flushed with success.

There was no sign of the dog or the ferret, but the twins were standing before the hearth, clutching each other's hands as they stared, aghast, at the slender, fair-haired gentleman who had paused just beyond the wreckage of the tea things.

Monty was there, too, sauntering across from his own quarters, and bowing politely to the fair-haired gentleman.

He cleared his throat, then waved one arm in the direction of the cascade of curtaining, from the depths of which Midge was still struggling to emerge.

'Allow me,' he said, 'to present my wife.'

The fair-haired gentleman's eyes swept the length of Midge's legs, which had emerged from the curtaining minus her skirts. Then, his nostrils flaring in a fastidious expression of distaste, he turned on his heel and stalked away.

Chapter Eight

'We didn't mean any harm, Vern!'

The twins were having a hard time keeping up with Monty as he strode out of the house and through the stable yard to the kennels.

'We just wanted to see what she was like!'

'That had better have been all it was,' snapped Monty, as he produced Skip from inside his jacket. 'I hope it was not the kind of devilment you have employed in the past, to rid yourself of every governess who has dared to set foot in your schoolroom.'

'We never meant—'

'Oh, didn't you! Well, even if you did not humiliate her on purpose, that is what you have done, with your wilful disregard of the rules. You know you are not supposed to bring animals indoors! You were lucky I heard Skip barking and got to him before father came in,' he growled, stuffing the wriggling bundle of fur firmly into his cage.

'You ain't…you ain't gonna put Skip in a sack and drown him, are you?'

Monty turned to his woebegone younger brother in surprise. 'Why in God's name should I do that?'

'Piers would've,' said the other sulkily, extracting the ferret from his own jacket, then thrusting his pet into his hutch.

'I am not Piers!' he grated, filled with loathing for the man who would have deliberately inflicted so much pain on two defenceless children. 'I hope to God I am nothing like him.'

The Earl of Corfe's firstborn had been spoilt from birth, and grown into a cruel and selfish young man. Every time he had come home from school, Monty had been the butt of his sadistic sense of humour. As, in their turn, had these two.

'The earl says you ain't,' declared Jeremiah.

'Says it all the time,' said Tobias.

And Monty could just hear the tone of voice in which his father said it. With a rueful grin, he leaned down and ruffled the boys' hair.

As one, they stepped back, out of his reach. But then Jeremiah glanced at Skip, snuffling happily round his pen, squared his shoulders, and declared, 'We'll tell her we're sorry.'

'Yes, we'll make it up to her!'

'I hope so,' said Monty. 'Because she is your sister now. And she is here to stay.'

Two sombre footmen came to the sitting room, armed with stepladders, to re-hang the curtains.

'I slipped on the floorboards,' said Midge, red-faced,

as one of them climbed to remount the curtain pole. 'And grabbed the curtains to prevent myself from falling.'

The two men exchanged meaningful glances as they re-positioned the set of ladders by the chimneybreast and carefully began to replace the delicate ornaments in their correct positions.

Knowing she had done all she could to prevent the boys from getting into trouble, Midge retreated to her bedroom to get changed for dinner.

She did not see Monty again until just before it was time to go downstairs. He emerged from the door to his own room, strode across to her and took both her hands in his.

'Are you angry with me?' he said.

'Me? Angry with you?'

If anything, she would have thought Monty would have been furious with her for having made such a spectacle of herself.

'It was imperative I got the dog out of here before father realized what the twins had done,' he explained. 'When I got down to the kennels and learned their punishment for breaking the rules would have been to see their pets drowned, it made me sure I had done the right thing. But the hell of it was, I did not have time to ensure you were unharmed.'

'Oh, never mind that!' exclaimed Midge, horrified to think of anything so dreadful happening to that dear little dog. 'I was not hurt. Only embarrassed.'

He smiled with relief. Then linked his arm with hers, saying, 'Come on, time to go down and face the music.'

Oh, Lord, she swallowed. However was she going to look her new father-in-law in the face? The last time he'd seen her, she had been lying on her back on the floor, completely covered with curtains. Apart from her legs, which, she recalled with chagrin, had been waving around in the air.

The earl was sitting on a comfortable chair by a roaring fire, in what was otherwise quite a chilly reception room. He accorded Midge a cool nod of recognition when he saw them enter the room, but did not deign to rise to his feet. At first she was somewhat taken aback by such a lapse of manners, but then she remembered he was reckoned to be something of an invalid.

Though as she eyed him more keenly, a frown gathered on her brow. He had a spare frame and a weary look to his eyes, but his fair hair was still abundant and his skin, though pale, not unduly lined. In fact, he did not look in the least ill to her.

Then he turned to Monty, and the temperature in the room dropped by several degrees, the look he accorded his son and heir was so frosty. Monty returned the look with equal *froideur*, took her arm and led her towards an ascetic-looking cleric, who *had* got to his feet.

'Allow me to present my father's personal chaplain, the Reverend Norrington,' said Monty as the cleric made his bow. 'And my father's private physician, Dr Cottee.' A rubicund gentleman, who had been taking a glass from a salver held out by one of the footmen, nodded to her affably.

'Now that you are here, we shall go in,' announced the earl dryly, getting to his feet with a fluidity of movement that was surprising for a man she had been told was an invalid.

The menu gave her pause, though. Every dish that was presented seemed designed to tempt the appetite of an elderly, sickly man. A delicate, transparent consommé in which she could just detect the flavour of chicken, was followed by steamed fish and a selection of boiled vegetables, and rounded off with an assortment of milk puddings.

Not that she managed to eat much of anything. She had been a bundle of nerves before even coming down. Now, the coldness of the earl, the haughty demeanour of the footmen and the blandness of the food completely robbed her of her appetite.

Worse still, nobody talked! Not that she would have dared say anything, had anyone attempted to strike up a conversation. She was quite sure that if she opened her mouth for any reason, she would only give the earl an even worse impression of her. And her hands were shaking so badly that, when she reached for her wine glass, she decided she had better not attempt to drink anything either. She was bound to spill her wine over the pristine white drapery! She withdrew her hand and tucked it in her lap.

'We are not used to entertaining females at Shevington,' remarked the earl as he discarded his napkin and signalled for the removal of the cloth.

It took Midge a few seconds to realize that this was the signal for her to go to whatever drawing room was designated for use for the rest of the evening.

But as she got to her feet, he added, 'You will retire to your own rooms.'

Midge couldn't help herself. She just gaped at him as she realized she was being dismissed! Not that she was not relieved that her ordeal in the earl's company was at an end, but still, it was not pleasant to think he could not tolerate one second more of her company either.

There was a scraping of chairs as the other gentlemen got to their feet, expecting her to meekly quit the field.

'W-well, good night then,' she stammered, blundering towards the door.

'I shall come with you,' said Monty, flinging his napkin onto the table.

'I wish *you* to remain here,' snapped the earl. 'I have several matters I wish to discuss.'

'I don't think that would be wise, do you Dr Cottee? Considering the delicate state of my father's digestion.'

The doctor's smile froze as his eyes darted from one implacable aristocrat to the other.

'Oh, if your father wants you to—' Midge began. Monty grabbed her by the elbow and propelled her towards the door.

'Silence!' he hissed into her ear. And then, with a cold smile at his father, 'I assure you, my response to those matters you wish to discuss would be bound to give you indigestion. Far better to talk in the morning.'

'As you say.' The earl's thin lips twisted into a sneer. 'Run along after your wife, then, boy.'

Monty marched Midge to their rooms in silence. Only when he had kicked the door shut behind him did he round on her. 'Do not argue with me in front of my father, ever again!' He spun away from her, running his fingers through his hair.

'I...I did not mean to. I just thought—'

'Well, don't think! Just follow my lead. And for God's sake, let me do the fighting in future.'

Midge was sorely tempted to sketch him a salute.

She settled for merely saying, 'Yes, Major! Any further orders?'

'Dammit.' He seized her by the shoulders and gave her a little shake. 'I am trying to defend you, here. Keep you out of trouble! Can't you see that?'

The trouble was, she could. She had not been here five minutes before she had demonstrated how out of place she was. Dinner tonight had confirmed he had not made the wisest of choices in her. His father had obviously been dying to get him alone, and give him a trimming for bringing home a girl who was so gauche and awkward and clumsy. Leave alone being a daughter of scandal.

'I fear that task is even beyond you, Major Claremont,' she said, her whole body drooping with the realization of how badly she was bound to let him down.

'No,' he growled. 'It is not. It must not be.' Something like desperation clouded his features before he took her face in his hands and kissed her.

There was something about the way he kissed when he was angry that thrilled her to the core.

Her despondency vanished as she poured back all her own hurt and loneliness and wounded pride into the kiss. She clamped her hands behind his head when he would have broken away. For she had been waiting for him to kiss her all day. Ever since he had set her ablaze by merely lifting her out of the coach. And now that she had him exactly where she wanted him, it felt as though, somehow, she had to…beat him at his own game!

His hands swept down her sides, paused to measure the span of her waist, then slid round and down, squeezing her bottom hard.

Midge felt a victorious thrill as he ground his hips

against her stomach, for he was definitely, hugely, aroused.

This time, when he tore his mouth from hers, she let him go. Knew she had been right to do so when he trailed hot wet kisses all the way down her throat. He let go of her bottom, but only so he could push the material of her bodice out of the way of his questing lips.

Not about to be outdone, she yanked his shirt from his breeches and ran her hands up the satiny smooth muscles of his back.

And then totally forgot what point she had been trying to make. She only knew she had to feel his naked skin against hers. And was grateful that for once, they were in complete accord.

They tore away each other's clothes and fell together onto the sofa, their need equally fierce. When Monty plunged into her, she strained up against him with all her might. He groaned. She whimpered. They both clutched at each other as hard as they could.

And in minutes, it was over.

Midge froze. She could not believe they had fallen on each other like wild animals, in the elegance of this formal sitting room!

'Are you all right?' said Monty, lifting his head from the crook of her neck, and looking down at her with concern.

She was not sure. She was shaking all over. Covered in sweat. And more than a little shocked at herself.

'That was selfish of me,' said Monty, hastily withdrawing. 'But I really needed that.'

She had needed it just as much as he had, but something about the guilt in his voice made her doubly certain a lady should never admit it!

'You look tired,' he observed with a frown as he pulled up his breeches. 'I shall just go and see if your maid is in your room.' He strode off while he was still speaking. And then returned, his shirt half in and half out of his waistband, scooped her up, and carried her into her bedroom.

After depositing her on the bed, he crossed to the fireplace and tugged on the bell pull.

'She will be up here soon,' he said. 'I suggest you get her to bring you something up to eat. You must be hungry. You hardly ate anything tonight.'

And then, having brushed a perfunctory kiss on her cheek, he strode out of her room, shutting the door firmly behind him.

And *then* Midge knew what she felt. Empty and used. Because now he was done with her, he couldn't wait to get away from her. She sat up quickly. It made her feel worse, somehow, to be sprawled limply all over the bed like that while he beat such a hasty retreat.

Especially now she recalled him saying, 'I needed that.' Not 'I needed you.' But 'that.'

She tugged her bodice into a slightly less uncomfortable position, loathe for Pansy to find her in such a dishevelled state, and swung her feet down to the floor, all remaining residue of pleasure ebbing away.

She had not placed any great significance on waking alone in her bridal bed that morning. Monty might have had a dozen reasons to have risen early, since they were going on a journey. But he had spent hardly any time with her at all today. And just now, he had shown he could not even bear to lie down with her for a few minutes after getting what he wanted from her.

It was just as well her aunt had warned her what men

could be like during the first weeks of marriage. Or the way he had practically sprinted out of her bedroom, the moment he had disposed of her body neatly back where it belonged, would have *really* hurt her.

She had to remember that though lust was an integral part of a man's nature, it was very far removed from anything like love. Or liking. Or even respect.

She smiled bitterly. A woman could be as bad. She only had to remember the first time he had kissed her. She had thought she hated him. Yet the intimacy he had imposed on her that night had thrilled her to the point where she might almost have thrown caution to the wind.

She wrapped her arms round her waist, as a chill shot through her.

She would be a complete idiot to mistake this passion they shared for anything deeper.

She should be grateful to him for the care he was taking not to mislead her. She had no wish to end up like her mother, broken-hearted because she had fallen in love with a husband who was never going to love her back!

Somehow, she must learn not to hanker for more than Monty was willing to give her.

The next morning, she woke to the sound of two voices conferring in subdued tones, somewhere beyond the end of her footboard. When she sat up, she saw Monty's two little brothers sitting on the rug, deep in discussion.

'Good morning,' she said, pushing her unruly hair out of her eyes. 'What are you doing down there?'

They looked at her warily for a moment or two, clearly not having expected her to be awake.

Then one of them, and for some reason, she was almost certain it was Skip's owner, explained, 'We wanted to thank you for keeping quiet about us having Skip in here yesterday.'

'Yes,' said the other, who she recalled, had taken his cue from the more dominant twin the day before, too. 'Cobbett told us you made up a story about falling over, so's we wouldn't get into trouble. So we brought you a present. We thought you would like to find it when you woke up.'

On the rug between them were what looked like a starling's nest and a very inexpertly dissected frog, spread out on a piece of warped card.

'Why, thank you,' she smiled. They really were the most utterly adorable little scamps. 'Would you like to tell me your names?' she added, feeling glad now that, as a reaction to that torrid interlude on the sofa, she had covered herself up with the most modest nightgown she possessed. 'Nobody introduced us properly yesterday. I'm Midge,' she said, reaching over the footboard to shake hands.

'Jem,' said Skip's owner, standing up and bowing from the waist.

'Tobe' said the other, accidentally stepping on the starling's nest as he rose to make his own bow.

'Do you ride?' asked Jem.

'Yes, I do. Only I have no horse at present.'

The twins exchanged a look.

'If you come down to the stables after breakfast, we can get Charlie to find you a horse.'

'We...we could show you our den,' offered Jem with a noble air. '*Nobody* else knows about it.'

'And just the other day we found a badger's set,' put in Tobe, as though not wanting to be outdone by his twin.

Midge's spirits lifted. It sounded as though not all her time at Shevington was going to be comprised of sitting about pretending to be a grand lady, after all!

It took only a week for her days to fall into a routine. In the mornings, after consuming a substantial breakfast, in her room, she roamed the estate with the twins, mounted on a lively mare called Misty, returning to the house to change for lunch.

She spent the first couple of afternoons going all round Shevington Court with Mrs Wadsworth, who took great pains to explain that things were running with such efficiency, no input would be expected from her. Midge came away with the conviction that the woman was warning her that she would heartily resent any suggestions she might make.

She would have felt that a girl like her had no business living in the midst of such grandeur, had she not begun to notice how friendly most of the lower staff were towards her.

Their reaction, she later learned from Pansy, stemmed from the way she had taken to the twins. The footman, Cobbett, had reported how she had taken the entire blame for the curtain catastrophe on her own shoulders. And thus, without even knowing she had done so, she entered into the confederacy of all those at Shevington who habitually covered for any boyish pranks the twins got into.

The stable lads were keen to find her a suitable mount,

and the cook handed her biscuits when she took the short cut through the kitchens to the stable yard. The under housemaids grinned at her like co-conspirators, and Cobbett took it upon himself to bring up her post every day, so that he could make sure she had whatever she needed.

She spent the afternoons dealing with her correspondence, before letting Pansy dress her up for the evenings.

Pansy was in her element, relishing the challenge of turning her mistress out in such style that Midge always went down to dinner knowing she at least *looked* the part of daughter-in-law to an earl. Not that she stayed looking stylish for long. The minute they regained the privacy of their rooms, Monty would fall upon her like a starving man.

Or did she fall upon him? It was hard to tell. Because making love with Monty was definitely the highlight of her day. Everything else she did was just marking the time until they could be alone together.

'Ah! Thought I might find you here!' Monty strode towards the stall where Midge had just led Misty. 'I should like to discuss a few things with you, if you have a moment?'

She looked round to thank the boys for the morning's adventure, but they had scuttled away the moment Monty showed up.

She frowned. They did not appear to like their older brother all that much. When they spoke of him, which was not all that often, it was with the resentful air reserved by small boys for authority figures. The one her stepbrothers had applied to the parish constable. It seemed so unfair, when they hardly knew him. From what she had gathered, he had been away campaigning for almost the entirety of their young lives, only returning for brief furloughs.

'I wanted to know how you are settling in,' he asked, inadvertently making her hackles rise. But she swallowed back the retort that had sprung to mind, that he would have known had he made any effort to spare her a few minutes during the daytime.

'You go out riding every day, I hear,' he said now, his eyes shooting past her, to the mount which was tossing its head impatiently, and looked concerned. 'Who put you up on Misty?'

'The stable lad Charlie picked her out for me,' Midge answered, patting the mare's neck affectionately. 'She's perfect!'

'Hmm,' Monty mused. 'I would not have said such a bad-tempered creature was a fit mount for a lady myself…'

Midge clucked her tongue as she handed the reins over to another one of the grooms. 'She is a bit spirited, I'll grant you that. But I cannot bear the kind of horses usually deemed fit for ladies to ride. I have no wish to feel as though I am trundling round the park on a sofa!'

Monty grinned. 'No fear of mistaking Misty for a sofa, that's true! Well, I am glad you like her.'

'She is a wonderful mount,' Midge answered.

'And my brothers? They have been behaving themselves?'

If it were not for his two little brothers, she would have been left entirely to her own devices since her arrival. 'They have been behaving like perfectly normal little boys,' she replied with a fond twinkle in her eye.

'Good,' he said, looking relieved. 'I did wonder, that first day, whether they had some plan to make things so hard for you here, you would pack up and leave. And I can see you are wet through. Was half-afraid the little devils might have pushed you into a stream.'

'They did no such thing!' she retorted. Then admitted ruefully. 'I managed to fall in all by myself. Tobe made it look so easy, and I can remember doing it as a girl...'

'Falling into streams?' he teased her, recalling Rick's description of her unfortunate habit of falling into or off things as a girl.

'No—' she giggled '—tickling trout. Only of course, this is not the right weather for messing about in streams, nor am I quite as well-acquainted with the terrain as your brothers.'

'I was going to suggest going for a walk, while we talked,' said Monty, taking her by the arm and leading her across the stable yard towards the house. 'But I think I had better get you indoors and into some dry clothing. Don't want you catching cold.'

'I would not catch cold so easily as that,' she scoffed. 'Besides, my habit is only wet to the knees.'

'I remember. Rick told me you were as healthy as a horse!'

Monty opened a door Midge had not previously used, which led to a corridor flanked by glass-windowed offices. She saw the estate manager, sitting at a desk, almost hidden behind his enormous pile of ledgers.

'Why,' Midge determinedly returned to the subject Monty had first raised, as he led her along the passage, 'would you think the twins might be trying to make me leave?'

'Because you are *my* wife,' he said grimly. 'And they neither like nor trust me.'

'They do not even seemed disposed to try,' she mused. 'Why is that? What have you done—'

'It is nothing I have done!' he retorted. 'But they have known so little kindness. Piers always went out of his way to make them as miserable as he possibly could. When you couple that with the way my father has treated them, because of his suspicions about their origins, it is hardly surprising they have such a deep-seated mistrust of any member of their close family.'

'How sad.'

'They ought to be at school, of course,' he muttered darkly, opening a second door, which opened onto the back stairs that led up to the main part of the house. 'They have too much time on their hands, and nobody appointed directly with their care.'

The same thought had occurred to Midge. In fact, she was really quite concerned for their welfare. It could not be good for them to be so comprehensively ignored by their father, whilst being so totally indulged by the staff.

'But father will not send them to school,' he said, 'And the little devils make it a point of pride to drive every single governess and tutor he has ever appointed from the premises.'

She bit down on her lower lip, considering what a thankless task a governess or a tutor would have, trying to bring some order into their lives. The staff, ranged against them in defence of the twins, would block every move they made.

'They really *should* be sent to school,' she agreed. 'They are both very bright boys. With a lot of energy that is not being given a proper direction.'

She only had to think of that frog Jem had so painstakingly dissected. He had an interest in natural history and the sciences, that was not being properly developed. Neither of them would reach their full potential if the current regime continued.

'I only wish there was some way I could persuade father to send them to school. But he will not listen to a word I have to say on this, or any other matter!' he said grimly.

Once in their room, she rang for the maid and asked for hot water to bathe.

'Wait!' said Monty as the girl prepared to leave. 'Get cook to send up some hot soup as well. And cake.'

She looked her enquiry at him.

'I feel as though I have not seen you since we got here,' he explained. 'I still have a lot of ground to cover, but if a man cannot take a nuncheon with his own wife...' He growled, flinging himself onto the sofa and stretching his legs out in front of him.

'You see, I was not born to the position,' he said, spreading his arms along the back of the sofa. 'Father concentrated on training Piers to take up the reins as the seventh earl. Whereas I was packed off to school. So now, I have a lifetime of training to cram into my skull in the shortest time possible. Not just running the estate, you understand, but all the rest of it. My standing in the county, my eventual duties in parliament...'

She folded up the muddy skirts of her habit, carefully tucking them up round her thighs before kneeling on the floor at his feet. It was the only way she could think of to prevent her dirty clothes from ruining either the carpet or the upholstery.

'I suppose your father feels the case is urgent,' she mused. 'My aunt told me he is not expected to live long…'

Monty let out a bark of laughter. 'Does he look ill to you?'

She frowned. 'No. And that has puzzled me from the first. But then he has a doctor always in attendance…so I suppose…'

'He has had a doctor in attendance ever since I can remember. He has always kept them in a chamber close to his own, so that he can call on them any time of day or night. Along with the chaplain. So that they can minister to either his upset stomach or his troubled conscience. Dr Cottee has lasted longer than most, because he claims to be an expert on the kind of nervous disorders suffered by men of excess sensibility, such as my father.'

'Nervous disorders?'

'Oh, yes. Dr Cottee has had the cunning to prescribe an atmosphere of complete tranquillity. So that my father's delicate nerves are not overset.'

She looked up at him, her head on one side, recalling the petulant cast about her father-in-law's mouth. 'You mean, nobody dares cross him, in case they make him ill?'

'Clever girl,' he said, reaching down to tuck a strand of hair behind her ear.

'Does he really get ill if somebody opposes him?'

'Well, my opinions on the way I should like to see this estate run give him a headache,' he remarked sardonically. 'On the one occasion we discussed politics, since I am diametrically opposed to his position, he had what looked like a genuine apoplectic fit.' He grimaced. 'And the fact that I am to be the next earl at all gives him lengthy bouts of insomnia.'

Her frown deepened. 'Why does he not like you, Monty? I would have thought you are the kind of son any man would be proud of!'

The sardonic expression intensified.

'I think—' he sat forward, clasping his hands between his knees '—that whenever he looks at me, he sees my mother. You see, it was not a love match. His parents picked her out for him, and he was still so morose about losing his first wife, whom he really loved, he put up no resistance. But my mother had her pride. She was not the sort to stay about and listen to him wax lyrical about the woman who died giving birth to his heir. After giving birth to me, she took herself off to town pretty smartish and lived her own life.'

'So…he sent you away and can feel no warmth for you because you are the son of a woman who defied him,' she said, reaching out and tentatively touching his knee. She knew exactly what it felt like to be judged by who your mother was! 'And the twins?'

'Ah, yes, the twins,' he said, sitting forward and taking her hand between his own. 'Piers never liked my father's third wife. He made her life as uncomfortable as only the spoiled heir to a fortune, who had the first place in his father's affections, could. Before long, rumours about her affairs began to circulate in the district. Then she died bringing those boys into the world. With the result that my father positively hated them from the very start! Not only did he suspect they were not his, but he blamed them for robbing him of a wife that I think, from what I can remember, he did feel some genuine affection for. At least all he has ever felt for me is indifference. But those poor little beggars…hidden away here as though their very existence is shameful…' He shook his head ruefully. 'If we cannot do something to help them, Midge, they are going to end up turning into complete savages!'

'Is he blind?' Midge blurted. 'I mean, it is perfectly obvious that they are his children. When I went through the portrait gallery I could see those green eyes and the dimpled determined chins they have on Claremonts going back centuries.'

'Quite,' he said dryly. 'But as I said, whenever he looks at them, he sees their mother.'

'Well, it is quite wrong of him to punish the children for their mother's faults!'

The door opened then, and Pansy came in, leading a procession of maids with all the items they had requested.

'I-I had better go and get changed,' said Midge, standing up with regret. She resented the interruption to one of the most meaningful conversations she'd ever had with her husband. It had explained so much.

Pansy helped strip her out of her muddy habit, and as she settled into the warm, scented water, she thanked her lucky stars she had not complained about what she had perceived as his neglect of her so far that week. He had enough people making life hard for him without her pitching in!

'What is taking you so long in there?'

She had heard Monty pacing up and down in the sitting room, but was startled to see him standing in the doorway, staring down at her. Her face flamed as his eyes roved over what he could see of her protruding above the soapy water.

'Towel!' she squeaked, flapping her hand in Pansy's direction.

But Monty got to it first.

'I can take over from here,' he said, not taking his eyes from where Midge cowered, her hands now folded over her breasts.

With a giggle, Pansy scuttled from the room, pausing only to scoop up her mistress's dirty clothing.

'Come on, out you get,' he said, invitingly spreading the towel out wide.

Somehow, without Pansy there, she felt less shy. Taking a deep breath, she stood up, her eyes drinking in the expression of naked desire on his face. He took a step forward, but rather than wrapping the towel round her, he painstakingly dried every inch of her. Then stooped, scooped up a handful of soapy water, and let it trickle over her breasts. So that he could dry them again.

Somehow his own clothes got wet and had to be removed too. By the time he tossed the towel to the floor and laid her down on it, Midge was on fire for him.

Afterwards, he rolled to one side and held her in his arms.

He had done that, once or twice, she observed drowsily. After making love with her, he sometimes held her until she fell asleep. Though he was never still with her in the morning.

'What is that?' she asked, idly running the tips of her fingers over a mass of knotted scar tissue on his shoulder.

'Bullet wound,' he replied, sitting up and reaching for his shirt.

She rolled onto her side, dragging the towel over herself. She felt shy again, now that he was finished with her. Especially since it was broad daylight! If she could see scars she had not been aware of before, what must he be able to see!

He glanced down at her, and seeing her concerned expression riveted on his scar, he said, 'You knew I had been wounded. You sent me wishes for a speedy recovery.'

She sat up, and on a spurt of daring, kissed the scarred flesh just as he was thrusting his arms into his shirtsleeves.

'Rick never told me how you got wounded. Or what the nature of your wounds were.'

'Sniper,' he said tersely, pulling the shirt over his head. 'Officers make easy targets, perched up on their horses.'

When she gasped in shock, he turned to her, explaining ruefully, 'It is a good strategy—to shoot officers from their horses—to attempt to reduce the ranks to chaos. War is a dirty business. Each side does whatever is expedient to beat the other. Come on—' he grinned, getting to his feet '—our soup must be getting cold.'

He finished dressing, and strolled into the sitting room, where the table was now laid out with lunch for two.

It took Midge a few minutes to secure the towel successfully and stumble after him to the sitting room.

Monty looked up from dunking a wedge of fresh bread into a bowl of steaming soup and whistled in appreciation.

'I shall make time to have lunch with you more often—' he grinned '—if you will promise to come to table dressed like that!'

Chapter Nine

After he left, Midge got properly dressed, then went to her writing desk, which Cobbett had placed under the window in the green sitting room. But after trimming her pen and smothering a series of yawns, she had to accept she was in no state to write anything sensible.

And, though it went against the grain to lie down in broad daylight, Midge was too tired to do anything else.

It had been worth it, though, she thought drowsily, toeing off her shoes and tugging back the coverlet. That conversation had made her feel much closer to Monty than ever before. She hoped they would have more conversations of the same sort, even if she did end up like this.

Though it was not the talking that had worn her out, but what came after, she smiled sleepily to herself.

She was just nodding off, when the term 'criminal conversation' popped into her head, and her whole body jerked awake. That was a term used to describe having an adulterous affair. The kind which were probably carried out in snatched moments during the daytime. Like the affair her mother had with the Earl of Leybourne when things with her father went sour.

She came wide-awake. The earl must have made Amanda feel like this, ready to cast her modesty aside, and roll about the floor on a heap of wet towels, in broad daylight. Did she have the potential to behave even more scandalously than her mother? For at least her mother had believed she was in love with the Earl of Leybourne when she had taken him to her bed. And love had no part in the marriage she had entered into with Monty.

But then, what sort of woman enjoyed marital relations so much, without being in love with her husband?

She went hot all over, until she remembered that since she had taken a vow to obey him, it was positively her *duty* to let Monty have his way with her, whenever and wherever he wanted.

She had no call to feel guilty!

She told herself that, time and time again over the next week or so. Whenever Monty initiated snatched 'conversations' during the daytime, which he did with increasing frequency. He tried to come back from wherever he had been to have 'lunch' with her almost every day. And once, when he had spent the morning in the estate manager's office, he had watched out for her returning from her ride, and totally shocked her by tugging her into an empty stall and 'conversing' with her swiftly in the hay.

And the worst of it was, it never occurred to her to refuse his advances. The moment he came striding towards her, that purposeful gleam in his eyes, her entire body melted into a pool of lust.

The passion that flared between them would have been easier for her to accept, if she could believe that they were growing closer in other ways. But Monty paid her so little attention, she could not help feeling a bit used. Oh, she knew he was busy during the daytime. But why was he so averse to spending a whole night in her bed?

She began to take a nap in the afternoons, so that she could stay awake after they had made love and prolong the time she could spend in his arms. Because she knew that the moment she fell asleep, he would leave her bed. At least he waited until she had fallen asleep before leaving, so that his departure was not like a slap in the face. But no matter how hard she fought to keep her eyes open, she would invariably fall asleep before he did. And he was never there when she woke in the morning.

But if, she reasoned, she could manage to stay awake after they had made love, she could at least coax him into having the kind of conversation which engaged their minds, as well as their bodies.

At first, they only talked about trivial things. But then one day in March, news reached England that Bonaparte had escaped his island prison and was advancing on Paris, recruiting support along the way. Both of them began to search the newspapers daily after that, avidly following his progress.

Midge's concern was all for how Bonaparte's return would affect Rick, until Monty, who had lived and breathed the war with France for all his adult life, gave her a broader perspective on the situation. Before long she was entirely in accord with his view that there was no point in trying to negotiate a peace treaty with the upstart Corsican.

'The Prussians have got the right idea. Declare war on him now and stop him before he regains too much power,' he told her one night on the way back up to their rooms after dinner.

'I wish it were possible for me to leave Shevington and…oh, I don't know,' he said moodily, opening the door for her. 'I know I cannot rejoin my regiment, but if I went up to town, there might be some way I could be of use…'

'Well, why don't you go?' she asked tentatively, kneeling down next to him as he crouched down on the hearthrug. Cook had developed some mysterious means of knowing how much she ate at dinner, and would send up a supper tray if she deemed it had been insufficient. Tonight, it contained crumpets for them to toast over the fire.

'What about you?' he asked, spearing one of the crumpets on a toasting fork. 'I would not be able to spend much time with you.'

Midge bit back on the retort that she hardly saw him as it was. There always seemed to be somewhere more important for him to be.

Unless she was on her back, with her legs open.

She bit down on her the surge of resentment, recalling the advice her aunt had begun to slip into her letters lately. She knew she had been more than a little indiscreet, but when she sat at her desk, in that empty room in the afternoons, the temptation to pour her heart out quite often overwhelmed her. And her aunt's responses clearly came from years of learning to cope in a marriage that was far from perfect. Only the day before,

Lady Callandar had reminded her that it was essential to guard her heart. That it would be a grave error to think that the level of intimacy a man instigated in the early days of marriage was an indication he might be falling in love with her. No, she sighed, she ought to be grateful that Monty was taking great care, by distancing himself physically the moment he had got what he wanted from her, not to mislead her into thinking *that*!

She had also added, *'Persons of quality have the luxury of enjoying privacy, not granted to the lower orders. Very few husbands and wives would share a room, let alone a bed, were they given a choice.'*

It had been a shock to realize just how much information she must have relayed to her aunt. Although she was glad she had let slip that she was concerned about the ramifications of their sleeping arrangements. Because her aunt's reply had certainly made her look at that particular issue in another light. The fact that Hugh and Amanda had shared a bed certainly had more to do with lack of space at the Brambles than any desire they might have felt for each other. Her three stepbrothers had all had to share a room, and she had been tucked away in a tiny space under the eaves. And Amanda had been so scared by the Gypsy's curse that she would never have consented to remarrying if there had been any risk of getting pregnant again, only to see her baby die.

She pulled herself back to the present with an effort, smiled brightly and said, 'I could visit my aunt.' She had no other female relative in whom to confide, and she was beginning to think there was much more she could learn from Lady Callandar, could she only discuss her concerns face to face. 'We could do all that shopping you deprived her of before the wedding,' she joked. And then added, more seriously, 'Honestly, Monty, do you think I would expect you to dance attendance on me when the future of Europe is at stake?'

He set the loaded toasting fork onto the tray, pulled her into his arms and hugged her tightly. 'It is useless even talking about it,' he breathed into her hair. 'My duty lies here now.'

Midge's fleeting feelings of loneliness and resentment were swept aside by a surge of sympathy for him. He had done his duty all his life. But nothing he did ever seemed to satisfy his father.

'I am not ready to give up yet.' He smiled sadly. 'The tenants, at least, are beginning to believe that I am nothing like Piers and that I won't turn a blind eye to their petitions. And every day you spend with them, I see the twins becoming more like civilized human beings and less like savages.'

She reached up to smooth her hands over the bunched muscles of his shoulders, kissing his throat, his jaw, the corner of his mouth.

'Tease,' he growled, turning his head to take control of the kiss.

Then, just when she was beginning to think they were going to make love in front of the fire, he surged to his feet, swept her into his arms and carried her into her bedroom where he disposed of her clothing with an efficiency born of much practice.

Midge had not had to send for Pansy to brush her hair, or unhook her gowns or untie her stay laces since the night she had got married. Monty was extremely keen to perform all these services for her. And get her into bed.

But not to stay there, once he had got what he wanted.

She knew she ought not to let his reluctance to spend an entire night with her bother her so much. She told herself that he was just not the kind of man who would want to hold anyone close all night. His mother, who her aunt had said was a cold, proud woman, had abandoned him at Shevington by all accounts. And then his father had packed him off to school, while keeping his older brother close. Experiencing that kind of rejection as a little boy must have made him harden himself.

Army life, too, must have made him become even more self-sufficient. A soft-hearted man would have been in agony watching friends and comrades dying all around.

But she just could not shake the yearning to get closer to him. To break through all those barriers he had built around himself, and become, well, if not the love of his life, then at least his bosom friend.

He *was* beginning to open up to her, about his past and what had made him the way he was.

She had also heard, from Pansy, who'd got it from Cobbett, who had got it from a parlour maid who'd been just outside the door, that Monty had demanded that his father show her more respect. There had been a heated argument, apparently, but the outcome was that the earl did now accord her the common civilities any gentleman should extend to a lady.

All that had to mean something, did it not?

Summoning up every ounce of courage she possessed, she waited until Monty had stripped her completely naked, and was backing her towards the bed, before ducking out of his embrace.

'Where are you going?' he asked, mystified, as she darted over to her bedroom door.

She looked at him coyly over one shoulder. 'I should like to try something different, tonight.' She crooked her finger, beckoning him to follow her as she sashayed across the sitting room.

'My God, Midge,' he croaked, tugging off his cravat and tossing it aside as he stalked after her. 'What you do to me!'

She opened his bedroom door, and nervously entered his domain for the first time since their marriage. She could hardly believe she had brought herself to walk around stark naked, but she had been sure that only acting so brazenly would excite her husband to the point where he would not argue about the spot she had chosen for their coupling.

What happened afterwards would be another matter. She knew that she might still be wanting more from him than he was willing to give. But she just missed him so much every second they were apart, waking or sleeping.

The worst that could happen would be that he would carry her back to her own bed once she had fallen asleep, and she would wake alone, as she had done every morning since she had married him, with the feeling that yet again, she was not quite good enough. That she was not the kind of woman a man would want to hold close to his heart all night.

He caught up with her, put his arms round her and drew her back against his chest. On the way through the sitting room, he had got rid of his shirt. She flexed her spine against the hair-roughened skin, butting her head up against his chin like a cat, as she gazed round his room.

There were no candles lit, but an enormous fire blazed in the hearth.

'It is—' she gasped, as he nuzzled the nape of her neck '—very warm in here.'

'And it is about to get even hotter,' he promised, taking one breast in each hand and squeezing rhythmically.

For the next few minutes, she lost the power of rational thought entirely as she gave herself up to Monty's ministrations. And it was not until a long time later, when they lay, sated and panting on his bed, that she reflected, with great relief, that he had not seemed to mind her invading his sanctuary at all.

Perhaps all she had needed to do was ask. He was the product of a loveless marriage. Perhaps it had simply not occurred to him that a wife might want to sleep in her husband's bed.

'May I stay?' she murmured drowsily, as he tucked her into the crook of his arm.

'Hmm?' He was dozing himself, now.

She raised herself on one arm, propping herself on his chest so that she could look into his eyes.

'All night. I want to stay here. With you. May I?'

'Not a good idea,' he grunted, reaching up and twirling a strand of her hair round his forefinger. 'I am bound to disturb you.'

'What do you mean?'

He sighed, and squeezed his eyes shut for a moment. When he opened them, his expression was defensive. 'I do not sleep much these days. Not for more than a few minutes at a time, unless I have all the windows wide-open. Which is why my valet insists on building up such an enormous fire every night.'

'Oh,' said Midge thoughtfully. Whenever Rick had come home on furlough, he always wanted to keep the windows wide-open at night as well. It had caused no end of arguments with his brothers. Often, she would come down in the mornings to find him rolled up in his greatcoat, on the hearthrug in the parlour, with an empty brandy bottle at his side.

'Do you have nightmares?' she asked softly.

'Not so much now, as when I first got back to England,' he admitted, looking downright uncomfortable.

She lay down, with her head on his chest, and he wrapped both arms round her. Rick had always denied having nightmares too, even though she had heard him crying out in his sleep. Men hated anyone seeing they had any kind of problem that might be construed as a weakness.

'You might not have any if I stay with you,' she offered tentatively.

He chuckled. 'You will freeze in here, once I open the windows.'

'No, I won't,' she declared stubbornly. 'Not with you to keep me warm. And not if we have plenty of blankets. Please, Monty, let me stay. What harm can it do?'

'If it means so much to you,' he said with a shrug, then set about re-arranging the blankets so that most of them covered her.

She watched his silhouette, backlit by the firelight as he crossed the room and began systematically to fling open all the windows. And she sighed with pure contentment. He had not been leaving her bed every night because he did not care about her. Quite the reverse! He was attempting to be considerate.

It was almost as if he was trying to make this marriage as real as it could be, under the circumstances. What more could she ask for?

It was light when he carried her back to her bed. And as he set her down, she noted that he was fully dressed.

'I did not think you would want my valet to come in upon you in that state,' he said, covering her naked body with a sheet. Midge sleepily returned his kiss, rolled over and shut her eyes. Things could only get better from now on. He cared about her welfare. He really did. He had stood up to his father on her behalf and was beginning to talk to her as though her opinion mattered.

Her day followed its usual pattern. Though the sun shone brighter, the colours of the spring flowers were deeper, and she had far more energy, now those niggling fears over Monty's feelings towards her were easing.

She did not worry she might have done something to displease him when he did not put in an appearance at lunch. Since last night, she was better equipped to accept that he had many calls upon his time.

She was sitting at her writing desk, poring over the latest letter from her aunt, when he surprised her by coming into the room so quietly she had no notion he was there, until he said, 'What news have you received to make you frown so?'

'What? Nothing!' The letter was full of hints as to how to cope with the demands of 'a lusty young husband.' If he caught sight of some of the things her aunt had written, he might easily misconstrue the nature of the original questions. Guiltily, she crumpled the page and tossed it into the sitting room fire.

'Midge,' he said reprovingly, 'I thought we had got to the stage where we could talk about anything.'

He sighed, taking her hands between his own. 'If something is troubling you, I want you to tell me. Perhaps I can help?'

Well, she was not going to admit she had been writing to her aunt about the most intimate details of their married life!

But as for the other matter...she caught her lower lip between her teeth and searched Monty's face.

She would, dearly, love to ask him what she ought to do about Stephen. For, not two days earlier, while she had been out riding with the boys, she had seen a man on a black stallion, on the brow of the hill, just on the borders of Shevington land. When he had doffed his hat to her, and she had seen his dark hair and the gleam of gold at his ear, she had instinctively started towards him. But then she had remembered Monty saying that Stephen only wanted to cause trouble.

She wanted to please Monty. It had not taken her long to see that he was nothing like her father, Kit Hebden. His handsome looks had not made him vain or cruel. He got no pleasure from deliberately shocking or hurting people. And he had been inordinately kind to her, since she had become his wife. Though she only had to think back to the scornful way he had spoken to her before he had discovered she was Rick's sister, to know she was not the bride he would have chosen in a million years. He ought to have married someone who matched him, at least in looks, if not in wealth.

No, she sighed, he had enough to contend with in her, without her deliberately flouting his wishes.

And Stephen had quite deliberately ruined her wedding day. If he was here, it was because he wanted to cause more trouble. Sadly, she had shaken her head and turned Misty around.

'Is that a friend of yours?' Jem had asked, craning his neck round as they cantered away.

'Why don't you want to talk to him?' put in Tobe.

She *had* wanted to talk to him, that was the trouble. Even knowing he had probably only come down here to disrupt the life she was slowly establishing for herself, she could not forget he was her brother.

'Monty would prefer me not to,' she had said sadly.

'We won't tell on you, Midge!' Jem swore.

'It will be our secret!' added Tobe.

'It would not be right,' she said sadly. 'Monty is only trying to protect me. He—' she turned and looked over her shoulder wistfully '—is not a good person.'

Stephen's stallion reared on its hind legs, pawing at the air. When he turned and galloped off, she had felt raw inside. He might not be a good person now, but she could not shake off the memories of how she had always been able to run to him, before the days of the murder and his banishment. Now that he was here, her impulse was to run to him again.

For he was her brother!

That very morning, she had seen Stephen again. Though she had deliberately got the boys to ride out in a different direction, Stephen had found them. And this time, he had been on Shevington land.

And that really worried her. She already knew Monty considered him a menace. She was fairly certain that this was one topic on which the earl would be in total accord with his son. She had learned the way titled, landed gentry thought of Gypsies from her grandfather and then her uncle.

Stephen had escaped detection so far. But if she told Monty he was in the area, would he feel compelled to have him hunted down and arrested for trespass? She knew that Monty would only consider he was protecting her. But she had no wish to precipitate an action that would hurt the man who had already suffered so much because of her family. No matter why he had come here.

And so, though she longed to be able to be completely honest with Monty, she mustered up a brittle smile and waved her hand airily towards the letter smouldering in the fireplace.

'It was just some marital advice from my aunt that made me a little embarrassed.'

'Oh?' He glanced at the letter, then back at her troubled face. 'Now I am truly intrigued.' His face took on a purposeful look. 'In fact,' he growled, 'I demand that you tell me.'

With one swift movement, he had her flat on her back on the floor, on the hearthrug, her arms pinned above her head. The demonstration of superior strength was so unexpected, so very forceful, that if she had not recognized the gleam of mischief in his eyes, she might have felt afraid. As it was...

'Tell me,' he growled low into her ear, 'or I shall...'

'What?' she gasped, squirming with excitement. 'What will you do to me?'

He raised himself a little, and ran his eyes slowly along the length of her body.

'Dreadful things…' he warned her, lowering his head and biting gently through the material of her gown, at a nipple that was sitting up and begging for his attention.

'You promised to obey me,' he said with mock severity. 'So, if you won't tell me this instant what was in that letter, then I shall have to punish you.'

'H-how?' She panted eagerly.

'By making you suffer,' he promised her, sweeping her skirts up to her waist and subjecting her to a few moments of sensual torment.

'By making you beg,' he warned her, stopping what he was doing just before she went over the edge. 'And finally, by making you scream.'

'You wouldn't,' she said a little uncertainly. He had not even wanted her to sleep in a cold bedroom. He would surely do nothing to hurt her! 'You d-do not want to make me scream.'

With a wicked grin, he lowered his head and set his mouth to what she considered a most inappropriate place, kissing her where…

'No!' she whimpered.

This could not be right! But she could not stop him. His hands were clamped hard round her wrists, and his shoulders pinned her thighs apart.

'Please…' she begged, arching up against his mouth. 'Stop it!'

But he did not stop, and before much longer, just as he had predicted, she was screaming out her shocked pleasure.

And then soaring to the heights all over again when he made love to her in the more conventional mode.

She did not recall him carrying her to her bed, but

he must have done, because she did not wake up on the hearthrug, where she had expired from exhaustion when he had finished with her.

That night at dinner, she could not stop looking at his mouth and wondering how on earth he had learned that it was possible to do such extraordinary things with his tongue.

'You ate hardly anything tonight,' he observed, when they entered their suite later. 'Were you not hungry?'

'You know very well why I could not eat anything,' she whispered, backing away from him as he stalked towards her in a purposeful fashion. 'I am still far too shocked by…' She bit down on her lower lip, shaking her head.

'Your punishment?' He chuckled, catching her up in his arms and carrying her to her bedroom.

'Yes— No…' She pushed a hank of hair out of her eyes, looking up into his face with exasperation. 'I cannot imagine how you could have known how to do that to me…I mean…' She felt her cheeks go hot, and knew her face must be bright red. It was such an odd thing to decide to do, if he had not known what the effect on her would have been. But if he had known what it would do to her, then he must have done it before. To some other woman.

She wondered if that other woman had screamed, too. And felt sure she must have done. Or Monty would not have warned her that *she* would.

'Oh, this is hopeless,' she grumbled as he set her down at the foot of the bed, spun her round and deftly began to undo her gown. 'You know so much about all this, and I know virtually nothing!' She had even had to write to her aunt to find out if it was normal for newly married men to want to sleep in a different bed from their wife!

'What do you want to know?' he said, nuzzling at the nape of her neck.

So many things! But mostly, 'If I am supposed to enjoy this quite so much!' she blurted out.

Her aunt and uncle had convinced her that she came nowhere near the standards of behaviour expected from a proper lady. And she was half-afraid that enjoying this aspect of their marriage proved that she was only one step away from being a complete wanton. Heavens, she would let him do just about anything to her. Anywhere! In a stable. On the hearthrug. She had even cavorted naked across the room last night to entice him, like the veriest light skirt!

It would be nice to hear him say something reassuring. Instead he made a strange choking sound against her neck, before beginning to chuckle.

'What is funny?' she asked, a little hurt. She had asked a perfectly serious question!

'You!' He chuckled. 'I never know what you are going to say next!'

Oh, well, she sighed. That was what came of fishing for compliments. She supposed she ought to feel grateful that at least he found her amusing. Her mother must have been so hurt whenever Kit told her she was boring.

Besides, a lady never gave way to her emotions, she could hear her aunt telling her. In a marriage such as theirs, the last thing her husband would want was an emotional scene. Their…marital conversation…was one area where so far, they seemed to be in harmony. She would be a fool to turn it into a bone of contention and needlessly drive a wedge between them.

'That first afternoon you were here, do you remember?' Monty said, his arms snaking round her waist. 'I left you to your own devices for five minutes, and while my back was turned, you managed to turn the stuffiest, most oppressive room in the whole place into a scene of utter carnage!' Even now, the memory of her struggling up out of the curtains and declaring proudly that she had not broken anything, made him want to chuckle.

She was the sunniest, brightest thing that had ever come into his life. Shevington was not a cold, inhospitable place while she resided under its roof. Even when faced with one of his father's most chilling lectures, he only had to think of the warm welcome waiting for him up here in these rooms to feel a smile welling up inside. Naturally he could not keep his hands off her. Not when she responded with such unfeigned enthusiasm. No matter what he did.

His conscience had troubled him after the way he had fallen on her, ravishing her on the sofa the first night they had arrived. Only the night before that, she had been a virgin! He should have been gentle and considerate. The rough way he had taken her had left her shaking with shock. He had paced up and down his room that night, cursing his lack of restraint and wondering how he could make amends. Though, with her typical generosity of nature, she had made the aftermath easy for him.

Every day, he thanked God he had found her. He loved the way her heart raced, just because he touched her. He loved that look of shocked gratitude in her eyes whenever he brought her to the heights of pleasure. And he loved watching her vainly struggling to stay awake, before eventually falling into a sated sleep in his arms.

He loved the fact that he was no longer on his own. He hugged her tight. She was his. Wholly his. To cherish and protect.

And speaking of which…

'Midge,' he said solemnly, turning her round in his arms to face him. 'You make me forget what I wanted to say to you.'

He was perturbed to see her looking quite upset, and suddenly realized it had not been very tactful of him to laugh at the naiveté of her earlier question.

'You are a delight,' he said, kissing the frown line between her brows. More than that. He was coming to the conclusion that he was becoming addicted to her. He had certainly never suspected he was capable of making love quite so often. She only had to look at him in a certain way…just as she had done earlier, making him forget the reason he had come up to talk to her in the middle of the afternoon.

Which he had to bring to her attention now.

'Sit down, will you, Midge,' he said, leading her to the dressing-table stool, waiting till she had sat down, then deliberately distancing himself by walking away and leaning against the bedpost. 'There is something I should like to ask you. I have been wondering if you have already written to your aunt about it…' he conjectured, raising one eyebrow in enquiry. Then, receiving nothing in return from Midge but a blank look, he stuck his hands in his pockets and said, 'Since we have been married, you have not refused me once. And you should have done, should you not? In the normal course of things?'

Midge's insides hollowed out. She knew it! Her behaviour was not what a husband wanted in a wife at all!

A true lady would have feigned reluctance, she expected. And made him work a bit harder before yielding. Pretence, she thought bitterly. That was what being a lady entailed. And she had never been any good at it.

She swallowed down a feeling of nausea. It was so unfair. He had taken full advantage of her wanton nature, after all!

'You had better explain what you mean,' she said mutinously. Because she was blowed if she could understand what he was complaining about!

A faint flush swept across his cheeks. 'To be blunt, my dear, you have not experienced your monthly courses, have you, since we married. I would have thought, after six weeks, that you would have been… um…out of commission at least once…'

The relief that he was not about to tell her she was better suited to the position of mistress than wife was so acute that, for a moment or two, Midge went quite light-headed.

'Dammit, Midge, are you going to faint?'

'I never faint,' she said weakly as the room spun round her.

The next thing she knew, Monty had scooped her up off the stool and was lying her gently down on the bed. Then he knelt on the floor at the bedside and laid his hands over her stomach.

'You are carrying my child,' he breathed, in awe. 'So soon!'

This was so typical of Midge, to charge full tilt into whatever she did! No holds barred.

She would be a wonderful mother. She was so loving; she would never abandon her child to the rigid regime at Shevington and seek her own amusements in London.

Nor shame it by taking a succession of lovers, no matter how disappointed she might be in her husband.

'A baby?' Midge breathed, her own hands fluttering over where his rested on her stomach. 'Do you really think so?'

Her whole world tilted on its axis. It had never occurred to her she might be pregnant. And yet, now he had put the idea in her head, it seemed so obvious. It certainly explained why she had been feeling a bit off-colour the last few days.

Monty looked at her slightly dazed face and felt a rush of protectiveness towards her. Midge was normally healthy and strong, but already carrying his child was taking its toll on her. It was not referred to as being in 'a delicate condition' for nothing!

She looked a little pale. Come to think of it, these last couple of weeks, she'd taken to going to bed every afternoon. Had she felt unwell and not told him?

When it was all his fault she was in this condition at all! Because his seed was growing inside her, the girl who was never ill had just almost fainted.

And suddenly, his father's words rang in his head. *'If she should die in childbirth, you will feel like a murderer...'*

He leapt to his feet, running his fingers through his hair. Two of his father's three wives had died in childbirth. And he had never really recovered from the loss. Especially not from the first. The love of his life. And suddenly, he knew exactly how the old man must have felt. The prospect of carrying on living without Midge was too ghastly to contemplate!

And more than that, he knew that if the worst should happen, it would indeed be all his fault. He clenched his fists, a streak of resolve running through him. He would just have to make damn sure nothing happened to Midge!

'I will get Dr Cottee to come and look at you in the morning,' he decided. She must have the best of care. Stay in bed all day every day if that was what it took to keep her safe!

'What is it? What's wrong?'

Midge was staring up at him with her huge grey eyes clouded with anxiety.

'Nothing, nothing at all,' he lied, his stomach roiling with fear.

'Then why ask Dr Cottee to look at me? Does he even know anything about having babies? I thought you said he was an expert in nervous disorders?'

'Well, I feel nervous,' he admitted, then immediately felt a pang of contrition. He should be reassuring Midge, not spelling out the dangers and terrifying her too.

Though what he most wanted right now was to clutch her tightly and never let her go!

Instead, he had to get away from her, fast, before she picked up on his fear.

'You need your rest,' he said grimly, backing away from the bed and the temptation Midge presented, lying there looking so achingly vulnerable.

He hardened himself against the hurt look she gave him as he fled from her bedroom. If he stayed, she would winkle his deepest thoughts from him. She had the knack of doing that. He had told her things he had never confided to another living soul!

He slammed his door behind him, and leaned back on it, his whole body shaking.

He hated to have to admit that his father was right about anything, but he was already learning how painful it was for a man to be so much in love with his wife.

Chapter Ten

Monty knew, the moment he set foot in his father's study, why he had been summoned. The doctor's gloating expression said it all, even before the earl offered his congratulations.

Dr Cottee bustled over with a glass of what looked like the best brandy in his hands. His father lifted his own glass towards him in salute.

'To the Claremont heir,' said the earl with blatant satisfaction. For once, the faint tint of disapproval that always hovered at the back of his eyes was entirely absent.

Monty mechanically swallowed the contents of his glass and sat down heavily in the nearest chair.

'You know I thought you had made a mistake, marrying that girl, given her family history,' said the earl. 'For a long time, everyone believed Lady Framlingham was barren. You are most fortunate that she has not inherited that particular weakness. But,' he continued, a peevish tone creeping back into his voice, 'there still remains the question of whether she will be able to carry a son to full term. Her mother was singularly unsuccessful in that respect.'

The doctor got to his feet, folded his hands over his ample stomach and adopted what Monty supposed he thought was a professional demeanour.

'We will need to be extremely careful of her ladyship's health.'

Monty felt all his fears from the night before swarm up and wrap their determined fingers round his throat.

'You have to put a stop to her careering all over the estate with those boys,' snapped the earl. 'Especially on that damned horse! Most capricious beast in the stables!'

Monty had a vision of Midge's body flying through the air, to land with a sickening thud on the turf whilst Misty galloped off into the distance.

'No more riding.' He nodded. 'Definitely no more riding.'

'Also—' the doctor cleared his throat '—it has not escaped our notice that you and she engage in marital relations with rather exceptional frequency.'

Monty hung onto his temper with grim determination. It felt as though the doctor had been spying on him! And what the devil did he mean by all this 'we' business?

'That will have to cease, of course,' said the doctor.

Much as he would have liked to tell the doctor it was no damned business of his how often he made love with his own wife, concern for Midge's health prompted him to ask, 'Are you saying it would be dangerous to continue?'

'In the early stages of pregnancy,' the doctor replied,

'any woman, no matter what her background, is particularly vulnerable to the risk of miscarriage. We would not wish to do anything that might jeopardize her health, or that of the heir, would we?' Dr Cottee then went on, at interminable length, about exactly what was, and what was not permissible for a woman in 'a delicate condition' to do.

'Naturally, I do not wish to do anything that might harm the unborn babe,' Monty snapped, though he refused to assume, as they were doing, that the child Midge was carrying was the male heir his father longed for. It might very well be a girl. He had a brief, intense vision of a pretty little thing with a thatch of unruly hair and a sunny smile, just like her mother's.

'Then you must make sure she behaves herself from now on,' bit out the earl.

Yes. Midge would never forgive herself if anything happened to her baby, because of any carelessness on her part.

'Then if you will excuse me,' he said, slamming the empty glass on the table and getting to his feet, 'I shall go up to her straight away.'

He stalked to the door without waiting for his father's permission to leave. Midge was pregnant. He had made her pregnant. So now it was his duty to keep both her and the baby safe.

Poor Midge. It was not going to be easy for a girl with so much energy to sit about all day, which was what the doctor's strictures would mean. He seemed to think the most strenuous thing she ought to do was take a brief stroll through the gardens. And as for him… he strode along the corridor that led back to the west wing, his brows creased into a scowl as he envisaged the torture of retiring to his lonely bed, which would seem far more empty now that she had shared it with him. He was going to spend night after night pacing the boards or wracked with the nightmares her soft and fragrant presence had kept at bay.

Hell, never mind the nights! How on earth was he going to keep his hands off her during the daytime?

Well, somehow he was going to have to find a way, if that was what it took to protect her.

He gritted his teeth as he thrust open the door to their suite, already mourning the loss of the intimacy that had made such a difference to his formerly bleak existence.

Midge's eyes widened with apprehension when she caught sight of the expression on his face.

'No need to look like that, Midge,' he snapped. 'It's not the end of the world.' Only the end of the freedoms they had enjoyed. 'I have just come from my father. Dr Cottee has confirmed my suspicion that you are going to have a baby.'

Midge glowered up at him. What had he got to look so irritated about? He had not been the one to undergo the most intimate and embarrassing examination any doctor could devise for a female patient. The moment Dr Cottee had left the room, she'd called for hot water so she could wash the feel of his slimy hands from her body.

It was only once she was fully clothed, when the feeling of revulsion had abated somewhat, that it occurred to her that he had not told her what the result of that examination had been. She had already been feeling hurt by the way Monty had left her to sleep alone, yet again, and puzzled by the way the news of her possible pregnancy had affected him. It was a further humiliation to find that the doctor had informed both the earl and her husband before anyone considered she had a right to know what was going on inside her own body!

Monty's eyes narrowed on her resentful expression. It was a far cry from the way wives of his fellow officers had looked whenever one of them had discovered they were increasing.

But then, women only married serving soldiers if they loved them enough to endure all the privations that following the drum entailed.

And Midge had never felt that way about him.

Theirs was not a love match. Far from it. He had bullied her into marrying him, selfishly wrenching her from that other man, the one she *did* care for!

No wonder she did not look radiant at the prospect of bearing his child.

A chill descended on him as he recalled an episode from his childhood.

His mother had been chatting with one of her bosom friends. She had startled him by throwing one arm around his shoulder and, for the only time that he could recall, kissing him on the forehead. *'How glad I am you are a boy,'* she had said, mystifying him. To her friend, she had then added, her lip curling, *'Now the earl has his spare, lest anything should happen to his precious heir, I have no need to carry on with that tiresome aspect of this marriage.'*

He felt short of breath. Something seemed to squeeze around the region of his heart.

No, dammit! Midge was nothing like his mother. She *enjoyed* making love with him. She did *not* regard having his child as a duty to be endured.

Did she?

Thrusting his fingers through his hair, he stalked over to the window and gazed moodily out.

'You may not go riding any more. The doctor has forbidden it. No strenuous exercise of any sort,' he finished bitterly, though he was now half-convinced that particular stricture was going to be harder for him to bear than for her.

As he spoke of horses, his eyes automatically followed the track that led round to the stables. And he saw his way out.

'I am going to London,' he declared, giving the window frame a thump.

It was extremely unhealthy for a man to be so totally obsessed with his wife. Getting breathless because he feared she might not care for him the way he cared for her! If he dithered about here much longer, he might find himself in the humiliating position of falling to his knees and begging for her love!

He heard her get to her feet.

'I am so glad.'

He could hear the smile in her voice without having to look at her.

'When do we leave?'

'I said *I* am going to London,' he said icily, turning round and glaring at her. 'Not you. You are to stay here and rest.'

The hurt look on her face almost had him weakening. Ruthlessly, he quashed the feeling.

The only way to preserve both her health and his sanity was to put a substantial distance between them. It would be madness to come anywhere near her again until he had got his feelings under better control. Better for her too. She would have a few days to get used to the idea of bearing the child of a man she…

A fresh wave of pain surged through him.

'Do not argue with me!' he snapped, as she took a breath to do just that. 'And do not think you can do as you please once I am gone. You are not to go out riding any more, do you hear me? And for the Lord's sake, don't let those demon twins lure you into any scrapes, either.'

He stopped short of relating the lecture that Dr Cottee had just given him. He had no intention of frightening her. He could already tell, by the look on her face, simply discovering she was pregnant was quite enough of a burden for now.

Midge sank back onto the sofa again, as though all the wind had been knocked out of her.

'I understand,' she said. 'I give you my word that after you have gone, I will not go out riding again or get in any scrapes with your brothers.'

'Dammit, Midge,' he began, instantly full of remorse for having hurt her. But then she lifted her chin and stared at him with such hostility that he bit back the apology.

Instead, he turned on his heel and stalked from the room, before he did what no man with an ounce of pride would ever do.

Get down on his knees and grovel at a woman's feet.

Midge would never understand men.

Yesterday, Monty had seemed pleased to think she might be carrying his child. But then his face had changed, and he had left the bedroom abruptly. Since then, he seemed unwilling to come anywhere near her.

He had been downright cross when he had told her he was going to London without her.

And then, this evening at dinner, while everyone else had been showering her with congratulations, he had looked positively gloomy.

Even the earl had unbent towards her enough to ask if there was anything he might do for her. When she had seized the opportunity to beg him to consider sending the boys to school, she had thought Monty would have been grateful. He was always saying he wanted them to have the education that was being denied them at Shevington. But when the earl, with a slightly mocking smile, had said he would grant her request, Monty had carried on staring balefully into his soup plate.

He had not risen from the table when she had, and though she had waited for him in their sitting room for hours, he had not come up to her. Eventually, when she heard the village church clock strike midnight, she had decided she might as well go to bed.

Her own. It was obvious by then that he was deliberately avoiding her. Nor had it taken all that long to work out why Monty did not want her to go to London with him. He knew her propensity for getting into scrapes. If he was going to get involved in politics, the last thing he needed was a wife who was a social embarrassment. The way he had lectured her about keeping out of trouble here at Shevington had hammered home what a liability he considered her.

But as the night wore on, her feelings of self-pity burned down along with her candle. As the new day began to dawn, so did her sense of resentment. Could he not at least have offered her his congratulations? After all, the whole purpose of marrying her had been to provide him with an heir. She had fulfilled her side of the bargain, and he ought to be grateful!

And what, exactly, was she supposed to do while he was in London being incredibly important? At least in London, there would be people she could visit.

There was nobody she could talk to at Shevington except the twins! And he had made her promise she would not ride out with them once he had left.

Not that he had left yet. She had not heard the coach being brought round. And it had to pass right underneath her window on its route from the stables to the front door.

Her heart thudding, she swung her legs out of bed, grabbed her dressing gown, tiptoed across their shared sitting room and laid her ear to the door of his room. She could hear somebody moving about. It sounded as though Monty was either getting dressed or his valet was packing up his gear. In either case, it meant he had not left yet.

She had just raised her hand to knock on his door, so that she might at least clear the air between them before he left, when a wave of nausea struck her. She took a deep breath, determined to fight it down. She wanted to bid him farewell in a dignified fashion. And determine whether it really was anything she had done that had put him in such a foul mood yesterday. He did have an awful lot of other problems, besides being married to a woman who was a walking disaster area. She wanted to tell him that…she gulped. With her head held high, she was going to tell him—

It was no use! She was going to be sick! Hitching

her nightdress up with one hand and keeping the other clamped firmly over her mouth, she ran to her room.

She made it to her bedroom just in time, grabbing the chamber pot from beneath the bed, and heaving wretchedly into it for what seemed like an eternity. What eventually got her to her feet was the sound of carriage wheels passing under her window. To her dismay, she realized that Monty was leaving.

Leaving without even bothering to bid her farewell.

Her legs gave out under her, and she sank into a disconsolate heap on the floor. That one night he had permitted her to sleep in his arms had meant nothing to him at all! He did not care. He truly did not care.

She did not think she had ever felt so wretched in her life.

The feeling of wretchedness stayed with her all morning. Pansy advised her, with a worldly-wise air, that some dry toast would make her feel better. And it did help settle her stomach. But no amount of toast could soothe a heart that was so badly bruised.

She did not even have the prospect of a ride out with the twins to cheer her up. She watched, enviously, from the window as they cantered away from the house on their scraggy little ponies, without so much as a backward glance.

The morning dragged interminably. She tried to read a book, but it could not hold her attention. She cast it onto the sofa cushions, and trailed to the windows to gaze longingly towards the woods where she knew the boys were playing. She was going to have to find some kind of sedentary occupation to while away the months of her confinement, she realized, or she would go mad.

Already, she was marking off the time until lunch would be served. And longing for the arrival of the mail.

It could not do any harm, surely, if she just went for a walk? The day was so mild. And, if she was not permitted to ride, at least she could go by the stables and visit Misty.

The prospect of getting out of the room that was beginning to feel like a cage, after only one morning, lifted her spirits no end. She paused to grab a shawl and drape it round her shoulders, so that nobody could accuse her of not taking proper care of herself, took an apple from the fruit bowl to console Misty for not being able to go out and get some exercise, and set off down the stairs.

She was going along the corridor that led past the estate offices, when one of the side doors flew open, and the earl emerged, looking thunderous.

'What do you think you are doing down here?'

She had never seen him with so much colour in his face. Not that it made him look any healthier than normal.

'I am just on my way to the stables,' she said, tugging her shawl more tightly round her shoulders.

'Thought you could sneak past me, did you? Flouting my authority by going riding though I have forbidden it!' He bore down on her, his eyes glittering with rage. 'Sly! Like all women! The minute your husband's back is turned, you think you may do just as you please! But you won't get away with it. I shall have the staff watching your every movement!'

It was a shock to see him act like this. Though Monty had described him as almost apoplectic with rage over a disagreement they'd had, she had assumed he must have been exaggerating.

'No,' she said in what she hoped was a soothing tone, and holding out the apple she had picked up for Misty, 'I was just going to…'

'The apple never falls very far from the tree, does it!' he said, before she could explain she had no intention of going for a ride. 'You are the product of the most notorious couple of my day. And you are just like them. Lascivious. Leaving trails of clothing all over the house. Luring your husband into the stables, so he can satisfy your itch in broad daylight!'

Midge was so shocked by the way the earl was berating her, the spittle flying from his mouth, that she simply backed away, open-mouthed. No wonder people put up with his cold, sarcastic moods, she thought as she fetched up against the wall, if crossing him could result in a scene like this.

'Mildenhall is a fool if he thinks you will not find some way to amuse yourself while he is in London setting up a mistress. Sauce for the goose, that is what women like you say, is it not? Plotting to get one of the stable lads to stand in for your husband, are you?'

She gasped in outrage, but the earl gave her no chance to refute the wild accusation.

'That is why I advised him only to marry a woman he could not possibly fall in love with. To spare him this sort of pain!'

He might just as well have struck her.

'He is not,' she cried, 'setting up a mistress!'

The earl flung back his head and laughed. 'Of course he is. Did you think a man like him could stomach staying down here, servicing a plain little baggage like you, when there are *pretty* women available in town? I told him so long as he married, and provided Shevington with an heir, I would frank his purchase of whatever woman he really wanted. Deserves his reward for doing his duty to the Claremont line,' he finished on a sneer.

'You are poisonous!' she gasped. Even if all he said was true, to fling it in her face like this was downright cruel.

'How dare you speak to me like that!' he hissed. 'Get back to your room!' He pointed down the corridor, and Midge, frightened by the malevolence that burned in his eyes, fled like a startled rabbit.

She did not stop running till she was safely in her room with the door shut firmly behind her. The man was unhinged! She had always wondered how on earth he could treat Monty and the twins so unkindly. Now she wondered if it was this kind of irrational behaviour that had driven his third wife into those affairs she was famous for having. Or whether he had imagined them all in some fit of insane jealousy!

And as for what he had said about Monty's reasons for leaving…they could not be true!

They just couldn't!

And yet, had she not always wondered why he was so reluctant to stay in her bed all night? He had let her think it was on account of the nightmares, but the minute there was a suspicion she might be pregnant… oh! She sank to the sofa, covering her face with her hands. Had he always looked on making love with her as a performance of his duty to the Claremont line? He had certainly ceased performing the minute Dr Cottee had confirmed there was no need for him to bother any more! And now that he had got her pregnant, he was off to London to find a *pretty* woman as a reward for having done his *duty* to the family name.

No wonder Monty had protested so vigorously when she had suggested accompanying him to London! It would be harder to trawl for a pretty mistress with a pregnant wife in tow.

Not that it had ever stopped her father.

She sat up straight, wondering what on earth possessed her to make excuses for Monty, even as he was on the verge of being unfaithful to her. What kind of idiot appreciated her husband for his discretion in setting up his mistress?

One who had always known he was far too good for her. One who had gone into this marriage knowing he was never likely to fall in love with her. One who…was about to be sick!

She retreated to her bedroom and her chamber pot, and when the maid came up with her lunch tray, almost ordered the girl to just take it away. She was in no fit state to swallow a single mouthful.

Though she was glad she had not done so when the twins came in a short time later. They took one look at the loaded tray and began to help themselves to her untouched sandwiches, stuffing some into their mouths and some into their pockets for later.

How often must they have been on the receiving end of one of the earl's tantrums? Many times, probably. She only had to think of the dread with which they had regarded him the day they had brought their pets into the house. No wonder they spent almost all their time out of doors or hobnobbing with the lower servants!

She tried to raise a smile for them, but it was an effort.

And the boys noticed.

'We know you're going to have a baby,' said Tobe, his disdainful gaze flicking down to her stomach.

'And that you don't want us here any more,' said Jem, resentfully.

'Oh, no!' She had not thought it was possible to feel any worse, but her heart sank as she realized the earl must have told them he was going to send them to school in such a cruel way that they believed it was some kind of punishment. She stretched out her hands, wanting to explain, but as one, they backed away from her.

'We only came to pass on a message from that friend of yours.'

'The one on the black horse.'

'He came smash up to us in the bluebell clearing where we showed you the badger's set.'

'Asked where you were. Told us to tell you he wanted to see you. And that he's staying at the Silent Woman down at Shevington Crossroads.'

'And then he clapped his hand to his head and went a funny colour and kind of hunched over the horse's mane.'

'Think he was going to be sick.'

'Anyway, we said we'd tell you he needed to see you, and we have.'

'But we ain't going to do you any more favours!'

'We thought you were our friend!' cried Tobe angrily.

'I am…' she protested, but it was too late. The pair of them had dashed from the room, slamming the door behind them. She buried her head in her hands again with a groan. The twins were all that made life at Shevington bearable. She had not expected they would give up their outdoor pursuits, to sit and keep her company. But now that the earl had turned them against her, they would go out of their way to avoid her. She would not see one friendly face, from one end of the day to the next.

When Cobbett arrived with the mail, she felt as though he had thrown her a lifeline. There *were* still people who cared about her. Her aunt corresponded regularly, and Rick wrote when he had time. Letters from Gerry were rare, and tended to come in batches, depending on the vagaries of shipping.

Today, only a single letter lay on the silver salver. She recognized the crabbed handwriting as that of her stepbrother Nick. It was with some surprise that she broke open the wafer. This was only the second time he had written since she had come to Shevington, and that had only been a polite little missive, in which he had expressed his gratification she had married so advantageously.

But the news he had for her this time dealt her such a blow, she did not know how she could bear it, coming as it did so swiftly behind everything else that had occurred that day.

Gerry was dead. Of a fever. Nick had written as soon as he received the news, but her stepbrother, it seemed, had already been dead for several weeks.

She could hardly take it in. How could Gerry be dead? She had sent him a letter only the day before!

She let Nick's letter drift to the carpet as the horrible truth sank in. Gerry would never read that last letter she had written to him. She would never see him again.

His life was over.

No more promotions. No more adventurous tales to enthral his little sister.

No more Gerry.

Eventually her eyes focussed on the opulent room in which she was sitting.

Alone.

There was nobody with whom she could share her grief.

Nobody who cared a rap about how she felt.

Though she had tried so hard to fit in. She had thought she was making some headway, but today she had learned just how little any of them cared about her. Today, they had all turned their backs on her, one after the other.

She had known she did not belong in the place, right from the very first moment she had set eyes on the outside of the buildings! Right from the first moment... her eyes lighted on the hideous vase squatting on the low table by the fireplace. She could not believe she had gone to such lengths to save such an ugly piece of porcelain. Or to have worked so hard to ingratiate herself with a set of people who had all let her down so badly.

Leaping to her feet, she picked up the vase that seemed to represent all that was ugly about Shevington, raised it above her head and hurled it into the hearth with a wild cry of fury.

It shattered into dozens of pieces with a resounding crash that went some way to consoling her.

But it was not enough. Not nearly enough.

Gerry was dead. Buried in some far-off land. So far away she would never have a chance to so much as lay flowers on his grave.

Even if Monty and his father ever let her set foot

outside the walls of Shevington Court again! For the earl had more or less threatened to keep her imprisoned here.

She could not stand it.

The walls felt as if they were closing in on her.

Tearing at the buttons to her high-necked morning dress, she ran to the door and flung it open, half expecting to find a guard posted outside. It was almost an anticlimax to find nobody there.

She lifted her chin and strode along the corridor to the stairs. There was nothing wrong with going for a walk if she wanted! Just let anyone try and stop her!

With her fists clenched firmly, she marched right out of the front door. In spite of the earl threatening to set his staff to watch her every move, she did not encounter a single soul as she ran round the side of the house and across the neatly mown lawns. She was in such a state that she scarcely knew where she was going. It was only when the acrid scent of crushed cow parsley assailed her nostrils that she realized she had left the formal gardens altogether and was entering the fringes of the woodland. And only then did it occur to her that what she needed was to reach some spot from which the walls of Shevington would be completely invisible.

She plunged through the bracken, ducking under low branches and skirting bramble thickets, until she reached a hazel coppice. Only then did she tilt back her head and let out the scream that had been building inside her since…since…she doubled over with grief. It was all of it, coming together that had so shattered her. Not just the news of Gerry's death, but the earl's attack, the twins defection and Monty's unfaithfulness, all coming so swiftly, one after another.

The clearing echoed with the panicked alarm calls of the flurry of birds which had risen en masse when she had screamed.

Then desolate silence descended through the still leafless branches.

Reminding her that she was on her own.

If only Rick were here…but he was not. His duties had carried him to a foreign land.

But even if he were here, things would never be the same between them. Not now that she had married his friend. She would never be able to confide in him completely. Not if her concerns related to Monty.

Now there was nobody, she gasped, not one soul to whom she could turn for comfort.

Nobody who cared one way or the other…

Except… She went very still.

Stephen had followed her down here. *He* wanted to see her.

And he *was* her brother. She lifted her chin and threw back her shoulders. If there was a chance, no matter how slim, that this last communication from Stephen might lead to some form of reconciliation, then she had to take it. She *needed* to take it. She had only avoided meeting him up till now out of respect for Monty's wishes. But what did his good opinion matter to her now?

He had deceived her and abandoned her…oh, very well, not deceived her. Not on purpose. It was her own fault if she had assumed his kindness and forbearance meant anything.

But in the long run, she sniffed, it might have been better for her if he had not tried to be kind to her. At least then she might not have fallen in love with him. And then his haste to leave her to find a pretty mistress as compensation for doing his repulsive duty with her might not hurt so much that she no longer cared if Stephen did plan to harm her!

Wiping her nose on the long sleeve of her dress, she cast a quick glance about the coppice, then set off in the direction she believed Shevington village lay.

Chapter Eleven

Midge was breathless by the time she emerged from the belt of woodland that bordered the road, but pleased with herself for coming out not a quarter of a mile from Shevington Village. Even if she was a failure at everything else, there was no denying she had a good sense of direction!

It did not take long to find the inn, either, since Shevington was barely more than a handful of buildings clustered around the crossroads.

She grimaced at the inn sign, depicting a woman in Tudor dress, her severed head laying at her feet, then walked through an archway broad enough to admit mail coaches, into its bustling stable yard. From the crowd standing outside the office, and the two floors suggesting an abundance of rooms for hire, she deduced it held a strategic position on the routes between Dover and London.

She sidestepped the queue, and went directly

to the man presiding behind the bar in the public coffee room.

'Excuse me, but I believe you have a man staying here by the name of Stephen Hebden?'

The landlord gave her a withering look, which reminded her she was not wearing either a coat or bonnet. Her long-sleeved, high-necked gown had looked perfectly respectable when she had put it on that morning. But since then, she had torn open the top buttons, wiped her nose on the sleeve, soaked the hem dashing through long grass, and scooped up a considerable amount of foliage on her headlong flight through dense woodland.

'Nobody by that name here,' he said. 'Perhaps I'll do instead, darling.' He leered, leaning over the bar, his beery breath gusting into her face.

Midge drew herself up to her full height, knowing her only defence would be her attitude.

'How dare you speak to me like that,' she snapped, imitating her aunt at her most frosty. 'The man I am looking for is my brother. He sent word that he needed to see me urgently.' She made a brief movement to indicate that very urgency accounted for the state of her clothes.

The landlord's eyes narrowed. 'Don't s'pose by any chance this brother of yours has long, black hair and wears an earring? Looks like he could be a Gypsy?'

'Yes! That's him!' she cried. All that mud and leaves stuck to her skirts had done some good after all. She obviously looked like the kind of person who lived outdoors.

'Room four,' the barman said, 'up them stairs—' he jerked his head to a narrow staircase that rose from a corner of the bar '—and along the corridor to the end.

And I hope you're going to be able to settle his shot,' he added sourly, 'if he sticks his spoon in the wall.'

She had not imagined Stephen could be that ill! Thank heaven she had come to him so soon after the twins had alerted her to his distress. Not, she admitted to herself guiltily, as she scurried across the bar and up the stairs, that it had been concern for him that had driven her here. But for whatever reason, she was here now, and she would do whatever she could to help.

She knocked gently on the last door at the end of the corridor, and when she got no reply, lifted the latch and tiptoed inside.

The curtains were drawn, making the chamber gloomy, but from the glimmer of light that spilled in over her shoulder from the passage, she could make out the form of a man sprawled out on top of the bed.

He was only wearing his breeches. And holding his crumpled shirt over his face.

'Stephen,' she whispered, shutting the door softly behind her and making her way across to the bed. From a new tension that seized his body, she could tell he knew she was there, but he made no sound. She reached out her hand to check for fever. But before she could touch him, his hand shot out and he grabbed her wrist.

'What do you want with me?' he snarled through clenched teeth, as though even the act of speaking caused him pain.

'To help you if I can,' she replied. He moaned, and let her go, pressing the shirt more firmly over his eyes. 'I know you probably only came here to cause me trouble…'

A ragged laugh escaped his pale lips. 'I am already

paying for what I planned to do to you. You can leave now.'

Instead of leaving, Midge went to the bell pull and tugged hard. She did not care what he thought of her. She would not abandon a chance acquaintance in an inn where nobody cared for anything but how his bill was to be paid, let alone her only true blood brother.

'Tell me what you need,' she insisted, pulling a chair up to the side of the bed.

'Nothing,' he spat, his eyes still fast shut. 'Nobody.'

Tentatively, she laid her hand on his shoulder. His body was warm, but not burning as though he had a fever.

'I can tell your head hurts,' she said. He could not bear to open his eyes, though he had deliberately darkened the room, nor speak above a hoarse whisper. 'I am going to order some coffee,' she said briskly. She did not usually have much sympathy for men who drank themselves into such a state. But he had nobody else to take care of him.

And there was nowhere else she wanted to be.

Nobody else who needed her.

When the chambermaid arrived, she ordered coffee and some oil of lavender so that she could bathe Stephen's temples with it. The maid looked past her at Stephen's prone body.

'How you plan paying for it?'

Midge took a breath, and counted to three before answering. 'I am Viscountess Mildenhall. I am certain that, should my brother not have the money on his person, a bill presented to the estate will be settled without question!'

The maid pursed her lips. 'Starting up again is it? Only 'twas the countess herself used to meet her fancy men here before.' She smirked, then lowered her voice, leaning in as though sharing a confidence. 'If'n you don't want this getting about, dearie, you need to bring the readies next time.' She sauntered off down the corridor, her shoulders shaking with laughter.

Midge shut the door, appalled by the chambermaid's assumption she was here to embark on a clandestine affair, *and* to learn that the twins' mother had, indeed, taken lovers. In this very inn! When it was so close to Shevington Court. And so very busy. She must have been determined to inflict as much pain and humiliation upon the earl as she possibly could.

Though, having endured that unwarranted attack this morning, Midge grudgingly admitted she could actually understand what had driven her to take such a drastic form of revenge.

'You have ruined your reputation in this locale by coming to me,' grated Stephen from the bed. She turned round, to see him staring at her, an unfathomable expression on his face.

She shrugged. The locals would have seen Monty's carriage passing by this inn on his way to London. They might very well assume she had taken the first opportunity after her husband's departure to fly to the bed of her lover.

The earl, she grimaced, most certainly would!

'I do not care,' she said defiantly. The earl had already decided she was wanton, without a shred of evidence. Accused her of crimes she would never have dreamed of committing, judging her on hearsay about her parents and condemning her to solitary confinement in her room.

What was one more crime, to add to all the other charges? *She* knew she was completely innocent!

'You are my brother. And that is all that matters to me.'

He stared up at her, his eyes dark with suspicion and hostility. But presently, he shut them, and said, 'Sometimes, I get some relief if my sister runs her fingers through my hair.'

Midge crept back to the bed, her heart bounding with hope. She stood quite still for a few seconds, gazing down at the proud, shuttered face, and then, taking all her courage in her hands, set her fingers to his temples, and swept them firmly across his scalp to the crown of his head. He heaved a sigh that was almost a groan. But he did not push her hands away this time. Again and again she ran her fingers through his dark, luxuriant hair, until she saw his great scarred shoulders sag into the pillows, as though he was letting go of some oppressive weight. It was only then that the import of his words struck her. He had another sister. One with whom he was on intimate terms. One that he went to, when he was ill.

'My sister,' he had said. Not 'my other sister.'

She stopped working on his scalp, imagining a girl who looked just like him. For somehow, she knew this other sister of whom he spoke came from his mother's people. The people he felt he belonged to. Else why would he take such pains to emphasize his origins? He could easily have cut his hair fashionably short. Nor was there any need to sport such a large, showy gold hoop in his left ear. Or wear clothes that were so colourful and cut in such an exotic style.

Stephen carried on breathing steadily, and she saw that the furrow between his brows was gone. He was asleep. She pulled his shirt from his slackened grasp, shook it out and draped it over the back of a chair, wondering if there had been anyone to do as much for Gerry in his last days.

The thought of Gerry sent an immense wave of grief crashing over her. And now that there was nothing more for her to do and nowhere else to run, she found the urge to break down and weep impossible to withstand any longer. She clenched her fists, and went over to the window which had a broad sill, upon which several frayed and rather greasy cushions were scattered. She took one and sat down, drew up her knees and buried her face in it. If she could no longer contain herself, the least she could do was muffle the sound of her sobs, so that she did not disturb Stephen. From time to time, she raised her head long enough to glance across at him. But nothing roused him. Not even the return of the chambermaid with the coffee, though not the lavender oil. Midge shrugged fatalistically. Sleep was probably the best remedy for whatever ailed him anyway.

She gulped down the coffee herself, between sobs, then drooped her way back to the window seat. She meant to keep watch over Stephen, but she could hardly keep her eyes open. Though that was not surprising considering she had hardly slept a wink the night before. And today, instead of taking her customary nap to make up for it, she had spent the afternoon smashing pottery, hiking across country and providing landlords and chambermaids food for gossip. And the bout of weeping had drained her of what little energy she'd had left.

She rearranged one or two of the cushions to pillow her head, and settled into a more comfortable position, feeling like a dish rag wrung out and hung limply over a line.

And woke with a start when Stephen reached over her, to yank the curtains open.

'Good morning,' he said dryly.

Midge rubbed her eyes, then winced at the pain that shot down her neck when she tried to move her head. The cushions she had so carefully arranged the night before were scattered all over the floor, and she had woken with her face wedged against the windowsill.

'Morning?' she repeated groggily. It seemed impossible, yet the sluggish grey light of a new day was definitely oozing through the grimy windows.

Stephen stalked to the washstand, poured water into a basin, and nonchalantly began to wash himself. Her shocked eyes roamed his naked torso, her heart welling up with pity. She had seen battle scars on her husband's body, so she recognized the suffering that all those criss-crossed silvery lines represented. If she had not known better, she would have thought he had been a soldier. A bullet had most definitely caused the ragged wound on his shoulder. It was so very like the one that Monty bore.

'Why did you come?' said Stephen, his back still towards her as he reached for a silver-handled razor.

Midge did not pause to think about her answer. She had been bereft and alone, and he had sent for her. 'I have nobody else.'

'What of your wealthy husband?' Stephen sneered, wielding the razor with frighteningly lethal speed.

'Gone to London.'

He dipped the razor in the water, rinsing away the soap.

'And what now?'

'I suppose,' she said hesitantly, 'you wish me to leave now you are well again. Though…' she pushed at one of the cushions with her toes '…you came down here to see me. Did you not? You must have had some reason for seeking me out.'

Oh, how she wished he would say he had regretted causing trouble for her at the wedding. And that, because he was her brother, he wanted them to be on good terms again!

But his face, as he turned to her, was harsh, not repentant.

'I wanted to know about what was said at the wedding.' When she frowned in confusion, he said impatiently, 'About your mother. That she told your stepfather to search for me. That when she heard I had died in the fire…' He turned abruptly, snatched up his shirt and dragged it over his head.

'She made me think she cared for me,' he snarled, jerkily doing up his shirt. 'That she thought of me as her son. And then she tossed me out like a piece of rubbish as soon as my father died!'

Midge leapt to her feet. 'She did not! When our father was murdered, she became very ill. Her father, my Grandpapa Herriard, came and took her back to his house to look after her. *He* was the one who sent you away. By the time she was well enough to come to the nursery to see us all, it was too late. You weren't there any more.'

She sat back down abruptly, her head spinning alarmingly.

'She begged him to tell her where you were,' she said quietly, leaning back and drawing in deep breaths to try to stave off the faintness. 'But he would not!'

'You remember all that, do you?' He sneered. 'What were you, about four years old?'

She shook her head, closing her eyes. 'I only remember flashes of things from back then. Being lifted out of my bed in the middle of the night, mother weeping, and then the misery of the nursery at Mount Street. Missing my mother, and—' she opened her eyes and looked straight at him '—you.' Stephen's absence had left a great gap in her life. A gap that nobody else had really ever been able to fill ever since.

'You were the one I always ran to,' she said sadly. 'I remember that.' She also remembered trotting after Hugh Bredon's sons in the same way she had used to follow after her adored Stephen. And being shocked to find her new big brothers did not automatically pick her up and cuddle her until she felt better. It had seemed like a long time before Rick had gradually begun to respond to her need for affection. Gerry had followed his oldest brother's example, eventually. Though Nick…

She pushed those unfavourable comparisons away, returning to the matter at hand. 'And then you were gone. And father was gone. And I was not allowed to go near mother—'

'At least she kept you!' he spat. 'Have you any idea what it was like for me, being sent to that place for children nobody wants? They told me I should be grateful for being taken in and fed, since my parents and friends had deserted me. Grateful! And every time I ran away and tried to get home, somebody would drag me back, and they would whip me in front of all the other boys and make me wear a red letter *R* pinned to my jacket!'

'I'm sorry,' Midge whispered, horror struck. How could anyone have been so cruel to a child that clearly needed love and reassurance? A boy who had just been ripped from the place he had been taught to believe he belonged? The scars on his body were as nothing compared to the scars that experience must have seared into his soul.

'There *was* a fire,' he said. 'You said, outside your fancy church, that you wondered if that had been a lie, too. Well, it was not! The chaos it caused gave me the chance I needed to escape.' He held out his hands and looked at the open palms for a brief second, before clenching them into fists and raising his dark head to glare at her again.

'Where did you go?' She looked at the hoop in his ear and the silver bracelet that adorned his wrist, and thought she knew the answer. 'You found your way back to your real mother's people.'

Something flashed across his face. 'Not immediately.' The expression settled into one so bitter, Midge knew she was not going to like what he was going to tell her next. 'I had to survive by begging and stealing for a long time before I found my way back to anyone who would offer me a home.'

'I am sorry,' was all she could think of to say. Though it was not enough. 'So sorry,' she said again, as a single tear slid silently down her cheek.

'So, you maintain she married an old man because he said he would search for me?' He laughed. The unex-pectedness of the sound, harsh and cold, made her flinch. 'But you and I both know he would not have given me a home. Had he found me. He would have taken one look at the wild thing I had become, and thrown me straight back in the gutter.'

Midge could not deny it was a possibility. Not now

she had seen through Hugh's facade to the coldness at his heart. He might well have said whatever he had deemed necessary to make Amanda marry him, so that he could have control of her fortune and his boys would have a loving mother. But he had not been much of a father to her.

'What does it matter now, what he might or might not have done?'

'What does it matter?' he exploded, his rage a tangible force she could feel battering her. 'I was torn from my home. Forced to live in a way you cannot possibly begin to imagine! And now, I—' he pulled himself up short. Drawing himself up to his full height, he threw his shoulders back and declared, 'I came to your wedding to spoil your day. Don't you know that? Don't you hate me for it?'

'No.' Midge looked him straight in the eye as she delivered that truth. 'And you have no reason to hate me, either.' She felt more tears sting her eyes. Stupid tears, that, since she had become pregnant, seemed to threaten at the least surge of emotion within her. 'None of what happened to you was my fault, Stephen. I missed you. I have missed you all my life.'

Stephen's eyes narrowed. 'What do you expect from me, Imo? That we can play at happy families again? As though these years, all the injustice of it, had never happened?'

Midge lowered her head, burying her face in her hands as she saw that that his life had been so harsh, he had been so convinced that everyone he had cared for had betrayed him, there might be no getting through to him. The embittered man who stood before her now was a complete stranger to her. The loving little boy she remembered was gone forever.

He was lost to her. As lost as Gerry.

'I do not expect anything from you, Stephen,' she sighed wearily. 'But I would like to ask you a favour.'

His face took on a sardonic cast that was very discouraging, but Midge decided she might as well ask anyway. He could only say no. And then she could simply walk back to Shevington Court and face the music.

'I came out yesterday in such a hurry, I forgot to bring any money. And I need to go to London.'

She needed to see Nick. He was the one person on earth who must, surely, miss Gerry as much as she did. With whom she could mourn the loss of that laughing, carefree young man. Oh, she knew it was a forlorn hope, considering the coldness he had exhibited towards her after Hugh's death, but any kind of hope for shared fellow-feeling was better than the certainty of the total isolation she would face on returning to Shevington Court. And she knew, too, that the earl would not permit her to travel anywhere for quite some time. If Stephen would not help her out…she choked back a sob, lifted her head and gazed up at him imploringly. Just a few days with Nick, that was all she was asking for. A few days away to come to terms with everything.

'Will you take me there?'

'Take you to London,' he echoed. 'After so short a time, you are ready to leave your husband? Or are you chasing after him?'

She flinched at the very notion she would demean herself by pursuing a man who had only ever feigned interest in her, and a chilling smile slashed across his face.

'If you are so set on ruining yourself, who am I to stand in your way? I will settle up and order a carriage. It will be my pleasure to take you to London.'

'Yes,' she said, regarding him sadly. 'I thought it would.' For Stephen did not care a fig for her reputation. In fact, the blacker he could make things look for her, the better pleased he would probably be.

Midge dozed in the coach, nearly all the way to London, while Stephen rode alongside on his magnificent black stallion. It was only when they drew up outside a house in Bloomsbury Square that she realized she had not made her intentions plain.

'I meant to ask you to take me to my stepbrother's lodgings,' she said as he opened the coach door.

His face closed. 'So, all that talk about missing me, wanting me to be part of your family, was just words! I might have known you were just using me!'

'No,' she protested. 'It is not like that…'

But he was striding away, shouting to the coachman to take her wherever she wanted to go. He mounted the steps of his house, and the door banged shut behind him.

Only then did she see that for all Stephen's apparent hardness, something about what had passed between them at the inn must have touched him. Because he was furious that she had not intended to make her stay in London with him.

She sank back into the squabs, reeling at her capacity for doing the worst possible thing on any given occasion.

But late that same night, Midge was back at Stephen's house, banging in desperation on the front door. If she had truly alienated him, she had no idea what she would do!

The dark-skinned servant who opened the door was

garbed in green, though Midge had never seen the like of the cut of his coat before. And he wore a turban wound round his head.

While she gaped at him, he said impassively, 'State your business.'

'I need to see Stephen. Please.' When he did not give a flicker of response, she added, 'I am Imogen Hebden. His sister.'

The Indian servant stood back and waved her into the hall. When she had entered the house, he closed the front door behind her and led her into a small parlour, in which a fire crackled cheerfully in the grate.

'I shall go and tell Stephen Sahib that you are here,' he said before melting away.

Midge made straight for the fire and sat on the chair closest to it, toeing off her sodden shoes. When she had put the dainty satin slippers on the day before, she had assumed she would only be sitting on a sofa all day, or at most, going down the stairs to dine. She had not thought she would tramp through woodland, take a coach to London, and then spend hours walking the streets. The soles had worn through hours ago. And then it had come on to rain, and she had not known whether it was worse to have shoes full of holes, or no coat or bonnet to keep out the wet. She felt, and was sure she looked like, a half-drowned rat, with her hair plastered all round her face and down her neck. She was surprised the servant had let her in. None of the houses she had ever visited before employed servants who would have shown in a woman in her condition without question, and sat them down in front of a fire.

She heard the door to the hall open again, and when she looked round, Stephen stood in the doorway, jacketless, his waistcoat still unbuttoned. He had brushed his long hair neatly back off his face. And removed his earring. And the quality of the evening garments was so fine, the style of what he was wearing so conventional that all in all, she decided, once he had donned a jacket, he would not look out of place at Almack's.

'What is it now?' he demanded brusquely as he stalked across the room towards her. 'What do you want?'

'I—' she swallowed nervously, and got shakily to her feet '—I am sorry to be so bothersome, but I need a place to stay for the night. Nick said…Nick said…' As her mind went back over the painful interview she had just had with her stepbrother, the room seemed to tilt around her. Just as the floor began to swim upwards towards her face, she felt Stephen's strong arms catch her, and she found herself lying, not face down on the hearthrug, but rather more decorously, upon a sofa.

She rather thought she must have fainted completely for a few seconds, because Stephen was pressing a drink into her hands, and she had no recollection of him going to fetch it.

'When did you last eat?' he demanded, his brows drawn into a scowl so tight she imagined he could very easily give himself a headache, without having to drink a single drop of brandy.

'This morning. At the inn,' she confessed. Stephen had been insistent that they breakfast before setting out. And although the last thing she had felt like doing was eating a mouthful, so anxious was she that word of her whereabouts might already have got back to Shevington Court, and someone would come to haul her back in disgrace, she had remembered how effectively Pansy's remedy for nausea had worked the day before. That plate of toast had kept her stomach calm all the way to London.

'You are wet through,' he said. 'What has happened to you? Why are you not with this other so-called brother of yours?'

'Well,' she sighed, 'he did not think it would be at all proper to have a married woman staying in his lodgings. Especially one who looked like she had been dragged through a hedge backwards.' She pushed a hank of wet hair off her face, and took a hefty swig of her brandy as her mind went back over that painful scene.

'I do not begin to understand what you thought you might accomplish by coming here,' Nick had said icily.

When she had began to stammer that it was because of the letter he had sent, he had pokered up, and stated, 'Germanicus is dead. There is nothing you can do about it. And if you think I am going to let a woman looking like that—' he had scathingly eyed her dishevelled appearance '—into my rooms then you are very much mistaken. I have prospects now, you know, Imogen. And I am not going to put my future at risk by letting you drag me into whatever scandal you are brewing. Now, I suggest you take yourself off back to your marital home, where you belong, and stop behaving like some kind of tragedy queen. *I* shall call on *you* there, at a more conventional hour.'

'You will do no such thing!' she had shouted at him, furious with herself for persistently refusing to admit how exactly like Hugh his middle son was. Totally self-centred and cold-hearted. All Hugh had cared about was books. And all Nick cared about was his career.

And she would rather die than go crawling to Monty's house in Hanover Square! She had immediately discounted any thoughts of returning to her aunt and uncle, too. Though her aunt might be sympathetic to her plight, her uncle was bound to be furious with her for coming up to London on an impulse, and alone.

'I shall go and stay with my *true* brother,' she had spat at Nick. Well, he had been upset that she had not intended to in the first place, hadn't he?

'Yes, that's right, the one who is half Gypsy. But let me tell you this,' she had said, jabbing Nick in his bony chest with her forefinger. 'He is twice the man you are. Ten times!'

Nick's thin lips had twisted into a sneer. 'The way you look I am sure you will fit right in with his camp on Hampstead Heath, or wherever they happen to be.'

'He,' she had boasted, 'has a very large house on Bloomsbury Square, as it happens.' And with her nose in the air, she had turned and clattered down the dingy communal staircase of the cheap lodging house where Nick had rooms.

It was not until she had got into the street that she remembered she had no purse. She would have done anything rather than go back into Nick's rooms and beg for the means to procure a cab. Besides, it was not that far. The coach Stephen had hired had not taken a quarter of an hour to take her to Nick's lodgings.

And so, in high dudgeon, she had set out to walk to Bloomsbury Square.

But those dratted indoor shoes! Ruefully, she rubbed at her wet and blistered feet. She had been limping before she had reached the first corner.

Stephen's gaze followed her movements. When he saw the state of her feet, he drew in a breath.

'I have to go out soon. It cannot be avoided. But Aktash will see to all your needs,' he said, crossing to the bell pull and tugging on it. 'You shall have shelter for the night. You stayed with me all night. You did your best to look after me. Now I do the same for you. And we are even,' he said fiercely. 'In the morning, we will discuss what your next move should be.'

Midge almost burst into tears again. She was safe, for now. But, oh, the problems she was going to have to face in the morning! Why, oh, why could she never think before charging off on one of her wild exploits? No wonder Monty was sick and tired of her. She was sick and tired of herself.

'What do you mean, she has disappeared?'

Monty glowered at his father, completely at a loss to understand how Midge could have vanished from a house that was teeming with so many servants.

'Somebody must have some idea where she is!'

Pansy, who had been summoned the moment Monty arrived at Shevington Court, wrung her hands. 'It wasn't till this morning, when I saw her bed had not been slept in, I got worried. Well, you know her routine. I only go up to her room now if she summons me special, excepting to take her breakfast up and help her dress for the day.'

Cobbett cleared his throat. 'I believe I was the last person to see her, my lord,' he admitted guiltily. 'When I took up her post.'

Monty drew in a deep breath, stifling the urge to hit the poor fellow. It was not his fault that nobody had organized any kind of search party. Ever since Pansy had reported her missing, everyone seemed to have begun blaming everyone else. It was a wonder anybody had actually had the presence of mind to send for him at all.

'I had not yet instructed the staff to organize a watch on her movements,' admitted the earl. 'She was too quick for me. It is the way with women like that. You made a serious error of judgement, thinking you could tame Framlingham's daughter.'

'What?' Monty whirled round to stare at him. 'What are you insinuating?'

'Am I not making myself clear enough for you?' He sneered. 'I had already caught her trying to sneak down to the stables, the minute you had gone. I put a stop to that, you may be sure. Told her I knew what she was about!'

Monty shook his head impatiently. 'Midge gave me her word she would not go riding—'

'Not four-legged beasts, perhaps. But there are other attractions to be found in the stables for women like her.'

It was all Monty could do not to fly at the dirty-minded old man, casting aspersions on Midge's character, with servants present, too! Clenching his fists, he growled, 'Do you mean to tell me you accused her of plotting to seduce one of the grooms? Is that it? I would not have thought even you could stoop so low.'

The earl collapsed into his chair, his face growing pale. 'You should have been here to keep her under control,' he said querulously. 'I should not have to deal with such a termagant.'

'Gave you back as good as she got, did she?' said Monty with satisfaction. 'Good for her!'

'I should have known you would somehow ruin my plans for the next generation of Claremonts,' muttered the earl peevishly. 'Bringing a creature like that to Shevington. I am supposed to have complete peace and quiet!'

'Well, don't worry!' snapped Monty, turning on his heel. 'Once I find her, you may be sure neither of us will be returning to this benighted place!'

Muttering under his breath, Monty took the stairs to their suite two at a time. He did not know what he expected to find when he got there. It was just that that was where he pictured her. And the last place anyone had seen her.

When he strode into their sitting room, the first thing he saw was the vase, which she had taken such pains to save, lying smashed to pieces in the fireplace. So many pieces—it must have been hurled to the ground with some force!

Midge had been furious. And who could blame her? His father was the outside of enough.

And far more unstable than even he had suspected. The earl had been so pleased Midge was pregnant. Monty would have thought that would have been enough to protect her from falling foul of one of his father's irrational outbursts.

Apparently not, he thought bitterly, nudging at some of the larger pieces of pottery with the toe of his boot.

Then something else caught his eye. A single sheet of writing paper. He picked it up, scanned it swiftly and screwed his eyes shut against the clipped, formal language informing her of her stepbrother's death.

My God! He sank to the sofa, his head in his hands. Just when she had needed him most, he had not been here. He had gone running off to London, in a stupid attempt to preserve his own pride.

But what good was his damned dignity if he had lost her?

He could picture how it must have been. The scene with his father, and then getting news like that. She must have been beside herself to have hurled the vase into the fireplace with such force. And then what? Knowing Midge, she had probably gone charging off without giving a thought to where she was going. Unless there was some particular spot on the estate she had grown fond of. Where she might go to find some kind of solace.

But then, why had she not returned at nightfall?

His stomach clenched as he pictured her stumbling down the main stairs, weeping…running out into the woods she loved so much…falling…lying injured and so badly hurt she was unable to rise. And he cursed himself for not spending more time with her. For working so hard to prove himself worthy of the position he would one day fill. For putting his father's demands before her needs. Now the only people who might know where she might have gone were the twins, with whom she had spent the majority of her time.

The twins! His father was sending them away, any day now, but they had not gone yet.

Shooting to his feet, he charged along the corridor and up the stairs to the set of rooms in the attics they inhabited.

They looked up from where they were kneeling on the floor packing their trunks, when he burst in upon them.

'Do you know where she might have gone?' he blurted.

They both looked at the screwed-up piece of paper he was still clutching in his hand.

'Doesn't it say in her note?' said Jem, at the exact same moment Tobe said, 'Just like our mother.'

'What?' Monty looked from one to the other, in complete bewilderment.

'We're sorry, Vern,' said Jem, getting up and wiping his nose on the sleeve of his jacket.

'She betrayed us, too.'

'Getting us banished from Shevington, coz there's only room for one baby in the nursery!'

'And then running off with her fancy man!' said Tobe indignantly. 'If she was gonna do that to you, there was no need to get us sent to school!'

'She has not run off with a fancy man!' Monty protested. 'She must have met with an accident. She is out there somewhere.' He waved his arm towards the window that overlooked their beloved woods. 'Does she have a favourite place? Somewhere she would go if she was upset?'

The twins looked at each other and he could see some message pass between them, before Jem looked him straight in the eye and declared, with touching sympathy, 'Vern, we *told* you, she's gone to the Silent Woman to meet her fancy man!'

'Hanging around here for days, he was.'

'And she pretended she didn't want to see him.'

'But as soon as you left, she went straight off after him like a shot!'

A new fear gripped Monty as he recalled the dreamy expression on her face, the night he had assaulted her on Lady Carteret's terrace. Her insistence it had been produced by thinking about some other man. How, a few days ago, she had thrust a letter into the flames and lied about its contents. And how her face had closed up when he had forbidden her to go to London with him.

He strode towards the window, running the fingers of one hand through his hair, whilst crumpling the letter from her stepbrother in the other.

He was constantly running up against the spectre of that Other Man!

But surely, Midge would not just run out on him? She was too honest, too direct to behave in such a sneaky way. And now that she was expecting, too…hell, she knew how much this child meant to everyone at Shevington!

No, he could not believe she would be so deliberately cruel. She did not have a cruel bone in her body.

And what was more, he could not believe she could have made love with him with such wild abandon, if any other man was of the least importance to her. She was not the wanton his father painted her! Why, when he thought how embarrassed she became whenever he attempted to take their lovemaking to a new level…

He rounded on the twins, his eyes narrowing. For some reason, they were lying to him.

'Tell me what has really happened,' he growled, seizing each of them by one ear. 'Or so help me I will make you rue the day you were born!'

'Ow, stop it!'

'Let go!'

'Not until you tell me the truth!'

'We have! We have! She's gone to the Silent Woman!'

'She must have,' whined Tobe. 'We took the message

from the man on the black horse, and then we saw her running off in the direction of the village!'

'Man on the black horse?' he said, abruptly letting them go. 'There really was a man asking to see her? What,' he asked, dreading their answer, 'exactly does he look like?'

'Like a Gypsy,' said Jem without hesitation.

'Yes, he's got an earring and a dagger in his boot and everything!'

A chill tied his guts into a knot as he saw, finally, why she had not come back.

He had not been able to believe Midge could be unfaithful. But he could believe that, in her naiveté, she had gone running off to meet Stephen after the dreadful day she'd had! For she had no idea how dangerous the man was.

Because he had never warned her.

He had thought he was shielding her from distress by not telling her how the fiend had abducted Marcus Carlow's wife. He had not wanted her upset by learning how the devil had plotted to ruin Stanegate's sister Honoria, either.

But when he thought of the silken noose Stephen had sent her, as a warning of his intentions, his stomach turned over.

Dear God, if any harm came to her…

With a face like thunder, he thrust the twins aside and made straight for the stables. She had already been in his clutches for over a day. But he would find her.

And heaven help that Gypsy bastard when he did!

Chapter Twelve

Midge did not wake the next day until nearly noon. And then only because a thin, sallow-faced maid came bustling into her room with a breakfast tray.

She also brought water for washing, and a complete set of clean clothing. When Midge tried to thank her, she just shrugged, and said, 'Master's orders,' in a dismissive tone.

Once Midge had settled her stomach with a plate of toast and washed and dressed, the girl led her downstairs to a room she described as a library, although it did not contain many books, and handed her over to Akshat.

'Stephen Sahib regrets he has to attend to some business today. He will return about seven this evening. If you are still here when he returns, he will dine at home. In the meantime, my instructions are to provide you with whatever you require,' he said, and bowed respectfully.

The trouble was, she had not been able to think of anything she did need. She was already feeling overwhelmed by the extent of Stephen's hospitality.

'Th-thank you,' she eventually managed to stammer. 'If I think of anything…'

The Indian manservant had indicated the latest issue of the *Times* spread out on a table under the window. 'Perhaps you would care to read. But if there is anything else—' he made a graceful gesture towards the bell pull by the fireplace '—you have only to ring.'

Midge had meekly walked over to the table and looked down, but her eyes only flicked over the closely packed columns of newsprint without registering a single word.

She was reeling from the thinly veiled message Stephen had delivered via Akshat. Stephen would put off whatever he had planned to do this evening if she was still there when he got home. But he more than half expected her to shake the dust from her feet the moment she woke up.

She shook her head. How could he think she would just leave and waste this heaven-sent opportunity to get to know each other? He was the only real sibling she had. Nick's attitude had brought it home to her, as nothing else could have done, that she had to stop regarding Hugh Bredon's sons as her brothers.

Though even if she *had* wanted to leave, she had nowhere else to go and no means of getting anywhere. She was *not* going to turn up on Monty's doorstep, in only the clothes she stood up in, and grovel to him for admittance! Not when she knew she was the very last person he wanted to see.

She took a sharp breath, raised her head and stared sightlessly out of the window. She had hoped that after a good night's sleep, she would have come up with some notion of what she ought to do next. But the sad truth was that she had no idea how she was going to get out of this fix.

The same tree that obscured the view from her bedroom window grew right outside this room. But by pressing her nose against the windowpane, she could make out an area of greenery in the centre of the square. That was what she would do! Take a walk: maybe that would clear her mind. At least it would be better than moping about indoors, feeling sorry for herself.

But when she opened the door to the hall, she found Akshat standing right outside.

'Are you leaving, Mem Sahib? Is there any message you wished to leave for Stephen Sahib?'

'N-no!' she denied hotly. 'I just thought I would get some fresh air. It is such a lovely day, and there seems to be a sort of little park area just outside?'

The servant's stance relaxed. 'Please wait here, Mem Sahib, while the girl fetches your bonnet and coat.'

'Oh, but I don't have a coat with me!'

'Stephen Sahib has provided all you may need,' he stated firmly.

He certainly had! Midge's throat felt thick with emotion as she backed into the library to wait for the maid who brought her some very serviceable outdoor clothing. Surely, this must mean that his attitude towards her was mellowing?

'I am to accompany you, Mem Sahib,' Akshat informed her, as he opened the front door.

'Oh, I am sure there is no need for that. I am only going to take a turn about the square!'

'Stephen Sahib has ordered me to guard you with my life while you are his guest.' His hand made a slight movement towards his waist, and she saw, with astonishment, the jewelled hilt of an oriental-looking dagger tucked into the belt.

Midge blinked. His statement and his gesture towards the knife belt seemed rather melodramatic to her, but she had no intention of wounding the sensibilities of a servant who was so determined to carry out his master's orders to the letter. Besides, she *had* read recently that two people had been killed by soldiers when a mob had attacked a Tory minister's home. She was not certain how far from this area that event had taken place, but she supposed it might have left Londoners a little nervous.

It felt unreal, going down the front steps, carefully wrapped up against any chance breeze, and duly escorted by such an exotic armed bodyguard. She stifled the urge to giggle. Why, her own aunt had not had her chaperoned so zealously!

Though the area was not a fashionable one, all the houses that stood round the square, Stephen's included, looked as though they belonged to prosperous families.

He must, she thought with some surprise as she craned her neck to look up at the window of the room she'd slept in the night before, be quite a wealthy man.

So why had he turned up at her wedding, wearing clothing that made him look like a vagrant?

She could not understand him at all. One minute he was wrecking her wedding, the next he was providing her with a bodyguard. He dressed like a Gypsy, yet lived in a house fit for a gentleman.

She shook her head, feeling suddenly overwhelmed by it all. And she was so tired! All she wanted to do was crawl back to bed, pull the covers over her head and shut out every single one of her problems. Akshat shadowed her back to the house and handed her over to the maid.

She fell deeply asleep the moment she laid her head on the pillow and did not wake until the maid came clattering in with a can of hot water.

Midge sat up, rubbing her eyes and pushing her hair from her face.

'What time is it?'

'Time to be getting dressed for dinner, Miss,' the woman replied with a hint of reproach in her voice. 'Mr Stephen is back from work and waiting for you.'

The woman clearly adored Stephen, she thought, rather startled, as she got out of bed and stumbled to the washstand. She seemed to think Midge should have been eagerly awaiting his return, not lounging about in bed.

Stephen had provided her with another outfit, this one suitable for eveningwear. When she looked at herself in the mirror, Midge thought she could have dined anywhere in such a beautifully tasteful garment. The underskirt was of pale blue satin, with a gossamer-fine silk overdress in an even lighter hue. She caught a wistful expression on the serving woman's face, as she set about brushing her hair, and wondered if she was the one who had been sent out to buy the gown.

Only, how would a woman who worked in a bachelor household know what to buy for a lady? She looked at the woman out of the corner of her eye with misgiving. Although she spoke politely enough, her voice was quite coarse, her accent reminding Midge of the women who sold flowers and fruit outside the theatres she had attended whilst staying with her aunt.

Better not ask too many questions, she decided as the

maid draped a matching shawl about her shoulders. A man as blatantly virile as Stephen was bound to have a mistress. Though, she frowned, this gown had surely been purchased for a lady of quality, not a lady of the night.

Stephen was sitting in the small parlour Akshat had taken her to the previous night, tapping one forefinger irritably against the arm of his chair.

'I must thank you for your generosity, S-Stephen,' she stammered as he got to his feet. 'For taking me in last night, when I was in such distress, and having me cared for today with such kindness.'

'It is no easy matter to ignore blood ties,' he said gruffly, gesturing towards the open dining-room door impatiently. Midge could see a table had been laid for two.

He held her chair for her, and when she was seated, took the place opposite her and flicked his napkin across his lap with a snap.

'I find it significant that our paths should cross at this time,' he said enigmatically as a young footman in smart green-and-gold livery ladled soup into her bowl.

Midge stared at Stephen. He spoke as if their meeting had been some kind of chance event, but he had deliberately revealed his existence on her wedding day.

'Where does your destiny lie now, I wonder,' he said, once the servant had departed soundlessly. 'You have run away from your husband. Do you now wish to make your home with me?'

Midge dropped her spoon into her bowl with a splash. She had *not* run away from Monty. Not intentionally. But, oh, dear, that was how it was going to look. She felt her cheeks heating as she clumsily tried to retrieve the spoon without getting soup on her fingers. Her aunt had always chided her for acting without thinking, warning her that one day her impulsive behaviour would lead to disaster.

She rather thought this might be a disaster of some magnitude. She had already decided she had too much pride to go round to Hanover Square. Slinking back to Shevington Court, knowing what she knew, would be even more demeaning.

But if she stayed here with Stephen, everyone *would* assume she had left her husband!

Which was a totally outrageous thing to do. Her aunt had warned her that the heir to the Earldom of Corfe would expect his wife to look the other way when he began to have affairs. Walking out of a marriage of convenience, on the flimsy pretext that she could not bear to think of Monty with a mistress, would create a scandal that would make his stepmother's affairs pale into insignificance.

She extricated the spoon and held it, dripping, over the bowl, her mind whirling.

'You may do so, if you wish.'

She looked up, startled. 'I had not thought that far ahead,' she admitted, worrying at her lower lip. As usual, she had not been thinking at all. Only reacting to the news that Gerry was dead, and she was all alone. Her instinct had been to fly to the only person in the district she felt she had any connection to. And then, when Nick had repulsed her, she had done the same thing again. Exhausted, distraught, all that was in her head was the knowledge that Stephen was nearby.

A smile tugged at the corner of Stephen's mouth.

'If you lived with me, I would let you do whatever you wanted,' he murmured seductively.

She set down her soup spoon firmly, her heart sinking as everything suddenly became clear. Everything he had done, from the moment they had met, had stemmed from a spirit of hostility! He was not inviting her to stay because he had suddenly developed fond feelings for her. He was just thoroughly looking forward to watching Amanda Hebden's daughter scandalizing the Ton.

By coming here, she had played right into his hands.

She picked up a napkin to wipe her sticky fingers clean, her appetite ruined. His attitude hurt her almost as much as Nick's rejection.

'I wish I could stay with you, but not like this!' she said. 'I only want to get to know you. Because you are my brother. Even though you harbour so much bitterness towards me. Stephen—' she reached her hand out towards him across the table '—none of what happened to you when we were children was my fault! And it makes me want to weep to learn of the terrible things you have been through—'

He reared back from the table so suddenly that his chair overturned.

'I do not want your pity!'

'What *do* you want then?' Why was it that she always seemed to be the one holding out her hand, reaching out to others, and they always, in the end, recoiled from her like this? 'Why did you contact me again, after all these years?'

He turned from her as he righted the chair. When he spoke again, his voice was flat. 'I have a destiny to fulfil. Justice must be done.'

'What kind of justice is there in conniving at my ruin?' She sighed. 'I could understand you wanting to hurt my grandfather for taking you away from the only mother you had ever known and committing you to that horrible place, but he is long dead. What have I ever done to deserve your enmity?'

'You were brought up in luxury,' he said in a voice so cold it sent a shiver down Midge's spine. 'And now you have married a rich and titled man. You have never gone hungry one day of your life or had to steal just to stay alive.' He leaned forward, his palms flat on the table. 'Your grandfather stole everything from me! I should have been brought up just like you. Oh, I know I would never have inherited our father's title. I will never be anything but a bastard in the eyes of the society that has taken you to its heart. But he could have made sure I had a decent education and the kind of patronage that would have ensured a respectable career. Instead, I have had to claw my way out of the gutter…'

'Oh, Stephen,' she sighed. 'Our father's murder left a shadow over us all. Not just you! You must let go of all these vengeful thoughts. Have we not all suffered enough because of what our parents did?'

'Who has suffered? You?' He laughed at her mockingly. 'You have paid nothing!'

'Oh, haven't I?' Quite suddenly, she came to the end of her tether. Leaping to her feet, she swept the half-empty soup bowl to one side with her forearm. 'I have paid for being Kit Hebden's daughter all my life! You say you have had to claw your way up. At least you could! Because I am merely a female, I have had to exist on handouts, like the beggar you say you were. Yes, I have married a rich man, but only because he needs an heir to set his father's mind at rest. And because my stepbrother asked him to take me off his hands. And because he wanted some woman he would not shed a tear over, should I happen to die in childbirth. I have always been expendable. I am so insignificant in the scheme of things, your mother could not even bother to curse me!' She laughed a little hysterically.

'It is only sons that matter! Our parents fought ferociously over your fate! Did you know that? My mother told me that, not long after you were given to her, Grandfather came storming to the house, demanding you be sent back to your real mother. And my mother ran up to the nursery and held you while the two men went at it hammer and tongs in the hall. She wept because she feared Father would toss you aside as easily as he had tossed aside all the mistresses she'd known about to that date. And once you actually *had* gone, Mother just stuck me in a nursery, and forgot all about me. Married a man old enough to be her father, because he had three sons to replace the ones she'd lost. And because he promised to search for *you*. I trailed along behind my new brothers, doing all I could to earn the tiniest crumb of affection, working my fingers to the bone to earn my place in that family, but when it comes right down to it, nobody has ever cared if I am alive or dead!'

By the time she had finished, she was breathing hard and trembling all over.

'My, my—' a mocking smile tilted one corner of Stephen's mouth '—and you accuse *me* of being bitter.'

He went to the sideboard, poured two drinks and handed her one across the table. Midge had no idea what it was, but she took a most unladylike gulp of it before dropping onto her chair like a stone. Stephen sat too, sipping at his own drink with a thoughtful air.

'You have no more need to hang on the coat-tails of your rich husband, Imo. You could join forces with me.'

'In your vendetta, you mean?' She shook her head. 'Oh, no. I cannot feel anything but pity for all the children of the men involved in whatever it was that happened that night.'

Stephen's eyes narrowed.

'What do you mean, *whatever* happened? Leybourne murdered our father!'

Midge sighed, and pushed the hair back from her face wearily. 'I am not about to start arguing with you over that. What does it matter now?'

Stephen drained his glass and set it down with quiet deliberation before answering her.

'I came across a journal written by Lord Narborough. About the events leading up to that night and what happened afterwards. The pages dealing with the murder itself are missing.'

'Are you saying you think he has something to hide?' She set her glass down on the table with a frown.

He paused again before answering. 'You surely do not think he deserves to have done so well out of the whole damned business, do you? Just think, Imo. Out of the three men concerned with breaking the code and catching the spy, only Lord Narborough is left standing. What does that tell you?'

She shook her head in bewilderment.

'Narborough was the only eye-witness. What kind of man is so eager to give the kind of testimony that was certain to send his avowed friend to the gallows? We both know where Leybourne was those times he was supposed to have been consorting with enemies of the state. *In bed with your mother!* And Narborough knew that too!' He paused, a nerve jumping in his jaw. 'At least Leybourne was gentleman enough not to drag her name into it. Narborough had no such qualms!'

She sucked in a breath, a horrible suspicion forming in her mind. 'This is awful! Mother always said Lord Leybourne could not have done it! He was too much the gentleman to stab another man in a fit of rage…he might have fought a duel…' she pressed her hands to her forehead, breathing hard '…and then again, why would he have suddenly switched sides, when he had devoted his life to hunting down enemies of the state? He had no reason! And so much to lose…'

'Let us not get side-tracked by your mother's opinions,' he sneered. 'She was no judge of character, was she? She would not have *wanted* to believe she had taken a traitor and murderer to her bed. Just remember this, Imo. The spying stopped after they arrested Leybourne.'

'That does not prove anything!' she protested. 'Except perhaps that the real spy became more careful. He was close to being found out. Father told Mother that it was so obvious, a baby could have worked it out. He shook the rattle in her face, and said that was how he was going to break it to them.'

'Rattle?' said Stephen, mystified.

'Oh, he had bought a gift for the new baby,' she said, waving her hand dismissively. 'Lady Verity, as it turned out. But never mind that,' Midge continued. 'If Lord Narborough was really the murderer, and he deliberately sent Leybourne to the gallows to conceal his own crime…using his reluctance to bring my mother into the scandal… Oh, how wicked!'

'You think…Narborough did all that?' Stephen said, his eyes narrowing.

But she scarcely heard him. 'And his poor family! They lost everything! Who knows how they have been forced to live since then?'

'Oh, I do,' he said, a malicious smile playing about his mouth. 'I know where they all are, and exactly how they have been living. The depths to which the son has been forced to stoop. The humiliations that have been heaped on the daughters. Helena is out in the open now, protected by, of all people, Marcus Carlow. But the other girl is working as a paid companion to a titled lady. Under a false name. Imagine that,' he said with evident relish.

Midge went cold inside. 'Stephen,' she gulped, 'if her father was a murderer, then justice has already been done. And more than done. But what if he was innocent?'

Stephen's brows drew down into a fierce black scowl.

She waved her arm round the room, desperate to find some way of preventing him from persecuting a poor girl who had already suffered more than enough.

'You have done so well for yourself, in spite of all the obstacles fate has thrown in your way. You have the wealth you say should have been yours. And you have earned it all for yourself. You should be proud of what you have achieved. You could live a good life, Stephen, if you would only let the past go!'

'You understand nothing,' he snapped. 'I cannot leave

it until my part is played out. It is my destiny. The truth must come out!'

She pounced on that word. 'If the *truth* is that Leybourne was hanged for a crime he did not commit, then you must not try to punish his children!'

His scowl deepened. 'What right do you have to come in here and tell me what I should or should not do! You know nothing!'

'I know that you have to stop harassing the innocent, or you will somehow pay for it!'

He reeled back, as though she had struck him, his face going pale. But before either of them could say another word, they both heard the sounds of raised voices from the hallway.

One of them was all too familiar. 'Monty,' whispered Midge in horror. How on earth had he managed to find her? And more to the point, why had he bothered?

She clapped her hands to her stomach. The Claremont heir. Oh, how foolish she was to get her hopes up. It was all about the baby she carried, not her!

But her heart was in her mouth as the voices grew more indistinct, and were then replaced by the sound of scuffling boots, slithering on the hall's polished tiles. The manservant wore a knife in his belt! What if he used it! The sound of a body falling with a dull thud to the floor sickened her.

But when the door flew open it was Monty who strode in, tugging down his sleeves and straightening his cravat.

And even though the light of battle still burned in Monty's eyes, Midge sagged down onto her chair with relief.

'Evening, Hebden.' He nodded curtly to Stephen as

he advanced across the room. Behind him, Midge could see the Indian manservant laid out prone on the hall floor, blood streaming from his nose.

'How did you manage to find me so quickly?' Stephen replied, looking curious more than anything else, as though it was normal for vengeful husbands to fight their way in during dinner.

'Left a trail a mile wide,' replied Monty grimly.

Stephen eyed Midge with a frown. 'I must be getting careless.'

Midge had heard about Monty's many exploits on the battlefield, but until this moment, she had never really seen the warrior in him. Now, she quailed at the knowledge that he had fought his way into Stephen's house and disabled an armed opponent, as a direct result of her own misbehaviour.

'Are you all right?' he growled, his eyes flicking to her brother. 'Has he harmed you?'

'Who? What?'

And then he was crunching his way across the broken soup plate, and scooping her up out of the chair and crushing her in a great bear hug.

'I am so sorry I was not there,' he said, cupping her face in his hands and looking down into her face earnestly. 'It was selfish of me to leave you. You should not have been all alone when you received such news. My poor, poor love.'

He smoothed back the hair which had inevitably escaped its pins at some point during the evening. In his eyes, she could read nothing now but concern.

And she felt suddenly very guilty.

She had assumed he would be angry, but when had

he ever actually berated her for anything she had done since they had married?

'I smashed the vase,' she confessed. 'On purpose.'

'Don't blame you. Hideous bit of porcelain,' he said in between the kisses he was peppering her face with. 'Daresay you needed to smash something, getting a letter like that. Especially after what my father put you through.'

'He told you about that?'

Monty nodded. 'I would never have left you alone, believe me—' he gripped her upper arms tightly '—if I had thought he would turn on you like that. But his attitude towards you, that last night, convinced me he would take the very greatest care of you.'

Something inside her melted as she gazed up at him. He was the only person over the past few days to have understood what made her act as she did. Or even be interested in what drove her. No wonder she loved him!

Stephen had asked her to be his ally, but only as a tool in his twisted quest for what he termed justice. He was fettered by what had happened twenty years ago.

And as for Nick, his mind was so fixed on the glittering career he believed was in his sights, that he had only seen her as a hindrance.

But Monty was here for her, right now.

She leaned into his chest and sobbed, 'I have been so miserable!'

'I know, I know,' he said, rocking her.

'My God,' muttered Stephen darkly. 'This is turning my stomach.'

Monty started, as though he had forgotten there was anyone else in the room. His face hardened.

'You will stay away from Midge from now on, do you hear me! How dare you take advantage of her distress to spirit her away!'

'No! No, Monty, that is not what happened.' She reached up and turned his face towards her own with the palms of her hands. 'If you must be angry with anyone, it should be with me. If not for Stephen's kindness, I do not know what the result of my folly might have been. He hired a carriage to bring me to London, at *my* request. And then when Nick turned me from his door, he gave me a roof for the night—'

'I could not believe it when I learned about that,' Monty interjected. 'He did not even make sure you had the means to get a cab. Anything might have happened to you…a defenceless woman, in a great city like this…'

'It was not so very far to walk to Stephen's house,' she pointed out. 'And once I got here, I knew I would be safe. Not that I was afraid. In fact, all I could think of was…'

'The one remaining brother who was within striking distance.' Monty's face cleared. 'I understand.'

'So you see, I did not deliberately disobey you. At least, not yesterday,' she added miserably. 'And even when Stephen first came to Shevington, I *meant* not to go near him, but…'

'I know, I know, the twins told me he had tried to get you to speak to him before, and that you would not. I do not deserve such loyalty…'

Uttering an oath, Stephen picked up the decanter and made for the door.

'No, wait,' said Monty. 'It is we who should leave.' He tucked Midge in against his shoulder, and held out his hand. 'I apologize for misconstruing your intentions. Will you shake hands with me?'

Stephen eyed the outstretched hand with contempt, then levelled a strange look at his dishevelled, tear-stained sister.

'You did not misconstrue my intentions. Give that girl enough rope, and she will hang herself.'

Midge flinched and paled, but then lifted her chin and said, 'Thank you for your hospitality, anyway. I know that you have no great love for me any more, but…' She trailed off, her eyes wounded and confused.

'It was fated—'

'Stuff and nonsense!' said Monty. 'From my reading of the situation, you deliberately chose the worst possible moment to come forward and make yourself known to a woman who would have welcomed you with open arms at any time! Do you know what I think?' he said, picking Midge up in his arms and striding towards the door. 'Stephen, I think you are Kit Hebden all over again.'

He paused in the doorway, to look back at the shambles Midge had managed to make of what he could see had once been a neat little dining room.

'I don't know who killed your father, but I would not be a bit surprised to learn that there were half a dozen decent men queuing up for the pleasure of despatching the scoundrel.' Their eyes met and held for a few tense seconds.

Then Monty nodded, seeing the Gypsy had understood his veiled threat, and strode into the hall, pausing by the prone body of the Indian manservant.

'Your father had a beautiful wife,' he said, looking down at Midge, who had put her arms round his neck, 'who loved him, but he was so cruel that he drove her into the arms of another man. He had friends,' he said, looking at Stephen again, 'who admired his intellect, but he despised them, and went out of his way to do them down. Hal told me you used to play together as children. But now, you do all that is within your power to plague him and his family. It has to stop, Hebden, do you hear me?'

Stephen grasped the neck of the decanter a little more tightly. 'It is not as straightforward as that. I have a destiny to fulfil. My mother's dying words were—'

'Oh, not that ludicrous Gypsy curse again! Life is hard enough without bringing that kind of thing into it! Stop using it as an excuse, man! You could have reconciled with your sister any time. You *chose* to embrace your solitary bitterness…'

'No,' Stephen breathed between clenched teeth. His eyes were fixed on Midge's face, not Monty's as he said, 'I have *tried* to tread a different path. But whenever I do…' He shook his head. 'I cannot escape my destiny.'

With a last contemptuous snort, Monty turned on his heel, stepped over the unconscious Indian, and carried Midge out of the house.

Chapter Thirteen

Midge had been practically swooning with admiration at the masterful way Monty had marched in and dealt with Stephen.

It was only once he'd settled her on the seat of his carriage and climbed in beside her that all her insecurities regarding her place in his life came swarming back.

When he put his arm round her shoulders, she stiffened and turned her head away.

'What is it, Midge? Something still bothering you?'

'Well, yes, as a matter of fact,' she snapped. 'It may seem like a small detail to you, but I would—' she clenched her fists and lifted her chin '—I would rather stay with Stephen than reside in your house while you trawl the streets for a mistress!'

'Trawl the streets for a...' He crossed to the seat opposite her, and took her fists in his hands. 'Midge, I thought you knew I came to London to see if there was anything I could do, as a civilian, to join the struggle against Bonaparte. We talked about it...'

'Yes! And then you talked to your father about setting up a mistress or two as a reward for getting me pregnant!'

'Oh, my God. Is that what he told you? I only heard the part about you attempting to seduce the grooms the minute my back was turned.' He ran his thumbs over her clenched fists soothingly. 'As if that was not bad enough. No wonder you ran out on me.'

'Are you attempting to deny it?'

'Emphatically,' he declared.

She looked up at him, eyes narrowed with suspicion.

'You did not even say goodbye,' she accused him. 'The minute you could go, you just went. Without a backward look!'

'I came to bid you farewell,' he countered. 'But you were being terribly sick. And I felt—'

'Disgusted!' she spat.

He shook his head. 'Guilty. It is my child you are carrying. I am the one who made you ill. I did not know how to face you. What to say. I am so sorry for leaving you the way I did. For leaving you at all.'

He looked so contrite, she wondered if he might be telling the truth. 'If what your father told me was not true, where did he get such a horrible idea from?'

He looked more shamefaced than ever, which redoubled her wariness.

'Midge, please understand that all I was doing was trying to avoid a confrontation. If I had told the old man the real reason I was so intent on coming to London, he would most probably have flown into one of his rages. Well, now that you have been on the receiving end of one of them, you will perhaps more readily understand why I gave up arguing with him years ago. I confess, I just let him assume what he wanted about my reasons for saying I was coming to town. But believe me, I have no intention of setting up a mistress. When,' he continued with a rueful smile, 'would I have the energy to mount one, whilst I am married to such a handful as you?'

He had made the feeble attempt to tease her into a more cheerful frame of mind because he could not bear to see those tears that were running silently down her cheeks. Especially since Rick had told him she never cried.

So he was appalled when she looked as though he had just mortally wounded her.

'Don't mock me,' she gasped, as though it hurt her to breath. 'I know you have never taken me seriously, I know I am a figure of fun to you, and that you only married me because you were completely sure you could never fall in love with me, but—'

'What! Not fall in love with you? Where on earth did you get such a crazy notion?'

'Y-your father,' she sobbed. 'He said…'

He could tell what the old devil must have said, or she would not keep on crying like this. With an oath, he drew her across the coach and onto his lap, where he held her tight.

'Please, don't cry, love. And please put everything he told you out of your mind. It was all a pack of lies! I am sorry my way of dealing with my father has hurt you. I would never intentionally hurt you. And as for not taking you seriously, that is simply not true. You are the light of my life.'

'You say that now, but you would not take me to

London with you, would you? Because you feared I would embarrass you!'

'What? How could you think that?'

'What other reason could there be, for not taking me with you, if it was not so that you could search freely for a mistress?'

'Because I cannot keep my hands off you, of course,' he replied.

She frowned up at him in complete bewilderment. With a sigh, he explained, 'The doctor said we must cease from having marital relations, now that you are with child. Your mother's problems in that department are apparently very well-known. First they thought she was barren, and then she had miscarriages. Dr Cottee said you may be at risk, too. I had not wanted to alarm you by telling you what he said,' he grimaced, shaking his head. 'God, I seem to have made all the wrong choices where you are concerned.'

When she flinched, he knew she had misinterpreted his last statement.

'Oh, no. Not that. Not in marrying you. That is the only thing I do seem to have done right, lately.'

There was a lurch and a blast of cold air, and they both looked up in bewilderment to see one of Monty's footmen holding open the carriage door.

Rather than letting go of her, Monty attempted to clamber out of the carriage with Midge still held tightly in his arms.

'What are you doing?' she squealed. 'Put me down!'

'Not a chance,' he growled, once he had got both feet planted firmly on the pavement. 'I am not—' he planted a swift kiss on her parted lips —'going to let go of you until I absolutely have to. Have you no idea of what it did to me, when I thought I'd lost you?' His arms tightened convulsively round her. 'I imagined you lying hurt somewhere, unable to get home…' he grated, as he mounted the steps to the front door.

'I thought I'd lost you too—' she nodded, clasping him tighter round the neck as she saw exactly why he needed to maintain this physical contact '—to a mistress.'

'It is bad enough,' he panted as he climbed the stairs, 'that I am going to have to leave you alone once we get to your bedroom.'

'I don't see why,' Midge objected. 'It seems perfectly ridiculous to suppose that making love with you might harm the baby. After all, my mother had her affair while she was pregnant. And my father apparently saw nothing amiss with that.'

Monty came to an abrupt halt on the landing. Then he said, slowly, 'I have never had a very high opinion of Dr Cottee.'

And Midge finally stopped crying. The angry flush faded from her cheeks. The corners of her mouth lifted a little. She shifted her position, experimentally. Monty's breathing grew laboured. His eyes darkened.

And Midge smiled in very feminine satisfaction as she saw the truth.

'You want me?' She smiled. 'And only me? Even though…'

He saw another wave of doubts go washing through her.

'Even though what?' he prompted. 'Come on, out with it, so I can crush whatever maggot it is you've got in your head now.'

He strode through with her into the bedroom, and

gently laid her down. She pouted up at him as he moved away, but he shook his head, holding up his hands in a gesture of surrender.

'I cannot see you lying there, and not want to ravish you within an inch of your life. And apart from the fact Dr Cottee has warned me that would be an utterly selfish and possibly disastrous thing to do, I need you to talk to me.'

He seized a ladder-backed chair, reversed it and sat down with his arms crossed along the top, his chin resting on his hands, as though he was using it to shield himself from her irresistible allure. Midge could not help putting her power over him to the test. She wriggled a little and stretched her arms over her head, noting with pure satisfaction the way his eyes darkened and his breathing hitched in his throat.

'Stop that, you little tease,' he growled. 'It is not fair.' Then he frowned. 'Or perhaps it is. Perhaps you need to punish me, just a little, for the hurt you have endured on my account.'

'No!' she sat bolt upright, immediately contrite. 'I would never hurt you, not purposely!'

'No.' He smiled fondly. 'I knew that. Even when the twins told me you had run off with your fancy man, I knew you could never be so cruel. Even—' and his face fell abruptly '—even though you loved him…'

'Him? You mean Stephen?'

'No. That other fellow,' he said grimly. 'The one you were dreaming about, that night on Lady Carteret's terrace. The one your family made you give up, so that you could marry me. And look what a rotten husband I proved to be!' He ran his fingers through his hair.

'You thought I had run off with another man! Oh,

no!' It was her turn to look guilty now. 'Oh, Monty, you never had any cause to be jealous. It was always you. There has never been anyone else.'

'But you were drifting about with that dreamy look in your eyes. And you loathed me...'

'I loathed Viscount Mildenhall. I had always thought that Monty sounded like exactly the sort of man I ought to marry.'

He went very still for a second, then said, slowly, 'And you have been tortured at the thought of me taking a mistress. Does this mean,' he whispered, 'you love me? A little?'

She nodded, shyly, and lay back down among the pillows, revelling in the way he was looking at her. As though she meant the world to him.

'You did not like me much when we first met, either,' she pointed out, too scared to ask outright if he might love her a little, too. 'And you only married me as a favour to Rick.'

He winced. 'I should not have let you think that. For it was not the truth.'

'Not?'

He shook his head as though in annoyance. 'I was only in London because I had got to the end of my tether, down at Shevington. My father made me feel so useless! The only value I had in his eyes was as a means to produce the next generation. I did not bother argu- ing with him that time, either. We had already clashed enough, during the months I had been there. But—' and he speared his fingers through his hair in a frustrated gesture '—once I got here, the husband hunters came out in force anyway. I thought you were one of them. The scandalous Miss Hebden.' He smiled ruefully. 'But even though I believed so many bad things about you, I found myself looking out for you everywhere I went. Despised myself for wanting to catch a glimpse of you. And not being able to help myself. You were driving me out of my mind! After that scorching kiss, I knew I had to marry you. I made the appointment to see your uncle the very next morning. Before I knew you were Midge.'

'Oh!'

'But then, something wonderful happened. I met you at the theatre and found you were Rick's sister. Perhaps now would be a good time to tell you that I used to lie awake in my bivouac, after hearing one of those letters you used to write to Rick, dreaming of coming home to someone who would love me like that. Like you loved Rick. No—' he flushed slightly '—I don't mean as a brother. I mean unreservedly. Well, when I found out Rick's loyal, loving sister, Midge, was the same girl as the one who had kissed me with such passion on Lady Carteret's terrace, I was even more determined to snap you up before someone else got wind of what a treasure was on the market.'

'Oh,' said Midge again, going pink with pleasure. 'Why did you not just tell me all this?'

'And risk laying my heart at your feet for you to trample on? A man has his pride!' He hung his head, and studied his boots for a couple of seconds, before adding, 'I bitterly regret the way I held back.'

She sat up again, and reached for his hands. 'It is all behind us now. And I will never trample on your heart, Monty. Or your pride. I—' She took a deep breath. One of them had to be the first to take the plunge. 'I love you.'

'And I love you too,' he said, dazed. And then he flung back his head and laughed. 'We're in love!'

'So when are you going to stop talking and just kiss me?' asked Midge plaintively.

He took her hands that were trembling slightly and kissed her salty lips. And kissed her, and kissed her, until she truly felt like the most alluring woman on earth.

'Midge,' he groaned at last. 'We have to stop. Before I am unable to stop. We must not do anything that might harm our child!'

She sat back, completely abashed. He was still able to think clearly and consider the consequences of what they were doing. Whereas she…she laid her hands protectively over her stomach. Over the past couple of days she had hiked several miles across country in unsuitable footwear, then sat up all night in an inn nursing a man who wished her no good. She had fled to London in only the clothes she stood up in, and got soaked to the skin, all the while in a state of complete emotional turmoil. And her mother, she suddenly recalled, had lost a baby, simply because she'd suffered a terrible shock.

Her eyes flew to his guiltily as it suddenly hit her that any one of the things she had done over the last couple of days might have brought on a miscarriage.

'Oh, Monty,' she gasped, feeling slightly sick. 'I have behaved dreadfully, have I not? How can you ever forgive me?'

'There is nothing to forgive,' he said tenderly. 'I should have been taking better care of you. I know how impulsive you are. I should have been with you when you heard about your brother. You had nobody. Nobody.' His face hardened. 'And, God knows, I have always found Shevington a cold, inhospitable place. How could I have left you there alone, just because I could no longer make love to you? It was selfish of me.'

'You are the least selfish man I have ever met,' she breathed fervently.

He reached for her over the back of the chair, his expression wry as he rubbed his hands soothingly across her hunched shoulders. Who did she have to compare him with? The stepfather who had not bothered to make any financial provision for her? The stepbrother who would not open his door to her when she was in dire need? Or the half brother who had turned up at her wedding with the sole intention of ruining her day?

'Then you agree, for tonight, we must sleep apart? Just one last time?' he said, brushing a tendril of hair from her face. 'Until we hear differently from another medical man, I refuse to put you at risk.'

'Is it too much to ask that you just hold me?' she whispered.

He shut his eyes tight, as though he was in pain. 'I do not think you understand quite what you are asking of me.'

She relented. 'If you can be noble about it, then so can I. But after tomorrow…'

'I am looking forward to tomorrow.' He grinned. 'As I have woken up looking forward to every day since I married you.'

'Oh,' she breathed, misty-eyed. 'Have you?'

He nodded, laying his chin on his hands again and gazing at her with a fond smile. 'It is hard to credit, now, that I was afraid that civilian life would be a dead bore! No chance of that with you in my life.'

Her spirits sank. She knew he was only trying to

lighten the atmosphere between them, but the truth was, she still felt like something of a liability.

'If all the doctors say we must not sleep together for a while, I will go back to Shevington, and stay there, if you like,' she offered bravely. If he could make sacrifices, then so could she. 'I don't want to be a burden. And I know I will most probably get into some dreadful scrape if I stay in town.'

'First of all,' he said sternly, 'I have no intention of sending you back to Shevington! Nor returning for anything but brief visits for the foreseeable future. I have achieved all that I can, for now. The tenants know I am not cut from the same cloth as Piers. The steward knows I am onto him and that I won't tolerate that kind of behaviour once I hold the reins. If he wants to keep his job, he will have to clean up his act! The twins have been sent to school...'

'Oh, and how they hate me for it!'

'They may do now,' he said soothingly, 'because they have never known anything but the unhealthy atmosphere that prevails at Shevington. Once they have seen something of the outside world and made friends, they will understand why you acted to get them out.'

'Do you think so?' she said wistfully.

Monty nodded firmly. 'And we shall make sure we are there for them, during school holidays. Show them we are their friends. They are not fools, Midge. They will come round.'

But a frown still pleated her brow.

'And as for your propensity for getting into scrapes, well, I shall just have to stick to you like a burr. And you won't hear me complaining. You are an utter delight, to me, Midge, exactly as you are. Funny, and impulsive, and kind and brave and warm.'

'But,' she persisted, 'you said you wanted to get involved with politics. You will not be able to do much of that if you are babysitting me!'

He stroked one finger along the curve of her cheek. 'When I heard you had gone missing, Bonaparte seemed of less importance than a flea. There are plenty of other men arguing my point of view in the house. But I am the only husband you have. You and the baby, you are my family now.'

Something inside Midge felt as if it was melting. All her life, it seemed, she had been waiting to hear somebody say that. With tears streaming down her face, she knelt up on the bed and flung her arms round his neck.

'Oh, Monty,' she sobbed, 'I do love you so!'

'Funny way to show it,' he observed with a wry grin. And through her tears, Midge smiled back at him.

And he finally knew that his father was wrong. In his heart now, instead of just inside his head.

Midge loved him. For himself. It did not matter who his mother had been or how much money he had or what title he held. She was plainly willing to follow him to the ends of the earth. She would even brave Shevington on her own, if he asked her to.

And best of all, he was head over heels in love with her too. And he did not care what his father might say. Nothing had ever felt so bloody marvellous!

* * * * *

COMING NEXT MONTH FROM

HARLEQUIN®
HISTORICAL

Available October 26, 2010

- **REGENCY CHRISTMAS PROPOSALS**
  by **Gayle Wilson, Amanda McCabe, Carole Mortimer**
  (Regency)

- **UNLACING THE INNOCENT MISS**
  by **Margaret McPhee**
  (Regency)
  Book 6 in the *Silk & Scandal* miniseries

- **LADY RENEGADE**
  by **Carol Finch**
  (Western)

- **THE EARL'S MISTLETOE BRIDE**
  by **Joanna Maitland**
  (Regency)

REQUEST YOUR FREE BOOKS!

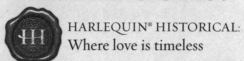

HARLEQUIN® HISTORICAL:
Where love is timeless

2 FREE NOVELS PLUS 2 **FREE GIFTS!**

YES! Please send me 2 FREE Harlequin® Historical novels and my 2 FREE gifts (gifts are worth about $10). After receiving them, if I don't wish to receive any more books, I can return the shipping statement marked "cancel." If I don't cancel, I will receive 6 brand-new novels every month and be billed just $4.94 per book in the U.S. or $5.49 per book in Canada. That's a saving of 20% off the cover price! It's quite a bargain! Shipping and handling is just 50¢ per book.* I understand that accepting the 2 free books and gifts places me under no obligation to buy anything. I can always return a shipment and cancel at any time. Even if I never buy another book from Harlequin, the two free books and gifts are mine to keep forever.

246/349 HDN E5L4

Name	(PLEASE PRINT)

Address	Apt. #

City	State/Prov.	Zip/Postal Code

Signature (if under 18, a parent or guardian must sign)

Mail to the **Harlequin Reader Service:**
IN U.S.A.: P.O. Box 1867, Buffalo, NY 14240-1867
IN CANADA: P.O. Box 609, Fort Erie, Ontario L2A 5X3
Not valid for current subscribers to Harlequin Historical books.

Want to try two free books from another line?
Call 1-800-873-8635 or visit www.morefreebooks.com.

* Terms and prices subject to change without notice. Prices do not include applicable taxes. N.Y. residents add applicable sales tax. Canadian residents will be charged applicable provincial taxes and GST. Offer not valid in Quebec. This offer is limited to one order per household. All orders subject to approval. Credit or debit balances in a customer's account(s) may be offset by any other outstanding balance owed by or to the customer. Please allow 4 to 6 weeks for delivery. Offer available while quantities last.

Your Privacy: Harlequin Books is committed to protecting your privacy. Our Privacy Policy is available online at www.eHarlequin.com or upon request from the Reader Service. From time to time we make our lists of customers available to reputable third parties who may have a product or service of interest to you. If you would prefer we not share your name and address, please check here. ☐

Help us get it right—We strive for accurate, respectful and relevant communications. To clarify or modify your communication preferences, visit us at www.ReaderService.com/consumerschoice.

HH10R

See below for a sneak peek from
our inspirational line, Love Inspired® Suspense

Enjoy this heart-stopping excerpt from
RUNNING BLIND
by top author Shirlee McCoy,
available November 2010!

The mission trip to Mexico was supposed to be an adventure. But the thrill turns sour when Jenna Dougherty and her roommate Magdalena are kidnapped.

"It's okay. I'm here to help." The voice was as deep as the darkness, but Jenna Dougherty didn't believe the lie. She could do nothing but lie still as hands slid down her arms, felt the rope around her wrists.

"I'm going to use a knife to cut you free, Jenna. Hold still."

The cold blade of a knife pressed close to her head before her gag fell away.

"I—" she started, but her mouth was dry, and she could do nothing but suck in air.

"Shhh. Whatever needs to be said can be said when we're out of here." Nick spoke quietly, his hand gentle on her cheek. There and gone as he sliced through the ropes on her wrists and ankles.

He pulled her upright. "Come on. We may be on borrowed time."

"I can't leave my friend," Jenna rasped out.

"There's no one here. Just us."

"She has to be here." Jenna took a step away.

"There's no one here. Let's go before that changes."

"It's dark. Maybe if we find a light…"

"What did you say?"

"We need to turn on the light. I can't leave until I know that—"

"What can you see, Jenna?"

"Nothing."

"No shadows? No light?"

"No."

"It's broad daylight. There's light spilling in from the window I climbed in through. You can't see it?"

She went cold at his words.

"I can't see anything."

"You've got a nasty bruise on your forehead. Maybe that has something to do with it." His fingers traced the tender flesh on her forehead.

"It doesn't matter *how* it happened. I'm blind!"

Can Nick help Jenna find her friend or will chasing this trail have Jenna running blindly again into danger?

Find out in RUNNING BLIND, available in November 2010 only from Love Inspired Suspense.